THE *W*IDOWS' *C*LUB

Center Point
Large Print

**This Large Print Book carries the
Seal of Approval of N.A.V.H.**

THE *Widows' Club*

joyce livingston

CENTER POINT PUBLISHING
THORNDIKE, MAINE

This Center Point Large Print edition
is published in the year 2006 by arrangement with
Barbour Publishing.

The text of this Large Print edition is unabridged. In other
aspects, this book may vary from the original edition. Printed in
Thailand. Set in 16-point Times New Roman type.

ISBN: 1-58547-863-6
ISBN 13: 978-1-58547-863-7

Library of Congress Cataloging-in-Publication Data

Livingston, Joyce.
    The widows' club / Joyce Livingston.--Center Point large print ed.
        p. cm.
    ISBN 1-58547-863-6 (lib. bdg. : alk. paper)
    1. Large type books. I. Title.

PS3562.I9435W53 2006
813'.6--dc22

2006016293

Dedication/Acknowledgment

I dedicate this book to every woman who is a widow, who may become one in the future, or who has a mother, sister, aunt, or friend who is facing widowhood.

Why did I decide to write a book about widows? Because I, too, am a widow, having lost my own precious husband in late 2004. I know firsthand the horrendous life changes caused by losing your beloved mate. Don Livingston picked me up off the ice, where I fell while skating at the neighborhood rink, and carried me through life, protecting me, providing for me, taking care of me, and, yes, spoiling me. I miss him more than words can express. He was my everything.

But—life goes on. And so do we. And while we may continue to grieve, we also find joy in the many things that make us laugh and the love lavished upon us by friends and family.

It is my hope that you will laugh and cry with Valentine, Sally, Reva, Bitsy, and Wendy as these women face the ups and downs of life and join together to become *The Widows' Club*.

If you enjoy this book, be watching for my next book, *The Widows' Club Invasion.*

CHAPTER 1

I was standing in the open sliding glass door that led to the balcony of my upstairs bedroom, watching a pair of geese fly overhead and wondering what I was going to do with the rest of my life, when a moving van pulled into the driveway of the empty house next door. Finally, I was going to have new neighbors. That house, which I felt had been terribly overpriced, even for this upscale neighborhood, had been on the market for months.

I was sure whoever bought it would immediately do a complete makeover, especially repainting the living room and dining room walls, which the former owner had painted purple. I liked purple, but this wasn't even a nice shade of purple, but a garish, dark, almost-black version of the color. They would probably also want to eliminate the heavy velvet drapery that covered nearly every main floor window and go for something that would let in the light. Something more like the lacy white curtains I had at my windows. And they'd definitely take out that ghastly purple and sage green carpet that covered nearly all of the rooms on the main floor. I wasn't sure what they'd do to the upstairs. The former owner had never allowed any of us neighbors that far into her house. Plus, there was an unkempt growth of vines that nearly covered the exterior of the house. Or, I suppose the new owners could have the same tastes in decorating as the old owners and simply leave things the way they were.

Ideally, my new neighbors would be a nice young professional couple with children, people who took pride in their surroundings. I had visions of us visiting over the backyard fence, sharing plant cuttings and chitchat. Maybe, if the family was looking for a church home, I could invite them to visit Cooperville Community Church. I knew they'd love it. What a treat it would be to have next-door neighbors who shared my faith.

I watched as the driver and another man crawled out of the truck, moved around to the back, opened the big overhead rolling door, and began pulling out boxes— sealed boxes, which didn't tell me anything about the new tenants and their likes.

Still clad in my favorite pajamas, the silky white ones with dozens of huge red hearts emblazoned on them, the ones Carter had given me for Valentine's Day, I moved out onto the balcony and breathed in the early morning air, feeling much like Juliet as I stood there. But there was no Romeo smiling up at me from below. God had taken my Romeo and, like it or not, I was alone.

"Why?" I asked for the umpteenth time, lifting my face and hands heavenward. "Why Carter?" No answer came. Then, with an occasional glance at the boxes being unloaded and carried into the house, I said, "My husband was the gentlest man I'd ever known, and he loved You. He loved serving You. I'm trying to understand why You would do such a thing, but I just don't get it. Didn't You know I needed him? We had so much of life to live yet. I'm only fifty-two, for goodness' sake. We had so many things still to do together. So many plans left undone."

My thoughts went back to the day I met Carter Denay. I had been popular, one of the in-crowd in high school. Aside from being the only child of a well-to-do family, I wore the latest, most expensive fashions, had my own checking account—a real rarity for a girl my age at that time. I made straight As, though many times undeserved—I knew how to work the teachers and was great at apple-polishing. I was head cheerleader, prom queen, and voted the most likely to succeed. There was only one other girl who was any competition, but she was kind of a rebel with a slightly tainted reputation, though I never believed she deserved it. Barbie Baxter. From the fourth grade through high school, we had competed in everything—from who had the better grades, to excelling in sports, to who dated the most popular boys, to who won the prom queen title.

Though we didn't have an actual name for the group of girls I hung around with, we could have been called The Spoiled Rotten Brats—the name would have been most appropriate. By my senior year, I had dated every boy in Nashville High who was anybody, and had found them all immature, and not the least bit worth my time. At seventeen or eighteen, boys were so much more immature than girls were.

Well, anyway, my mom and dad were quite happy with my fickleness, and especially happy that I hadn't found Mr. Right. They had big plans for my future. The last thing they wanted was for me to get serious with some guy and end up married and pregnant. Some of my friends were engaged by their senior year, wearing gold bands with diamonds so small a person needed a magnifying glass to spot them. Not me. I was going to go to college and belong to the best, most affluent sorority, of course. I would make the cheerleading team and date only the most attractive boys, but none of them seriously. I would graduate with honors—to keep my parents happy—then head to New York City to study fashion design. I envisioned myself walking into Saks, Neiman Marcus, or even Dillard's, and seeing labels that bore the name VALENTINE'S ORIGINALS embroidered in beautiful red script lettering, sewn into the neckline of expensive, upscale women's fashions. I could even picture embroidered red hearts replacing the dots above the three *i*'s in my name. Yes, I was going to make it—big time. The world of fashion would bow at my feet. My plans were set in stone, until the day I walked into a grocery store and saw the most beautiful blue eyes I'd ever seen on a man, glancing at me from behind the counter as I prepared to pay for my soft drink.

To this day, I remember what I was wearing. A pair of scanty white shorts, white tennies without socks, and the absolute barest of halters. I could have put the entire outfit, except the tennies, into my small purse without even making it bulge. It was a horrifically hot day—about ninety-four degrees, if my memory serves me right. Normally I don't perspire much, but that day, despite the nearly nonexistent outfit I was wearing and my antiperspirant deodorant, I did. Profusely. Probably because I'd been driving all over town with the top on my convertible down.

"Hi," I'd said to Mr. Blue Eyes. I smiled demurely and flipped my long blond hair back over my shoulder. "Hot, isn't it?"

Did he answer? No. He simply nodded. Normally, guys went out of their way to speak to me, but not this guy. He didn't even smile. "Will that be all?"

Was this guy dead?

Didn't he have any testosterone?

"No," I said, cocking my head coyly and putting on my best smile. "Do you have any nail clippers? I've broken a fingernail and I seem to have lost mine." I thought the guy would come out from behind the counter and lead me to the aisle where I already knew I'd find the nail care products. But instead, he motioned to a big number mounted on a sign above the personal care section and said in a monotone, "Aisle seven."

Mumbling under my breath, I made my way to aisle seven, picked up the first nail clipper I saw, which turned out to be a toenail clipper, and took it back to him, only to find two other customers had moved into my place in line, one of them a football jock from high school. I couldn't even remember his name. He was one of those kind of guys I expected to scratch himself in public. Definitely not my type, though he did ask me for a date once. I turned him down flat.

"Hey, I saw that winning touchdown you made at the game last Friday night," Mr. Blue Eyes told Mr. Jock, grinning, his face actually showing excitement.

"Yeah, that touchdown was the greatest. I came so close to losing that ball, but I held onto it and lunged right over the top of those linemen. Touchdown! You play football?"

Mr. Blue Eyes shook his head. "Naw, I'd like to, but I have to work." No explanation. No info if he was saving his money for college—although he looked old enough to be graduating from college. No word about having to support his mother or a wife—though I'd already checked to make sure there wasn't a ring on his left hand. Nothing. Which made me that much more curious. Though why, I didn't understand. There were plenty of good-looking boys around. Why did his blatant indifference bother me so?

Finally, Mr. Jock paid for his items and moved out the door. Mrs. Silver Hair stepped up to the counter with three items. Two bags filled with doughnuts and a bottle of juice. "Do you happen to have anything for sore muscles?" she asked, rubbing at her shoulder. "I looked but couldn't find anything."

Mr. Blue Eyes left his sacred place behind the counter and moved toward the number seven sign. Now I was really miffed. Why would he go to all that trouble for a woman who was old enough to be his mother and not even bother to find the nail clippers for me?

After the woman left, I casually ran my fingers

through my hair and started to move up into her place, determined to at least get a smile out of this handsome hunk. But before I could get there, who wedged herself in between the counter and me?

Barbie Baxter!

And she was wearing short white shorts and a halter much like the skimpy one I was wearing!

How dare she crowd in front of me?

Immature teenager that I was, I was so mad I wanted to yank on the dark curly ponytail that hung nearly to her waist and tell her to go to the back of the line.

"Hi," she told the clerk with that exaggerated, put-on smile of hers, the one she used on all the male teachers. "Nice to see you again." She flopped a five-dollar bill and a candy bar onto the counter, all the while batting her baby browns at the gorgeous clerk.

"Hi, yourself, Barbie. How ya doin'?"

He knew her name?

"I like your blue shirt. It brings out the blue in your eyes," she told him, twisting her head slightly and widening her already big eyes. Didn't that bimbo realize every clerk in the store wore the same blue shirt? It was part of their uniform.

"Thanks," he said. Looking slightly embarrassed, he counted out her change then handed her the receipt. "Come again."

As if she needed an invitation. *Grrr!* Why hadn't I seen him first? I hated to lose a guy to any girl, and usually didn't, but to Barbie? That was the world's absolute worst.

13

"You can be sure of it," she drawled out, her words dripping with honey. After a coy wave at him and a nod toward me, she sashayed her way out the door.

Grrr, grrr, and triple grrr! Barbie, of all people! I couldn't let her get ahead of me. I was determined to get to know this gorgeous creature.

I've never thought of myself as a snob, and I didn't want to be one then. We never actually had harsh words, never even gave each other a frown, but we just didn't *click*. I guess, in many ways, our outward appearance and our personalities—as much as I hate to admit it—were simply too similar.

Trying to put the incident with Barbie Baxter out of my mind and concentrate on the issue at hand, I turned back to the hunk. Well, maybe back then I hadn't thought of him as a *hunk*. I thought girls calling guys hunks came later in my life. Maybe *dude* or *male specimen* would have been a better term back then. As businesslike as ever, and still ignoring my overly exaggerated smile, he rang up my items: one soft drink and one toenail clipper, then, slipping the clipper into a small bag, told me the total.

"I so appreciate your help," I cooed, batting my eyes much as Barbie had as I pulled a ten-dollar bill from my pocket and attempted to mask my impatience. "Are you new here? I come in quite often, and I don't think I've seen you around."

"I'm filling in for someone. I usually work the graveyard shift."

Glancing around and noting there were no other customers making their way to the counter to pay for their selections, I peered at him over my soft drink and took a slow sip. The cool liquid felt good sliding down my parched throat. I struggled for something clever to say and thinking of nothing asked, "Oh? Do you attend college?"

He handed me my change, and for the first time a slight smile curled at his lips. "No, ma'am."

Fanning myself with the little bag he'd just handed me that held my lone pair of toenail clippers, I leaned against the counter. "My school counselor said it's really tough to get a good job without a college degree."

He turned slightly and began to methodically line up the specialty items on the counter in precise rows. "I'm sure your counselor is right."

"Then," I asked, my curiosity peaking beyond its limit, "why don't you want to go?"

He glanced around the store, probably making sure no customers needed help, before answering me. "College was too expensive for me. Instead, I opted to attend vo-tech school. I'm doing my apprenticeship program with a local electric company. In another year, I'll be a full-fledged electrician. That's why I usually work the late-night shift, so I can train for that during the days."

"So," I asked, putting on my most feminine smile, hoping he'd notice my dimples—Barbie didn't have dimples—that almost always drove men crazy and made other women jealous, "You really want to be an electrician when you grow up?"

He actually chortled. I was so shocked that I momentarily let my lips relax. Then, quickly garnering control, I tilted my head and broadened my smile.

"An electrician? Of course, but what I really want to do, eventually, is own my own company."

Amazing. Despite his earlier aloofness with me and his friendliness with Barbie, the man was actually carrying on a conversation. "Own your own company? That's a pretty lofty goal."

"I know but I'm willing to do whatever it takes."

His voice carried a certain strength, a resolve, that made me think he just might do it. I stared into his clear blue eyes. They reminded me of the almost-violet color I'd seen once in a double rainbow when Mom and Dad and I had taken a trip to Alaska and stayed in Denali National Park. I'd never seen such a vividly colored rainbow. I sucked in a breath and quickly said, "I'm having a few friends over Friday night for a barbecue. Would you like to come?"

He looked at me as if I had broccoli stuck between my teeth. "Ah—no—I mean—I can't. I have to work."

"I thought you said you usually worked the late-night shift." I couldn't stand being turned down. Especially when I knew Barbie Baxter was after him.

Another look of embarrassment wound its way across his face. "I do—work the late-night shift."

"Then," I said, lifting my chin proudly, not about to accept *No* for an answer, "you'll be able to come to my house, enjoy the fantastic barbecue my dad makes, and get back in plenty of time to report to work."

His eyes narrowed. "You don't even know me. Are you sure you want to invite me to your house?"

Having not put on my glasses that day—since I hated wearing them—I squinted in the direction of his nametag. "Of course, I know you, Carson."

He smiled a shy grin. "It's Carter, not Carson."

I felt like a dork, but muddled ahead anyway. "Carter? I like that even better." I stuck out my hand. "I'm Valentine."

Instead of taking my hand and giving it a shake, he eyed me quizzically. "You're kidding, right? I've never met a girl named Valentine."

"You have now," I told him proudly. I've always liked my name. And, you guessed it, I was born on February fourteenth, and my mom, being a romantic at heart, couldn't resist naming me Valentine. You have to admit Valentine is better than Cupid, which she told me she also considered. Can you imagine being named Cupid? Yuk.

"You're serious?"

"Yep, totally." Turning over the receipt he'd given me, I took the pen from the counter and wrote my full name, phone number, and address on it, adding, *Be there precisely at six,* and handed it to him. "My dad hates it when people come late. It's the big red-brick house on the corner with the circular driveway. You can't miss it."

"Maybe this isn't a good—"

I brazenly grabbed onto his hand. "Please, Carter,

17

you must come. It'll be fun, I promise. Dress casual," I called over my shoulder as I headed out the door, not giving him time to refuse. "See you at six on Friday!"

I nearly knocked down an incoming customer on my way out. I was sure Carter was standing there behind his counter, his eyes bugging out, wondering what had just happened. It probably wasn't everyday a strange new girl bopped into his grocery store and invited him to dinner. I really hoped he'd show up.

My next project? Inform my dad, who always cooked his famous barbecue on Saturday night. This week, he simply had to cook it on Friday night instead and plan for one more person to enjoy it. I wanted to leave Saturday night open in case Carter asked me to the movies.

A loud noise of some sort brought me back to reality. With a final glance toward the moving van, I stepped inside my bedroom and stared through misty eyes at the photograph on my nightstand. Though the man of my thoughts was much older and graying at the temples when that picture had been taken, Carter was still as handsome as that first day I'd seen him at the grocery store. And his eyes, his clear blue eyes, still held me captive. He and I were meant to be together. Barbie Baxter, despite her good looks and best efforts, never had a chance.

"I love you. I'll always love you," I told his image as I sat down on the edge of the bed and cradled the frame against my chest. "Why did you have to leave me? I wasn't ready for you to go. We were going to joyfully face our sunset years together, but now you're gone and I'm alone." Just saying the words aloud brought tears to my eyes and an ache to my heart.

A second noise, this one a sudden loud thump outdoors, brought back my curiosity and I hurried to the balcony again. A yellow Mercedes convertible had pulled into the driveway and parked next to the truck. I leaned over the railing, hoping for a glimpse of whoever was moving next door. There they were and, though their faces were turned away from me, I could tell they were a handsome couple. Him, in a dark suit, his short, cropped hair slicked back with some kind of gel, and her in a gorgeous yellow floral slack set, her long blond hair floating over her slim shoulders and around her face like a gypsy's wiry head of hair on a windy day. Even from the angle I was seeing her, she reminded me of a cover I'd seen on a romance novel at our local bookstore.

I sighed as the happy couple walked into their new home. Though I hadn't seen any children so far, at least it looked like half my neighbor wish list had been fulfilled. I envied them as they disappeared inside and the door closed behind them.

They have each other.

Me? I was alone.

All alone and I didn't like it one bit.

What am *I going to do with the rest of my life?*

CHAPTER 2

"This is one of those mornings," I grumbled two hours later, raking my fingers through my dry, frizzy hair. It was one of those bad hair days. I think my beautician botched up the mix when she bleached the highlights into my slightly graying hair the last time.

"Didn't sleep well?"

I lowered my coffee cup and eyed Sally Norton. My close friends Sally and Reva, who both became neighbors a few years ago, and I all live in a cul-de-sac called Morning Glory Circle. They, along with a few other friends, including Edna Fitzwilliam and Wendy Sinclair, who are both older and wiser than the three of us and also dropped by now and then, meet at my house every morning for coffee and chitchat. Raising a brow, I cringed as Sally leaned back in her chair and rubbed at her temples. I knew from her expression whatever she was going to say was not good.

"That daughter of mine is going to be the death of me yet. I told her to be home no later than eleven last night. Guess what time she showed up?"

"Eleven fifteen?" I asked off the top of my head.

Sally gave me a look that confirmed my ignorance. "She showed up at nearly one! Can you tell me what a fifteen-year-old girl could be doing until one o'clock in the morning?"

"Hey, you're asking the wrong woman," I told her

pointedly. "Remember, Carter and I never had kids. I haven't a clue, but from what I've seen on *Oprah* and *Dr. Phil*, I'd doubt she was attending a prayer meeting." I reached across the table and gave the drama queen's hand a patronizing pat. With Sally, everything was a crisis. "Sorry, sweetie, I guess that answer sounded a bit flippant. I can only imagine how worried you are about Jessica. She's such a pretty girl, and I—"

Sally stared at me. "Pretty? How can you tell? You can barely see her face with all that makeup, especially the black smudges around her eyes. She looks like a cast member in a Tim Burton film. I'm at my wits' end, Valentine. I don't know what to do with her. I've threatened to take away her cell phone, but she knows I want her to have it in case of emergencies. What else can I do?"

"Did you try to call her on her cell phone last night?" I asked, then realized any mother worth wearing the title of *Mother* would think to call her daughter on the cell phone if she had one.

"Yeah, I called her on the cell. About a dozen times. She claimed she'd left it in her friend's bathroom when she'd washed her hands so she hadn't heard it. How dumb does she think I am?"

I gazed sympathetically at the overwrought woman. Sally didn't need this. She still hadn't adjusted to losing Eric.

"Anyone home?" two voices sounded out back.

I jumped to my feet and rushed to unlock the storm

door for Reva and Edna. "Glad you girls made it."

Reva moved to the coffeepot and poured herself a cup of the delicious coffee for which I'd become famous. My own secret concoction of half regular, half decaf, and a scant pinch of brown sugar. Edna pulled out a stool alongside Sally. That was the way all my friends were—right at home. This place of mine had become the headquarters for emotionally needy women like us. It was comfortable and homey. A lot of people have a welcome mat at their door, but mine really means what it says. I liked it that way.

"I talked to Wendy earlier," Reva said. "She said to tell you she might not make it this morning. She has an appointment for her annual physical." Stopping mid-sentence she lifted the new bright yellow and white daisy coffee mug I'd picked up at a gift shop in St. Louis on my last bus trip and stared at it. "Where did you get this? I've never seen it before."

"St. Louis." I gestured toward the matching spoon rest on the range, the canister set on the counter, and the dessert-sized plates on the table. "You like them?"

Reva answered with a shrug. I knew that would be her reaction. Delicate and feminine were two words missing from her vocabulary. Sally, Edna, Wendy, and I were feminine to the core, but not Reva. If I wanted to describe her I could have done it with one word. *Plain.* I could count the times on one hand that I'd seen her in a patterned shirt. And frills of any kind? Not her. She was definitely a woman, and proud of it. She just happened to like plain things, from her short-cropped hair, her unembellished T-shirts, to her simple white tennies. Give Reva a plain pair of jeans, a blue chambray shirt, her white tennies, hand her a hammer, a screwdriver, a pair of pliers, or a roll of duct tape, and she'd be one happy camper.

She was our neighborhood Mrs. Fix-it. If the toilet stopped up, the handle came off the refrigerator door, the car wouldn't start, the bread maker wouldn't make bread, or any other mechanical problem reared its ugly head around our homes, Reva was the one we called first. She was a genius. And the best part of all? She was always willing to help.

"That wind is vicious. Must be a storm brewing out there." Reva plopped into a chair and smoothed at her mannish cut. "Don't know why I even bothered to comb my hair."

Sally fingered her own locks. "I should never have tried to give myself this perm. It fried my hair. Maybe I left the solution on too long." Pulling a long strand down over her forehead, Sally stared at it cross-eyed. "Do you think I should dye my hair? I hate this mousy color. Besides, I think I'm getting some gray hairs."

"I think you should leave it and let it turn gray like Valentine's." With her elbow, Reva gave me a teasing nudge. "You're getting grayer by the day, but on you it looks good, especially with those blond highlights."

I nudged her back. "You'd *better* add that last part." She'd said the truth all right. I was getting grayer by the day. If I was like my mom, by the time I reached sixty, I'd be one of those silver-haired ladies.

"I meant it, Val. I like your hair. It's one of your best features." Turning back to Sally, Reva said with a teasing grin, "Maybe you could dye it jet-black like your daughter's. That'd be dramatic."

Sending Reva a warning look, I nodded in Sally's direction. "Go easy on her, Reva. Jessica has been giving Sally fits." I said it in an almost whisper, knowing how even the most innocent comment could upset Sally these days.

Reva scrunched up her face. "Sorry, Sal. I was only joking. If you want to dye your hair, go for it. I'll even help you do it."

Sally slumped in the chair then let out a deep sigh that seemed to come from the pit of her stomach. "Girls, I really need a change in my life. I can't remember the last time I did something just for me. My kids take up my every waking moment."

"Tell me about it." Reva's face, too, took on a deep scowl. "Can you believe David was out until after one last night? Even though I had made it perfectly clear to that boy he was to be home and in bed by eleven?"

Sally's hand went to her hip. "Well, that explains who Jessica was really with. That girl didn't get home until one, either. I knew her story about falling asleep while watching a late night movie on TV with her friend didn't ring true."

I watched with concern as Reva narrowed her eyes. I'd been so afraid there would be trouble if my two friends' children kept dating each other. They both had a propensity for getting into trouble. Together they were downright dangerous.

"Those two were together?" Reva's scowl deepened. "After I warned David about keeping Jessica out so late? Wait'll I get my hands on that son of mine."

Sally grabbed onto her wrist. "You can't put all the blame on David. My daughter needs to share some of the blame. She knows better, Reva. To be honest about it, staying out that late was probably her idea!"

"I—I'm no one to be giving advice," Edna inserted cautiously, as if not sure how well her question would be received, "but exactly when did Jessica and David's rebellion start? I mean—has all this happened since—"

"Since their fathers died? Most of Jessica's started after we lost Eric. She has always been a rebellious child, but he was able to keep her under control. I can't."

"Jessica's hurting, too, Sally," Edna offered, showing genuine concern. "That girl loved her father. Perhaps she feels as lost without him as you do."

There was an awkward silence. I wanted desperately to say something to make Sally feel better, but what did I know?

After a moment, Sally looked up at Edna, her eyes taking on a sad expression. "She has a funny way of showing it. I'd think, since her father is no longer with us, she'd turn to me. I love her every bit as much as he did."

"Face it, Sal," Edna said kindly. "Your Jessica was daddy's little girl. There's a special bond between a girl and her father, especially a loving father like Eric was.

25

I'm sure she loves you, too, but that bond has been broken and she's having a hard time dealing with her loss."

I lifted the coffeepot then nodded in agreement. "You're a great mom but, no matter how hard you try, you can't fill Eric's shoes."

Reva nodded, too. "My husband rarely raised his voice to our son. Me? I yell. Which one of us do you think David listened to?" Taking the empty coffeepot from my hand, she moved to the sink and began filling it with water. "I sure wish that man were around now. It's tough raising a teenage boy alone. I wouldn't wish this job on my worst enemy."

The corners of my mouth turned up slightly at her words. "Worst enemy? You haven't got an enemy in the world. Everyone loves you."

Reva stared at the coffeepot, and by the expression on her face I could tell she, too, was frustrated. "Not David. He thinks I'm a tyrant. I sure wish I knew how to control him. I've prayed and prayed about that boy. He must have God stymied, too, 'cause God sure hasn't given me any answers."

I got up, pulled a paper coffee filter from inside the cabinet door and handed it to Reva before lifting the lid on the coffee canister and measuring out a scoop of my premixed regular and decaf coffee grounds. "I guess we all know from experience that God doesn't exactly answer our prayers the way we want Him to or when we want Him to."

"You can say that again." Sally pulled two packets of

sugar from the glass container in the center of the table then, changing her mind, put them back and reached for the pink packets that contained artificial sweetener. "God must be too busy these days to even hear my prayers. I'm sure not seeing any answers. Seems everyone I know is going through one kind of problem or another."

Reva gestured toward me. "Except for Val."

Surprised by her statement, I punched the On button on the coffeemaker then hurriedly scooted back into my chair. "What do you mean by that comment? I have problems just like the rest of you."

"Face it, Valentine, other than losing Carter, you've pretty much got the world by its tail."

"World by its tail? What does that mean?"

"You're gorgeous."

That remark, though undeserved, I appreciated.

"Have a great figure."

I wouldn't exactly say great, but not bad, I guessed.

"You're always dressed beautifully."

I have to admit, I do love clothes and have closets full of them, many of which were either presents from my husband or ones he helped me select.

"Have a standing weekly appointment at the beauty salon to have your hair and nails done."

Guilty, but they do both my hair and nails so much better than I can.

She gestured around my spacious kitchen with its custom-made oak cabinets, granite counter tops, marble floors, and the new top-of-the-line appliances

I'd purchased a few months ago. "If these things are problems," she said, "I'll be happy to take them off your hands."

Sally swatted at the air. "Reva! That isn't fair. Valentine's had her share of problems, too."

I struggled to keep my cool. "Those *things* you mentioned are material possessions, Reva. I'd give them all up in a nanosecond to have Carter back with me."

Reva reached out and patted my hand. I could tell by the look on her face that she hadn't intended to offend me with her words. They'd just been thrown out without thinking.

"I *meant* my careless-sounding remark as a compliment, Valentine. Your home is one of the loveliest I've ever seen, and I'm sure you deserve everything you have. You're one of the most unselfish women I've ever known. But, Val, not all of us are so blessed. Take Sally for instance. Though she doesn't say much about it, I'm sure she has to watch every penny."

Sally nodded. "Every dime and dollar, too, at least until I can sell our business and pay off the remaining equipment loans. Once those bills are taken care of, I'll be fine. Although I loved him for it, I wish Eric hadn't sheltered me so."

"Look, Reva," I said, turning my full attention toward her, wanting to make sure she understood where I was coming from. "My Carter was a genius. He came up with an idea to promote our first electric business and, with sacrifice and hard work, it eventually paid off. Until we were able to get that business on its feet, the two of us worked eighteen hour days, six days a week and, sometimes, even on Sundays. It wasn't until we sold that first business and Carter launched Denay Construction that we became financially independent and able to do whatever we wanted. The wealth we finally attained didn't just happen. No one *gave* us anything, Reva. Carter and I *both* worked for it."

She held her hands up in front of her face. "I'm sorry, Valentine. I didn't mean to come off sounding so harsh."

I took a moment to settle myself down before responding. I was sick and tired of people criticizing me for all my worldly possessions. "Look, Reva," I said, trying to keep my voice kind, "you're one of my best friends, but you weren't around when Carter and I were first married. There's no way you could have known the struggles he and I went through in the beginning. Even after we sold that first business and Carter formed his construction company and I no longer had to work, our problems didn't end. A former employee sued us and it nearly cost us everything. Fortunately, it was resolved in our favor but, for a time, it looked like we might even have to declare bankruptcy."

Her eyes trained on me, Reva swallowed nervously. "I—I didn't know."

"That's because she never talks about the rough times," Sally inserted with authority. "Only those of us who were around at the beginning knew about it. Even though we were aware Valentine and Carter were going through rough times, those two pretty much kept their problems to themselves."

Good ol' Sally. I could always count on her to come to my defense. She had been there right by my side, praying for me, comforting me, and trying to cheer me up when that awful lawsuit had happened. She'd witnessed, firsthand, what that trauma had done to us. I think my sweet husband aged at least five years that trying summer.

"It was a terrible time for both of them," Sally went on. "I've never seen Valentine so distraught."

Feeling ashamed for the way I'd snapped at Reva, I sent her a gentle smile. "You couldn't have known. You weren't living just two doors down from me like you are now, but a lot of people in the church knew and stood by us when everything hit the fan. But Sally was the main one. She was there for me twenty-four-seven. And Edna, too. I can never thank them enough for all they did."

"That's what friends are for." Sally reached across the table and gave my hand a squeeze. "I prayed for you night and day."

"Me, too," Edna added.

"Believe me, we could feel your prayers. I doubt Carter and I would have gotten through that horrendous time if it hadn't been for you, Eric, and our other friends."

Reva sent me a contrite look. "I—I'm sorry, Valentine. As usual, my big mouth got me in trouble."

"We might have had material things," I told her, still feeling bad for my sudden outburst, "but both of you have something we never had." I swallowed at the sadness filling my heart just thinking about it. "You have children. Carter and I longed to have a baby, but it was never to be. That sweet man spent a fortune taking us from one specialist to another but, despite the poking, prodding, endless blood tests and procedures, none of them were ever able to help us conceive." The lump in my throat nearly gagged me. Why hadn't God seen fit to give me that baby we longed for? I would have been a terrific mother. Surely He knew that.

Reva stood and wrapped an arm around my shoulder, leaning her forehead against mine. "Forgive me, sweetie. I had no business talking to you that way. I guess I'm a little unnerved. This has not been a good week for me. Today is the anniversary of Manny's death. I—" Pausing, she sucked in a deep breath. "I just came from the cemetery."

I threw my arms around her, hugging her tight. "Oh, honey, I'm so sorry."

Sally joined us in a group hug. "You shouldn't have gone to that cemetery alone. Why didn't you call one of us?"

Our normally strong Reva lifted sad eyes to meet ours. "I wasn't alone. David went with me."

"But you said he and Jessica didn't get in until one," Sally said.

"I rousted him out of bed at seven, which was a mistake. He didn't want to go and grumbled all the way there, caused a scene when we got there, and grumbled all the way back. I just hope his dad wasn't watching from heaven. It would have broken his heart."

"Do you think our husbands can look down from heaven and see us?" Sally asked wistfully.

It was a question that had plagued me ever since the moment I had first seen my precious husband lying so still in that coffin. "I don't know. I can't image either Manny or Eric looking down on you two and seeing the problems you're going through without feeling sadness."

Sally backed away from our group hug thoughtfully. "But—since there's no sorrow or sadness in heaven—would God allow them to see us?"

She had a point. "I honestly don't know, but I hope Carter can see me. Even hear me. I talk to him all the time." Releasing my hold on Reva, I began gathering up the dirty cups, spoons, and dessert plates from the table.

"How old did you say David was when Manny died?" Sally asked Reva, obviously trying to change the subject. "Eight?"

Absentmindedly, Reva picked up three of my new sunny yellow place mats and maneuvered them into a neat stack. "Yeah, eight. I can still remember his big round eyes as they lowered Manny's casket into the ground. It was so sad. For both of us." Reva collapsed back into her chair, her hands clasped in her lap. "Being just a kid, he didn't understand why his father was being taken away from us. He still doesn't understand. I'm sure that's the reason he tries to avoid going to church with me. That boy is angry, and I don't know what to do about it."

"I'm angry, too."

All eyes turned quickly toward Sally.

"Oh, not angry exactly. Maybe angry isn't the right word for the way I feel, but I am upset." I detected a slight tremor in her voice. "I can see no good reason why God allowed Eric to suffer so long and then took him from us. Those treatments drained every ounce of life from him. I wish he'd listened to me and never had them."

I stared at Sally. "You never told me you felt that way. I thought you were all for his treatments."

"Oh, Valentine, you think you know me so well, but you don't. Not the real me. I can put on a good face even when my heart is breaking inside. That's the only choice you have when three kids are depending on you to be both their mother and their father. Eric was the strong one, both physically and emotionally. He sheltered and protected me all his life. Do you realize I'd never even balanced my checkbook until after he was gone?" Sally hung her head, avoiding our eyes. "I—I was too ashamed to admit I was so stupid and naive. He handled everything in our family. I skipped through life singing, 'La de da, La de da,' as if I didn't have a care in the world. And, thanks to Eric, I didn't. I had my own charge card and a book of blank checks—that was all I needed. But now it's a different story. I'm it. The only one to manage those things and I don't like it at all. I want my husband back. I need him. My children need him."

Her hands gripping the edge of the table, she jutted her face toward us. "Can you give me one good reason why God would take my Eric? I don't know if our husbands can look down and see us or not, but I know God can. Didn't He realize how much my family needed Eric? How much I needed him?" Cupping her face with her hands, Sally's eyes filled with tears that tumbled down her cheeks.

I started to go to her, to wrap my arms around her, but what could I say to console her that I hadn't already said? Everything she was saying was true. We all knew it. Eric *was* Sally's life. We'd always kidded her about it. Though she was a great friend and fun to be with, she had no business sense at all which, to Eric, must have been part of her charm.

Blinking back her emotions, Sally looked from me, to Reva, to Edna, then back to me. "I—I'm sorry, girls. I didn't mean to lay all of this on you, but Jessica has me climbing the wall. I've never been so frustrated."

Her sorrow touched me deeply. I stared at my friend. Sally's pain was so real it was palatable. I'd known Sally had gone through some horrendous times since Eric passed away, but I'd had no idea things had been this hard for her. I was her friend. Why hadn't I noticed her struggle? Was I so caught up in my own grief, having my own pity party that I had no compassion for others?

"I'm glad that house down at the end of our cul-de-sac opened up when you decided to sell your big house. It's nice to have you and the children as neighbors," I told her, sincerely meaning it. "You need to be near those of us who love you and understand at least part of what you're going through. We need each other. You, me, Reva, Edna, Wendy. Though all of us have lost a spouse, we each have our own unique set of problems. We need to share those so we can be there to help each other."

I paused, pressing down at the sorrow that squeezed my own heart. "Life is strange. Carter had great plans for our future. He was going to sell his construction business eventually and we were going to travel and see the world. But, because of his busy schedule and his obligations at the church as deacon and part of the worship team, the farthest we ever got from Nashville was New York City. Once. Now here I am with all the time in the world and money to go wherever I want, and I don't want to go anywhere. Not without Carter. It wouldn't be any fun without him."

"All of our men were good men," Sally added.

I glanced from one widow to the next. Sally was right. Though all of us had been friends for years and had shared many of the same experiences, we didn't really know each other. Not with the kind of knowledge that reached deep into the innermost recesses of one's heart. There were things about me I hadn't been willing to share, not even with my beloved husband, and may never want to share with anyone. Sometimes the burden I carried nearly overwhelmed me.

"Well, do you think you will?" Sally asked, nudging my arm.

I stared at her. I'd been so deep in my thoughts I hadn't been listening to the conversation going on around me. "Will I what?" I asked, embarrassed I'd let my mind wander.

"Do you think you'll ever marry again?"

CHAPTER 3

Marry again? Me? Whatever for?" The thought of sharing my life and bed with anyone other than Carter sickened me. Though I'd only been a widow for three years, I could honestly say I had never seen a man, even the really nice, godly men at our church, who could have begun to compare to my Carter. "I could never find another soul mate like Carter. God threw away the blueprint after He made him. How about you girls? Will you ever marry again?"

Reva gave her head a vigorous shake. "Not me! I feel the same way. Manny is irreplaceable, but I have to admit I could sure use some male influence with David. Sometimes, he makes me so angry I'd like whip him with one of Manny's old belts like my father used to do me, but I know that would only make my stubborn child that much more stubborn." She crossed the room and picked up my worn Bible from the built-in desk in the corner and lifted it high. "I know God and the Bible are supposed to be the solution. I hear the pastor say it. I hear counselors say it, but somehow those techniques, the ones they say they've developed from the scriptures, don't seem to work with my son."

I smiled at my friend. "Maybe they haven't worked—*yet*."

Reva gave me a sheepish nod. "That may be true, Valentine, but it's so frustrating to see David wasting his high school years, his life. What if he doesn't make it into college? Manny had such great expectations for our son. I feel like I'm letting him down."

"I heard one of those TV pastors tell of a mom who bemoaned how she'd lost all control over her high school daughter and couldn't understand why. You know what advice he gave her?"

My three friends looked as me as if they were hanging on my every word and expected some kind of magic solution. "He told that mother, 'All you can do is all you can do.'" I shrugged, not sure I should be the one to elaborate.

Thoughtfully fingering her silver hair, Edna picked it up from there, "And he was right. There are so many influences in your children's lives. Think about it. You have your kids until they reach school age. Then what happens? By the time they ride the school bus to and from school, they're away from home anywhere from nine to ten hours. Add the time they spend with their friends, after-school functions, homework, and the myriad of other things kids do, and parents are lucky if they have one hour a day with them. And parents are the bad guys. The ones who make them clean their rooms, do their homework, dump the trash, feed the dog, and refuse to give them any advances on their allowance. Is it any wonder we lose control?"

Reva nodded while a faint grin settled on her lips. "When you put it that way, it's amazing we have any control at all. I love David. He's my only child, but I feel like such a failure. I had visions of rearing the perfect boy. Man, was that ever a pipe dream."

"We've all have that dream, Reva." Sally's fingers twisted at the wedding band she still wore on the third finger of her left hand. "Remember when we made those vows? For better and for worse? We were young and eager to get on with life, sure we could conquer anything, but I wonder if any bride or groom has any idea what they're saying."

Silence hung heavy in the room as we thought over Sally's words. Her abrupt change in subject caught us all off guard.

"Did any of you ever consider divorce?"

Sally, Edna, and I turned toward Reva.

"Manny and I did . . . once," she confessed, not waiting for an answer, her voice barely audible. "Looking back, I realize now it was all my fault. It was a money thing. I had my heart set on new furniture for our living room and had made it perfectly clear that's what I wanted for my birthday. Manny kept telling me we couldn't afford new furniture right then, but I thought he was just telling me that so he could surprise me. He was always doing nice things to surprise me." Reva's face held a wistfulness of remembrance.

Sally's big, round eyes widened. "So? Did he surprise you?"

"He sure did. I watched out the window all day, looking for a furniture truck to arrive. I was so sure it was coming I'd already shoved the old couch and chair into the dining room to make room for it. About three o'clock, I saw a truck coming down the street. I could hardly contain my delight. But as I stood waiting for the truck to turn into our driveway, my heart skipped a beat. It passed our house and continued on down the block. I raced out frantically waving my arms in the air, thinking maybe they'd gotten the wrong address, but they just kept going. I told myself they would make a U-turn at the end of the block, turn around and come back."

Caught up in her story, I hunched toward her. "Did they?"

Reva closed her eyes and leaned back in the chair, her shoulders sagging. "No. My new living room furniture, the furniture I'd been hoping for, never arrived."

"Oh, boy. I'll bet you let Manny have it when he got home," Sally said.

"I would have, but I got to thinking maybe Manny had decided to give me a birthday card, with a note inside, telling me when the furniture would be delivered."

Edna leaned forward in her chair. "Did he?"

"He gave me a beautiful card all right, and there *was* a note inside, along with something else. A fifty-dollar gift certificate to a local kitchen gadget shop. The note said he'd noticed my electric grill hadn't been working properly and thought I could buy a new one." Reva bit at her lip. "What an unromantic gesture that was! I'd never been so hurt in my whole life, and I let him know it. I tore into him, criticizing him for everything he'd ever done that I hadn't liked. My meek accountant husband just stood there with his jaw hanging low. Especially when I said perhaps it was time for him to move out!"

I gaped at Reva. I'd gotten plenty mad at Carter a few times, but never over something as inconsequential as furniture. But then, I knew our financial situation was a whole lot different than Reva's and Manny's. "Surely you wouldn't divorce that good man over a new sofa and chair."

Reva nodded her head in the affirmative. "I know it sounds silly now, but you have no idea how important a new sofa and chair was to me at that point in my life. From the time Manny and I married we'd been on a tight budget. Most of our furniture had been hand-me-downs, too, and not at all what I would have picked out if I'd had a choice. I pouted for three whole days, speaking to him only when necessary, thinking I was married to the worst, uncaring monster in the whole world. Though he tried to explain to me that, as an accountant, he'd seen too many people who had bought things before they had the money to pay for them, racked up high credit card bills, and ended up in financial trouble, I wouldn't listen. I was tired of living from paycheck to paycheck. Instead, I told him I wanted out."

Sally's hand flew to her chest, and she let out a gasp. "Out of your marriage? You didn't!"

Reva stood, walked slowly to the storm door and stood gazing out at my backyard. "Yes, out of our marriage. I told him I wanted a divorce and was going to look for a man who could give me nice things, instead of someone else's castoffs."

"What did Manny say? Surely, he didn't let you go," Edna said.

"He didn't say anything—just walked out of the room. Since I'd already asked him to sleep in the spare bedroom, I was all alone with my thoughts. By the time I crawled out of bed the next morning, Manny was gone. I'd realized what a fool I'd been and had decided to apologize to him, but when I called his office, they said he was out and couldn't be reached. I was heartsick. I was so afraid he'd taken a new job out of town that had been offered to him, and the next place I would see him would be in divorce court."

"He didn't even phone you?" Sally asked.

"No, but at exactly two o'clock a big truck pulled into our driveway. A furniture truck with not only the sofa and chair I'd wanted but also the new coffee table and two end tables I'd had my eye on. I couldn't believe it! When I opened the door, the man handed me an envelope. It was a card from Manny saying he loved me and would never let me go. Even if it meant going into debt—my happiness meant more to him than all the money in the world."

Sally clapped her hands with glee. "Oh, that is so wonderful! And you got your new furniture after all!"

A big smile blanketed Reva's face as she crossed the room and slipped back into her chair at the table. "Actually, no, I didn't get it. I told the delivery man to take the furniture back to the store. I no longer needed it. Up to that point, I'd been taking Manny for granted but, that day, by going against his personal convictions about money and debt, my husband had proven he loved me. Suddenly, that love and the sacrifice he was willing to make to ensure my happiness was all I needed. The furniture had lost its importance."

Sally dabbed at her eyes with her sleeve. "Oh, Reva, what a heart-touching experience."

Edna bobbed her head in agreement. "Sometimes men can be so thoughtful."

Reva's face brightened. "But that's not the end of my story. Manny and I had been trying so hard to have a baby. There didn't seem to be any physical reason to keep us from it; it just didn't happen. But eight weeks after I sent that furniture back to the store, I found out I was pregnant with David."

I swallowed hard, my emotions spinning out of control. "Your Manny loved you dearly."

"I—I loved him dearly, too. Remember the floral sofa and matching chair I have in my living room?"

The three of us nodded.

"Four years later, on my birthday, that even prettier sofa and chair arrived, but this time my husband had the cash to pay for it, so we were both happy." Reva hung her head and nibbled at her lip. "Can you believe I was ready to throw away our marriage over something so trivial as new furniture?"

Sally's lips pressed into a thin line. "I can. Been there—done that."

My brows rose in surprise. "You, Sally? No! I find that hard to believe. I've never seen a more godly man than your Eric."

"I'm afraid, like Reva, our problems were with me, not my husband. At one time, I—I thought Eric was cheating on me."

This time, it was me who gasped. "Eric would never cheat on you!"

"I was smart enough to finally figure that out, but it took me nearly a year. It happened when I was pregnant with Jessica and then after she was born, too." Sally turned to me. "Remember how big I got? Despite my doctor's warning, I gained nearly sixty pounds with that child. I literally ate myself into oblivion, using that eating-for-two thing as my excuse. I felt like a whale. Eric asked me—no, pleaded with me—to keep my weight under control, but I laughed it off, fooling myself by saying it would all come off once our baby was born. It didn't."

Avoiding our gazes, Sally fingered her place mat. "Eric had just started his plumbing company and was spending nearly sixteen hours a day trying to get it on its feet, so he was rarely at home. When he was home, he was either working on books or trying to catch a few hours' sleep. But knowing how awful I looked, and how tired I was having to take care of a newborn, colicky baby by myself, I let the green-eyed monster come between us, sure he was looking at other women. When I found a sticky note in Eric's pocket with a woman's first name and phone number on it, I flew into a rage and accused him of being unfaithful."

Though I was Sally's best friend, her revelation sent shivers down my spine. I'd known there was something going on in her life at that time, but nothing like that. Whenever I'd asked her about it and she'd deny having a problem, I'd simply attributed her roller-coaster mood swings to postpartum depression.

Reva rotated the sugar container between her hands meditatively. "That green-eyed monster has broken up many a marriage."

Sally bobbed her head. "I was too embarrassed to tell anyone, not even Valentine. I just sulked by myself. Eric explained that the phone number was the number of one of his key clients. He said she was old and severely handicapped, but she owned several large apartment buildings and depended on him to take care of any plumbing problems that arose. Do you think I believed him? Did I pray about it and let God handle it? No. Instead, I did something really stupid. I wasn't about to let that woman have my husband so I looked up her address in the phone book, dressed baby Jessica in her prettiest outfit, loaded her into her infant carrier, and marched right up to that woman's luxurious apart-ment, ready to confront her."

Both Reva's eyes and mine bugged out. Edna simply smiled. "You didn't!" I said.

"Yes, I did."

"What did she have to say when you confronted her?" Reva asked.

As we stared at Sally, a gigantic smile crossed her face and she began to laugh almost hysterically. "She said, 'Come in, my dear, and let me see that sweet baby.' The woman, though quite attractive, had to be in her late seventies and, as Eric had said, was confined to a wheelchair. He had been telling the truth all the time. I was so stunned I just stood there like an idiot, trying to come up with some reason for showing up at her door. I finally blurted out that my husband had said such nice things about her that I wanted to meet her. She actually believed me. I spent about an hour with her, having tea and looking at her photo albums; then I left."

"Was Eric mad when he learned you'd gone to see her?" Edna asked.

Again, Sally grinned. "Actually, once he found out I hadn't offended her by saying something I shouldn't have, he told me he was glad I'd gone. Knowing how naive I am, he was flattered that I had been so adamant about not letting some floozy break up our marriage and was willing to do battle to keep him. From that day on, Eric made sure to set aside a little time each day to be with me. His attention was all I'd really wanted, and once I got it, everything changed. That's when we began our Friday night dates."

Edna patted Sally's hand. "I'm so glad the two of you worked things out."

"Me, too." The smile on Sally's face told it all.

"My marriage to Warren wasn't perfect—" Edna paused, her expression turning into a shy grin. "But nearly perfect. At least, that's the way I remember it. Maybe I'm choosing to forget the bad times." She turned toward me. "What about you and Carter, Valentine?"

"If you're asking if we ever considered divorce, the answer is yes—but only one stupid time. Once we got through those first years and sold our electric company, finances were never an issue. However, we did have a few other stressful times. I've already told you about the lawsuit that could have wiped us out."

Sally slammed her palms together with disgust. "Someone needs to put an end to those—it seems anyone can sue anyone else for no reason whatsoever."

"Well, our lawsuit wasn't our only bad time. Not being able to conceive caused many tense moments between us. I was so sure it was Carter's fault, and he was sure it was mine. We argued about it all the time. When we were each finally tested and the results came in saying Carter's sperm count was way too low to allow for conception, it nearly killed him. I can't tell you how much we both wanted a baby. For a few weeks that man literally withdrew from nearly everything in his life. He even tried to talk me into divorcing him so I could find a man who could give me the children he knew I wanted. But, of course, I wouldn't hear of it. I couldn't imagine life without Carter."

I tried to tamp down the sudden rush of emotions that spilled over as I spoke about my beloved husband and the trials that nearly ruined our marriage, but a stream of tears flowed down my cheeks anyway. "But, here I am," I said, blinking hard, "a number of years later, without him, and I don't like it one bit. I've often wondered if this is God's punishment for all my complaining."

Edna's hand gripped my wrist. "Now, dear, you know our God is a loving God. He's not out to punish those whose hearts are turned toward him. You mustn't say things like that."

Sally gave her head a sad shake. "That was when Carter quit serving on the worship team."

"Yes, it was. For months after the doctor gave us that news, Carter refused to sing. His deep baritone voice was one of the things that attracted me to him in the first place. When we were courting, he sang me love songs." I wiped at my tears with the back of my hand. "Now he's singing love songs to God."

"And I know he's enjoying every minute of it." Edna patted my hand.

Picking up her purse from the floor, Sally rose and headed for the door. "I've got to go. I promised Michael I'd take him to the mall. That youngest son of mine desperately needs a new pair of shoes."

Reva stood, too. "And I've got to go home and yank David out of bed. He hit the sack as soon as we got back from the cemetery. If he thinks he can stay out all night and sleep all day, he's got another think coming. Thanks for the coffee and the chitchat. Tomorrow, I'll bring donuts. You gals are my lifeline. I don't know what I'd do without you."

I joined them in a second group hug. "I wish Wendy could have been here. I know her arthritis has been kicking up, and she's going to have to have a hip replacement soon, but she's always able to retain that cheerful attitude of hers."

"I wish she lived here on Morning Glory Circle like you both do," Edna added. "It would make it so much easier for her to come to our morning chats."

Sally frowned. "Umm, I'm not so sure about that. This cul-de-sac already has the reputation of being Widow's Alley. I think all the real estate salesmen in town must be bringing their widowed clients here to our little corner of the world."

Suddenly remembering the moving van and the couple I'd seen earlier, I gave my hands a clap. "Guess what, girls. We have new neighbors! The moving van brought their furniture this morning."

Reva flinched. "Not another widow."

"No, a great-looking couple. I only saw them from the back, but they were both tastefully dressed and looked to be nice people. I didn't see any children, but that doesn't mean there aren't any. There is certainly plenty of room—"

The doorbell rang, interrupting my sentence.

Reva gestured toward the hall. "Want me to get it?"

I nodded. From the front hall we could hear the

48

voices of Reva and one other person who didn't sound at all like Wendy or anyone else I knew. Finally, Reva returned to the kitchen, smiling as though someone had told her the joke of the day.

"It's your new neighbor," she said with the strangest look on her face—kind of a combination of total shock and amusement all rolled up in one. "She says she hasn't had a chance to go shopping yet and wants to know if you would loan her a bottle of gin or a couple of cans of beer."

Gin?

Beer?

Those words clanged through my brain like a fire truck racing to a four-alarm fire. What kind of neighbor was moving in next to me?

"Or vodka, anything strong to drink. I can't imagine how I'll get through this moving thing without it," a female voice said from behind my friend.

I spun around just as my new neighbor walked up behind Reva.

"Barbie?" I said, my jaw dropping as I caught sight of her.

"Barbie Baxter? You're my new neighbor?"

CHAPTER 4

Valentine! You live in this house?"
    I nearly didn't recognize the woman who'd rung my doorbell. Barbie. The girl I'd known in high

school, my nemesis, was standing before me. Her long, flighty bleached-blond hair—which used to be dark brown—flowed like a huge halo over the shoulders of an amazingly beautiful Hawaiian print tunic that reached clear to the floor. As a teenager, she had been attractive, but now she was absolutely gorgeous. From the surprised expression on her face, I realized her seeing me was as much a surprise as me seeing her. "Yes, I do, and you've moved in next door?"

"Just this morning. When the real estate salesman told me a single woman lived in this house, I had no idea it would be you. Does that mean you and Carter are no longer together?"

Sally, bless her heart, stepped up beside me and answered for me. "Carter died three years ago."

Barbie's face took on a contrite expression. "I—I'm sorry. I didn't know. I moved away from Nashville right after my first year of college. He was a terrific guy. I wish I'd caught him. As I remember, that boy was one stud muffin."

My Carter a stud muffin? I glanced at her flawless complexion, her meticulously applied makeup, her willowy figure, her—my eyes came to rest on the third finger of her left hand. No ring? Surely, Barbie was married. Didn't I see her husband with her this morning? The attractive man in the dark suit, with the graying hair?

Barbie crossed her arms and began to size me up. "Well, I declare, Valentine. Will wonders never cease? Here I came over to this house to borrow something to

50

drink and I find my old schoolmate is my new neighbor."

"I'm Sally Norton." Releasing my hand after giving it a squeeze, Sally stepped toward Barbie then gestured toward Reva and Edna. "And these are our friends Edna Fitzwilliam and Reva Billingham. Reva and I are your neighbors, too."

I continued to gaze at Barbie. Though I hadn't seen or heard of her since high school, she was one of the last persons I would have expected to move in next door. God certainly had a sense of humor when He allowed her to turn up after all these years and move next to me.

I guess I shouldn't have been too surprised when Reva donned a smile and blurted out, "Welcome to the neighborhood, Barbie. The four of us, and sometimes a couple of other friends, meet here in Valentine's kitchen every morning about ten. You'll have to join us tomorrow."

Reva! I thought to myself, *You said you had a big mouth—now you've just proven it. Whatever were you thinking? You should have asked me before inviting her to my home!*

I glanced quickly at Sally and found her wide-eyed and appearing as bamboozled by Reva's impromptu invitation as I was.

A broad red-lipsticked smile broke out across Barbie's flawless face, revealing a perfect set of sparkling white teeth any dentist would be proud to say he'd created. I swear they even twinkled, like on those tooth-whitening toothpaste commercials.

"What a lovely idea," she drawled out, batting her eyes at the clueless Reva. "I'll be here. I'm usually finished with my two-mile walk by nine. That'll give me plenty of time to shower and dress before coming to Valentine's home. May I bring anything? A fruit bowl? Fresh pineapple?"

Reva shook her head. "No, just yourself."

Finished with her two-mile walk? What did she need to do that amount of exercising for? Her body already looked emaciated. She was at least fifteen pounds lighter than when I'd last seen her in high school. And that drawl? The woman had never had a Southern drawl when I'd known her. Where did that come from? Without realizing it, I caught myself staring at her. She said she'd moved recently. She'd probably moved here from Alabama or Louisiana or some other Southern state where she'd picked up the local twang. Or, maybe she just liked the idea of trying to sound Southern.

Suddenly realizing I hadn't said a word since my initial, *Barbie? You're my new neighbor?* I knew what I'd *like* to say, but restrained myself.

"Reva's right. You needn't bring anything," I finally spit out, struggling to keep my words from tripping over each other. "Reva has already volunteered to bring doughnuts." A second glance at her willowy figure and I tacked on, "Or don't you eat doughnuts?"

She ran her hands down her slim hips. "I don't eat anything that contains sugar so, if you don't mind, I'll ball up a nice, fresh cantaloupe and bring it along.

Fresh fruit is so good for our complexion."

Sally and I exchanged glances.

I had to know. Was she married to the man who'd been with her this morning? Trying to make it sound like a casual afterthought, I pasted on a smile that I hoped looked realistic and asked, "Is your husband from around here?"

Barbie gave me a questioning stare. "Husband? Which one?"

Which one? What kind of an answer was that?

Without waiting for my response, which may have been a long time coming since I had no idea how to answer, she went on, "You remember that rich Dirk Banes we went to school with, don't you?"

Did that name ever ring a bell. "Oh yes, I remember him. Always acted as if he were hot stuff. He asked me out once, but I turned him down cold. Something about the guy just turned me off. Maybe it was the fact that he treated girls as if they were appendages instead of people, or maybe I just didn't want to compete for mirror time."

She uttered a slight huff. "I turned down his offers for dates, too, in high school, but I felt differently about him when we went to college, especially after he turned up with that expensive car and seemed to have all the money he wanted to spend when most of us were struggling to pay our tuition. He and I married during the summer between my junior and senior year in college. But that man was a bore. He made fantastic money working for his daddy, but all he wanted to do with his free time was stay home and watch sports on ESPN. That lifestyle wasn't for me. I'm a mover and a shaker. We fought all the time. He had a terrible temper. I divorced him one year later for incompatibility. Got a nice settlement, too, thanks to his daddy who seemed as glad as Dirk to get rid of me. He was as big a bore as his son. I even got to keep the big diamond Daddy Bigbucks had bought for Dirk's mother. That thing is huge!"

"I do remember how wealthy his family was. He talked about it all the time. Oil investments, wasn't it?" After hearing her divorce bombshell, it was the best response I could come up with.

"Yes, oil and a whole lot of other things. I always thought they were into something illegal, but Dirk would never talk about their business. Which was fine with me, as long as I had carte blanche with his money and his credit cards." She put a finger to her chin thoughtfully. "Then there was Skip Morrison. I married him about six months later."

Reva's face brightened. "Surely you don't mean the Skip Morrison who used to do the evening news on network TV?"

That man had to be at least twenty years older than Barbie. Why would she marry a man that old? Then it hit me. The notoriety and the circle of influential friends and associates that must have surrounded such a well-known broadcaster. She always loved being the center of attention.

Barbie nodded with a smile of satisfaction. "Yes, that

Skip Morrison. He was a much better husband than Dirk, but the poor man nearly drank himself to death. The pressure of the television business, I guess. I tried to help him—really I did—but he just wouldn't listen to me or to anyone. When the doctor said the booze was eating up his liver and he'd be a mighty sick man if he didn't give it up, Skip said he'd rather die than quit drinking. I decided right then and there—I wanted out. I was much too young to be stuck with someone who wouldn't listen to his doctor and do what needed to be done. I hate weak people, and I certainly didn't want to have to take care of one!"

Sally's jaw dropped. "You divorced him, too?"

"I certainly did," Barbie snapped back, as if she'd done something wonderful instead of something so callous.

I wasn't shocked by her words. Nothing Barbie Baxter did would surprise me, except moving in next door to me. That surprised me!

"So you're single again?" Reva asked, her expression showing as much shock as Sally's and Edna's.

"Actually," Barbie cooed almost proudly, "I married one more time after Skip. A big wheel I'd met at one of the National Broadcaster meetings. Milton Borden was the best husband of all." She rolled her eyes. "For a while. But that all changed when he decided to leave me for his beautiful, young secretary."

Reva gasped as her hand flew to cover her mouth. "You poor thing! Unfortunately, that happens to so many women your age."

55

Barbie gave Reva a look that could have killed. I knew those words *your age* were not going to be well received by this woman who obviously was working hard, hard, hard to appear at least ten years younger than she really was.

"Don't feel sorry for me," Barbie responded, smiling, or should I say smirking, and shrugging her slender shoulders. "He didn't want to divorce me. He begged me to stay with him. The man was crazy about me. He just succumbed to temptation one time, so he said, and made a baby with that bimbo. After I threatened to go public and ruin his career, he never even contested the divorce. He gave me everything I asked for. Thanks to his philandering, I came out smelling like the proverbial rose. I almost wish I'd asked for more."

She made divorcing husbands sound like an occupation. What was wrong with this woman? Even if she wasn't a Christian, where were her values?

Barbie snapped her fingers then glanced at the oversized, ostentatious diamond watch on her wrist. "I'd better scoot. My real estate salesman is supposed to pick me up in an hour, and I have to get dressed. He's such a thoughtful man and absolutely gorgeous. He came over with me this morning to meet the moving van and see if he could help me with anything. Wasn't that considerate of him?"

She paused with a mischievous wink. "Lucky me. It's going to be so much fun having you all for neighbors. You must come to my house once the decorators get in and get their job finished, and my new furniture arrives. My home is going to be fabulous. Thanks to Milton and his wayward tendencies."

Stunned by her comment about her former husband, the four of us watched as Barbie, with a wave of her hand, called out, "Toodles!" then spun around on her heel and disappeared into my front hall. We stood there, jaws dropped, eyes bugged, until we heard the front door click shut.

Sally turned to face me and let out an exaggerated sigh. "So that's the infamous Barbie."

I blinked hard, trying to remember if I'd just had a nightmare and it was all a dream, or if the real Barbie Baxter had stood in my kitchen bragging about her three marriages and talking about the house she'd moved into next door.

Unfortunately, it was all real.

Too real.

And she'd forgotten all about the gin and beer she'd come to borrow.

When the phone rang at about three that afternoon, I half expected it would be Sally, wanting to rehash Barbie's unexpected morning appearance but, instead, it was Pastor Wyman.

"How are you doing, Valentine?" he asked in that kindly voice of his that always made me know he cared. "I mean *really* doing?"

Even though I was on the phone, I shifted my shoulders and lifted my head, which was my usual stance when someone asked me that question. "I'm doing okay. Thank you for asking. I still miss Carter and always will, but I'm resolving myself to the fact that life goes on and Carter would want me to go on, too. "

"Carter was a good man." He paused then cleared his throat. "I asked how you were getting along for a purpose. The church board met last night, and we decided it was time Cooperville Community Church had a bazaar, as a fund-raiser for the new youth building we so desperately need for our kids."

The pastor's announcement set my heart singing. Seeing a youth center built for our church's young people had been one of Carter's dreams, but why was Pastor Wyman calling *me* about it?

"We need someone to head this thing up, Valentine, and we think you are the perfect person to do it."

I nearly dropped the phone. *Me?* I'd never done anything like this before. The job would be monumental.

"We want to do this thing up right, make it a two-day affair. If it goes as well as we think it will, we'd like to make it an annual affair. We see it not only as a fund-raiser but also as a means of getting new people into our church. It will be a sort of outreach to our community and the surrounding area."

I stood there listening, pondering. It sounded like such a good idea, and though I'd never worked on a bazaar before, I did have the organizational and delegating skills to put something together and make it happen. Hadn't I helped Carter establish our two businesses? Hadn't I handled the selling of our construction company and everything that went with it after his death?

"As the bazaar's organizer, you'll have full charge. The board has great confidence in you and your ability to make decisions, and will back you in every way. You can set the entire thing up the way you think it will work best, name your committees and appoint their chairpersons, decide on the date—all of it. It'll be your baby. We'll give you time to think it over and pray about it, but we're really hoping your answer will be yes. There's no one we'd rather have head this up than you."

Closing my gaping mouth, I clutched the receiver even tighter, my heart pounding in erratic thundering beats. *Me! They want* me *to head up the bazaar.* I knew Carter would want me to do it. A youth building had been his dream for as long as I could remember. Tingles of excitement ran up and down my spine as ideas crowded themselves into my mind. I wanted to do this. I really wanted to! For God *and* for Carter.

Trying to tamp down my enthusiasm a few notches so Pastor Wyman wouldn't think I had no idea what I was getting myself into, I slammed my eyelids shut, swallowed hard, sucked in a gulp of air and, trying to sound calm, said, "I don't need time to think it over, Pastor. I'm sure the Lord would say yes if I asked Him. I'll do it!"

"Good, Valentine. The board will be happy to hear you've accepted. But don't worry, we aren't going to leave you out there, stranded without help. We've appointed Robert Chase as liaison between you and the board. You can call him anytime you need assistance or have questions."

I was glad to hear it was Robert Chase. He'd only been coming to our church for about two years so I didn't know him well, but from what others had told me he was not only a devout Christian but also an all-around nice man. Though this was his first year to serve on the church board, he had come well recommended by the pastor of his former church in Atlanta. He was the kind of man Carter would have picked for a friend.

Pastor Wyman and I talked for another half hour, covering things like budgets, advertising, and the like, then, after thanking me and reminding me this was going to be a great, unselfish way to help our church, he said good-bye and hung up.

I wasn't sure if I should laugh or cry. I was so excited to be a part of this, especially since I knew Carter would want me to do it, but the responsibility was going to be awesome.

I headed for the desk in Carter's study, planning to make a few notes, but before I reached it someone rapped on my front door. Through the little peephole I could see a voluminous head of bleached blond hair topped by an exquisite wide-brimmed red hat, the kind I'd seen in old movies. A fancy big-brimmed one with a gigantic purple rose attached to one side of the crown. Barbie! What could she want? No gin or beer, I hoped.

When I pulled the door open, she rushed in and grabbed hold of my arm, her eyes pleading. "You've got to do me a favor, Valentine. Please say you will."

Me do *her* a favor? That was a new one. I suddenly realized she was wearing a purple dress and purple shoes—fancy high-heeled ones with red sequined bows on the toes—to go along with the red hat.

"I'm in a real bind," she said, not waiting for me to agree or disagree to her request. "I'm the queen— "

That I could understand. Barbie had always acted as though she thought of herself as a queen.

"—and as queen, at last month's Red Hat meeting, I encouraged every Red Hat lady to bring a guest to our annual Friends Dinner."

Red Hat, huh? I thought to myself. I had no idea she belonged to that social group, though I wasn't surprised. I was interested in joining a chapter myself.

"But Audra, a friend who used to live next door to me, just phoned and said she has a splitting migraine and can't go with me tonight. After that rousing speech I delivered, I can't show up without a guest. You have to come with me!"

"But—"

She tugged me toward the door. "I have a dozen purple dresses and a big selection of red hats. I'm sure there's something in my closet that will fit you. But you'll have to hurry. Our reservations at the restaurant are for seven."

I was curious to see what went on at those Red Hat meetings, but to go with Barbie? I was slightly flattered that she would even think of me. "Surely there's someone else you can call," I insisted, still reluctant to be her stand-in guest. I really didn't know her anymore, after all these years, and I wasn't sure being paraded by her in front of a bunch of strangers was the best way to start getting reacquainted.

She released my hand. "I've already called at least six people. You're my last hope."

So much for my being popular. Boy, did she know how to deflate a girl's ego.

I started to say no, but I heard that still, small voice. *You might be the one to reach Barbie for Me*, it said from the depths of my heart.

But how, God? my inner self asked. *She's a conceited twit.* Then the guilt came for thinking such a judgmental thought.

Before I knew it, I blurted out, "I'll go with you tonight, if you'll go to church with me on Sunday."

She snatched my hand again and gave it a shake. "Deal! Now grab your purse and come with me. I'm going to give you a makeover from head to toe. You won't know yourself when I get finished with you. You'll outshine everyone there—except me, of course. I'm the queen."

I sent up a quick prayer. *Lord, I know you want me to be a light to this woman, so please help me get through this evening without killing her!*

$\mathscr{C}$HAPTER 5

D o you really think she'll go to church with you?"
I tossed Sally a grin. "After what I went through last night for her? She'd better."

"And she really was the queen bee?"

Reva huffed. "I'll bet Valentine has the sting marks to prove it."

I had to laugh at their comments as we sat at the table in my kitchen. Anxious to hear how my evening had gone, they'd both come early, hoping to beat the queen to my house. Edna had called Reva to tell her she'd be too busy to join us today. Something about a blind date. I lifted an eyebrow at the news but let the comment go unexplored. I couldn't imagine Edna with any kind of date, especially a blind date. I doubted she'd dated anyone since her husband had died all those years ago. Maybe Reva was only teasing.

"Who named her Queen Bee?" Sally asked with wide, innocent eyes. "Is that some special mark of achievement?"

I shook my head. "Her title isn't really Queen Bee. She's Queen Barbie. The lady sitting next to me at the restaurant told me *Queen* is the title they give the one who forms the chapter. This chapter is made up mostly of friends and acquaintances of Barbie's. They haven't been meeting very long—less than a year, Barbie said. I guess she has been living in some plush apartment on the east side for the past year while her divorce from that Milton guy was going through. She attended a Red Hat group, enjoyed it, but wanted to be a queen, so she formed her own group."

Reva took another doughnut from the sack she'd brought and waved it at us. "So, were all the gals as high-falutin' as Barbie?"

"Actually," I admitted, "they were a very nice group. All clad in purple and red, of course, and with very elegant hats. Some even wore purple or red feather boas and those lace gloves. Dinner was at The Bistro. The manager seemed delighted to have us there—he came out and greeted us personally, flirted with the ladies as if they were teenagers. The tables were all beautifully set when we arrived with red baskets filled with cut purple chrysanthemums and red roses as centerpieces. We sure turned a lot of heads."

Sally pinched off half of a doughnut then dropped the other half back into the sack. "And you really wore Barbie's clothes?"

I giggled and covered my face with my hands, prominently displaying my purple-painted fingernails. "Right down to my bare skin. I even wore one of her new purple bras and new pair of purple undies! She had a stack of brand new ones, still in the packages. She let me keep the ones I wore. She said they were a gift to me, but I doubt I'll ever have a place to wear purple underwear, except to Red Hat meetings. Besides, they were way too small and nearly cut off my circulation. I could hardly wait to get them off. But I have to say, the evening was fun."

64

"So?" Sally said. "Details, dear, we want details!"

"Including guests," I went on, "there were about twenty-five of us, all clad in purple with red hats. Some were really decked out with official Red Hat rings, purses, jewelry, glasses cases, all sorts of things. After we finished a fabulous meal, there was a drawing for door prizes. I didn't win anything, of course, but a lot of the ladies did. They played a cute little get acquainted game which was interesting. Then the queen, or Drama Queen as I like to call her, took over, lavishing words of praise on those who'd been responsible for the planning of the meeting and the ordering of the centerpieces. She introduced me as her—get this—*best* friend from her high school days, then welcomed us all and made a few announcements as to the time and place of the next meeting. We visited and visited and visited until the restaurant was ready to close, then left, and Barbie brought me home."

"Did she invite you back?"

Unable to resist the heavily glazed doughnuts any longer, I reached into the sack and pulled one out. "Oh, yes. She not only invited me back, she invited me to become a member, right there in front of the whole group."

Sally's face filled with awe. "You're not going to do it, are you?"

I looked her square in the eye. "I already have. I'm officially a member of Barbie's 'Red Hat Babes.' Not only that, I promised to bring the two of you to their next meeting!"

65

I would have thought I'd said I was going to commit suicide from the look of astonishment on Sally's and Reva's faces.

"Yoo hoo!" a slightly Southern voice called out as the storm door to my kitchen opened and the queen herself walked in. "It's me. Barbie! Your friendly next-door neighbor!"

CHAPTER 6

Bummer. Barbie was early, and I hadn't yet had a chance to tell Sally and Reva about the bazaar. Well, it'd just have to wait. I didn't want to talk about it in front of her since I still didn't have a sense on where she stood spiritually, and I didn't want to offend her or make her feel awkward in any way.

"Lookie, lookie, lookie!" With her well made-up face exuding enthusiasm, Barbie crossed the kitchen. She wore a sheer pink and fuchsia floral chiffon blouse over a pink tank top and a pair of stark white, tight-fitting pants that clung to her body like a prime coat to Sheetrock. Excitedly, she waved a Tupperware carrier by its handle before settling it on the table in front of us. "Cantaloupe, honeydew, fresh pineapple, strawberries, red grapes, and orange wedges. Doesn't that sound yummy?"

With a flourish done only as Barbie could do it, she snapped off the lid, reached in with her purple-manicured fingers and popped a pale green honeydew

66

ball into her red, red lips. How could that woman be so chipper and look so good this time of morning? Her hair—which had a huge fuchsia-colored silk flower that matched the fuchsia of her shirt tucked into it—formed that abundant halo around her head and looked exactly the same as it had at the Red Hat meeting last night, as if her head had never touched the pillow.

I fingered my own hair. I'd had to use the curling iron this morning just to get it to settle down after sleeping on it. I glanced at her feet. Just as I suspected. A pair of stiletto fuchsia-colored heelless sandals cradled each foot and made her already slim legs look fantastic. I slid my well-worn flip-flops back beneath my seat, moving them slowly so as not to attract attention.

Without even asking where things were, she moved to my cabinets and began rummaging through them, opening doors and drawers until she located the small bowls and forks and a large serving spoon. Once back at the table she began to dole out her goodies.

Tacking on a plastic smile, I took the bowl and fork as she offered them to me then glanced at the big clear plastic container of fruit. I had to admit, it did look good.

Reva graciously accepted her bowl and fork, then looked at Barbie with an expression that said she was totally impressed. "You did all of this? It's beautiful!"

After releasing a high-pitched chuckle, Barbie gave Reva's shoulder a playful slap. "Sugar, would you believe me if I said yes?"

"Uh—I guess so." The look on Reva's normally

quick-to-respond face was priceless, a combination of bewilderment and naivety.

Barbie, who was now offering a bowl and fork to Sally, turned and gave her an almost mocking grin. "Of course I did. Haven't you heard? I'm a domestic goddess."

Poor Reva. From past history I knew Barbie was pulling her leg. She didn't.

With a toss of her head and a cackle that sounded as if she were about to lay an egg, the self-proclaimed domestic goddess slid into the only empty chair at the table. "I'm teasing, girls. The only domestic thing I'm good at is spending money! I bought the fruit medley in the grocery store deli."

Sally's widened eyes went back to their normal size and she smiled sweetly. "Well—it's just magnificent. Thank you for bringing it."

The halo-haired diva gave her an exaggerated from-the-waist-up bow. "I'm glad you like it." Barely missing a beat she turned to my friends and asked, her face shining with joy, "Did Valentine tell you about the Red Hat meeting I took her to last night?"

Sally speared a melon ball with her fork. "Valentine said you loaned her a beautiful purple dress and a magnificent red hat."

"I did, and she looked great in them. Everyone said so. Of course, I didn't loan her the new purple dress I'd purchased for myself." Barbie helped herself to a small serving of the fruit. "I try to never wear the same outfit twice. I'm the queen, you know."

Almost in unison, Sally and Reva said, "We know."

"It was nice of you to give Valentine that purple underwear," Sally said.

I felt my face flame. I could have wrung sweet, naive Sally's innocent little neck.

Barbie gave me a smirk as one perfectly waxed brow rose. "So? You told them about the purple undies? I kinda figured you would."

I felt like a dork. Trying to appear casual, I explained, "I told them about all the purple things you loaned me. The purse, hose, dress."

"And the red hat. One of the prettiest I own, I might add."

Actually, I wished she'd kept the purple undies and given me the red hat. It was gorgeous.

Sally leaned conspiratorially toward Barbie. "Where do you buy purple undies? I've never seen them where I shop."

"At a funny little boutique called Zazoo's Sexy Lingerie. You'd be surprised what they have there."

Mercy me. Just from the name, I hated to even think what that store might carry in the way of merchandise.

"But you must keep it a secret." Barbie tilted her head, muffling a laugh with her hand. "I don't want all my Red Hat friends running out and buying purple underwear like mine."

"I don't think you have to worry about the three of us letting your secret out, Barbie," I said, eager to change the subject for all our sakes. "I really did have a good time at your meeting last night. What a great group of women." I meant those words.

"Don't forget you promised to bring these two to our next meeting." Barbie gave me a smile. "Did you tell them the difference between the red and pink hats?"

I shrugged. "No, not yet. Why don't you tell them? You know more about it than I do."

Barbie edged toward them, seeming pleased for the opportunity to explain the difference to my friends. "Neither of you are old enough to become Red Hats yet—you have to be fifty—but you can attend all the functions as Ladies-in-Waiting until you reach fifty. But the Ladies-in-Waiting don't wear red and purple. They wear pink hats and lavender dresses or pantsuits."

Reva studied her for a moment. "Other than ball caps, I don't wear hats, and I sure don't have anything pink or lavender. I'm more a tan and beige kind of person."

Sally scrunched up her face with a distant look, as if mentally searching her closet. "I think I still have that pink hat I wore to my niece's wedding."

Barbie took center stage. "Don't worry about it. I'll loan you both something. Though neither of you are as slender as I am, I have a lavender caftan that would be perfect for you, Reva, and a pale lavender poncho Sally could wear over a pair of white pants. I'm sure I'll be able to come up with hats if you don't have them. I have an adorable pink sequined ball cap and a darling pink pill box covered with netting, kind of like Jacqueline Kennedy used to wear."

The visual image of Sally and Reva in those getups nearly made me laugh out loud.

With a quick glance at her watch, Barbie wadded up her paper napkin and tossed it into her bowl. "Sorry, girls, got to git. I'm having my roots touched up this morning and my nails redone. I'll catch you later."

"Whew! Whatever vitamins she's taking, I want a bottle," Sally told the others. "She must be on something."

Reva grinned a sarcastic grin. "Maybe it's all the fresh fruit."

"Could be!" I leaned toward them, both elbows on the table, and said, "Let's forget about Barbie for now. I have great news!"

For the next few minutes I gave them a nearly word-for-word repeat of my conversation with Pastor Wyman. Their reaction was just as I'd hoped it would be—wide-eyed and enthusiastic.

"And I want you two to head up the most important committees." I turned to Sally first. "Sally, you're a people person. Everyone likes you. I need you to head up the booth development committee. I figure with a church the size of ours and with the many talented, crafty women we have, we should be able to have at least thirty booths."

Sally nearly choked on her coffee. "Thirty booths? You really think we can get that many women to participate? That's a lot of booths."

I gave her a smile of encouragement. "Think about it. Thirty isn't really that many." Retrieving the notebook in which I'd already begun to jot ideas, I flipped open a page and shoved it across the table. "Look. See all those names? Each woman listed here is great at doing some type of craft."

After perusing the list, Sally lifted her face with a smile. "I might even make up a few of those stained-glass ornaments, like the ones I gave you two for Christmas a few years ago. Do you think those would sell?"

"Sell?" Reva pulled the book toward her. "I'll buy several myself, to give as Christmas gifts to my family. Everyone who comes to my house comments on them."

Sally's face took on a wistful expression. "Jessica helped me make those, but that was before she went off the deep end. Hopefully, she'll help me again. It'd really be nice to do a project with my daughter, if I could get her away from those freaky friends long enough to do it."

Reva looked up from the notebook. "What'd you have in mind for me, Valentine?"

I thought she'd never ask. "Well," I drawled out, knowing the job I was about to ask of her was going to be enormous, but definitely one she was qualified to undertake. "Your committee will be in charge of building the booths."

She sputtered and nearly choked on the glass of water she'd poured herself while Sally and I were discussing the crafts. "Thirty booths? You want *me* to build thirty booths?"

Turning quickly, I reached across the space between

us and gave her a sharp rap between her shoulder blades. "You, and as many committee members as you'll need to do the job. We'll use the Sunday school tables covered with drops for the front of the booths and across the back, but we'll need some kind of dividers on either side. I was thinking of maybe curtains or sheeting hung from poles, that sort of thing. I'll leave it up to you to decide what will work best."

You could almost hear the woman's brain clacking away with ideas, which was exactly the response I'd hoped for. "You could ask some of the men to help. I'm sure they—"

Her hand shot up between us. "No, no men. If the women of the church are going to put this thing on, I think we should leave the men out of it. I'm not the only woman in our congregation who is handy with a hammer, saw, drill and screwdriver. I think we can do it without them."

Remembering what the pastor had said, I shrugged. "Well, I'm sure they'll be there if you need them. I'll leave that decision up to you."

Sally pulled the book back toward her, her finger scanning the notes I'd made. "What about Wendy? I know she'll want to help."

"I'm saving her for the most important part, as prayer committee chairwoman. If this thing is going to be done up right, we'll need all the prayer we can get. No one can pray like our Wendy, and I'm sure she'll find others who'll want to join her. So many of our older ladies are confined to their homes most of the time but would still like to help in any way they can. I figure as we get into this thing, whenever we run into a problem we'll send an SOS call to Wendy, and she'll get her committee of prayer warriors on the job." I couldn't resist a smile as I thought of Wendy's saintly, wrinkled face. "How could God refuse those sweet old girls?"

"They're a force to be reckoned with, for sure," Sally said. "Wendy has counseled more women than we'll ever know about. Even with that frail, arthritis-ridden body of hers, she's always available to anyone who needs her." She stopped her scanning long enough to pop another melon ball into her mouth along with a single grape. "You know—these things are good."

"So?" I asked, feeling fairly confident the answer was going to be yes, "Can I count on both of you? Come on, girls, don't desert me now. I know you both have your hands full, but the change and having a new worthwhile project might be good for all of us."

Sally lifted her hand. "I'm in."

Reva did, too. "You know you can count on me. When is this bazaar supposed to take place?"

"I'm thinking of four months from today. I'd like to have it sooner, but the women who will be reserving booths will need time to make the items they'll be selling. Plus, there's a lot of preliminary work that needs to be done and many decisions to be made."

"What about signs for the booths?" Reva asked, her enthusiasm rising with each new question as we discussed it. "Do you want my committee to be responsible for those, too?"

74

"Sure would be nice if you could." Pulling the book back in front of me I checked my list again. "Baked goods always sell really well at all the church bazaars I've attended. I was thinking of appointing Dotty Pragel as chairwoman of that committee, and I was going to ask Ann Bonner to chair the committee in charge of the luncheons and dinners we'll be serving. Both are extremely efficient women and born leaders. And of course Edna will be our treasurer—since she used to work as an accountant's assistant, she's so good with that sort of thing."

They both nodded in agreement.

I paused long enough to spear an orange wedge with my fork. "You both know Bitsy Foster, don't you?"

Sally eyed my orange wedge then speared one for herself. "That adorable young girl whose husband is serving in Iraq?"

I bobbed my head. "It'd be bad enough having your husband in that awful place, but to be pregnant, too? And without any family nearby to help you? I'm not sure what I would do in her situation. I don't think I could handle it. Do you realize Bitsy is barely twenty?"

Leaving one lone melon ball uneaten, Reva pushed her bowl aside and shook her head. "How far along is she?"

I hurriedly did the math on my fingers. "Due in about eight, maybe nine weeks, I guess. I was thinking of asking Bitsy to co-chair the publicity committee with Trudy Simon."

Sally shoved the notebook back my way and sat up straight. "What a great idea, but won't it be difficult for her to co-chair that committee with a new baby on the way?"

"By cochairing with Trudy, it shouldn't be too hard. They'll need to create flyers. Those can be done right away so they'll be ready for distributing later on. And they'll also need to set up interviews. Most of that can be done over the phone before the baby comes. Trudy has already agreed to handle everything that comes up after Bitsy's baby is born. I just think it will be an easy way to get Bitsy involved in the church, even if it will be a short-term job."

Everyone present agreed, and it was decided that I would contact Bitsy and invite her to my house for the initial organizational meeting.

For the next hour we talked about others we thought would be good to serve as chairwomen of the various committees. As that conversation waned, I turned to Sally. "Things going any better between you and Jessica?"

"I'm afraid not. I got a call from the school principal yesterday saying if Jessica didn't get her grades up she was going to have to repeat this school year. She keeps talking about getting a job and moving out anyway, as if she could support herself on whatever kind of job a fifteen-year-old inexperienced girl could get." With a sigh, she folded her hands in her lap. "What if she just disappears and I never hear from her again?"

"That's a constant worry for me, too, Sal. I just

learned David got fired from his weekend job at the car wash. He and another guy put a big scratch in some man's new Lexus."

"I'm sorry, Reva," I said, hurting for her.

Reva let her shoulders droop dejectedly. "David's friends are as rebellious as he is. I wish they'd all wake up before it's too late."

Despite her efforts to hold them back, tears rained from Sally's eyes. "With all the peer pressure our kids face these days, they could get into real trouble."

"You're so right." Reva lowered her gaze and nibbled on her lip. "I—I found one of those tiny, expensive MP3 players stuffed under the mattress in David's room. He sure didn't have the money to buy it."

"Did you question him about it?" I asked cautiously.

"Sure did. He said exactly what I'd thought he'd say. Said he'd borrowed it from a friend."

All color drained from Sally's face. "Was the MP3 player a silver color with a little green neck cord attached to it?"

Both Reva and I turned our undivided attention toward her.

"I found one in Jessica's jewelry box. She told me the same borrowed-from-a-friend story David told Reva. Like an idiot, I believed her. You—" She paused, her hand going to cover her mouth as her eyes widened. "You don't suppose they stole those things, do you?"

"Oh, precious Lord, I hope not." I said it as much a prayer as a statement. "Being rebellious and messing

77

up on your grades is one thing, but stealing? That could get them in a whole peck of trouble and put a nasty blight on their record."

Reva gave her head a shake. "Having a record doesn't worry teenagers. They know as soon as they reach adulthood those juvenile records will no longer stand. That's why drug pushers can get teens to make the contacts and sell drugs for them."

Sally nodded in agreement. "I'm trying so hard to bring my children up the way I should, but Jessica thinks I'm old-fashioned and clueless. She sees *me* as the bad guy. She now claims God is nothing more than a fairy tale. I have to drag her to church. If she ran away, I wouldn't have any idea how to go about finding her."

Suddenly, though the planning of the bazaar had become the most important thing in my life, it took a temporary backseat. "I know you're both going through a lot of stress," I told the nearest and dearest friends I'd ever had. "If you'd rather not help with the bazaar I'll understand." Though there was no way I could do it, I wanted so badly to work out all their problems for them.

"No. I want to do it. I'm really looking forward to working on the bazaar," Reva said, lifting her chin. "I think it's exactly what I need."

Sally took hold of my hand and smiled up at me. "I feel the same way, Valentine. I think Jessica seeing me helping with the church bazaar would be a better testimony to her than all the words I could say to her in anger, which is about the only way we communicate these days."

"What about Michael and Charlotte?" I asked, hoping against hope Sally's younger children weren't looking to their older sister as a role model. "Serving as chairwoman is going to take you away from home quite a bit."

"I'm hoping to get Charlotte involved with me. She's a great little organizer and is as repelled by her sister's appearance and behavior as I am. And Michael? He and that nice boy who lives next door to us spend every afternoon together building model airplanes. His mother is a stay-at-home mom and has told me Michael is welcome to stay with them anytime I need to be away."

"That's really nice of her," I said. I was glad Sally had such a considerate neighbor.

Pushing her cup aside, Sally gave us a feeble smile. "Though she's a lovely woman, she's not a Christian—yet—but I'm working on it. I know she'll want to come to our bazaar."

We turned our heads in unison as the back door opened.

"Well, lucky you!" a female voice said brightly as a bleached blond, sans dark roots, ambled her way across my kitchen, holding up ten fingers newly manicured in a bright, bright magenta. "You get to see me one more time today."

Barbie was back.

"I forgot to ask you what time I should be ready in

the morning. To go to church with you."

Would wonders never cease? Barbie was actually going to church with me like she'd promised? I'd figured she'd find some way to wheedle out of it.

"The morning worship service starts at ten forty-five. I'll pick you up about ten fifteen." I decided it would be worth missing Sunday school just this one time to make sure she didn't have to drive to the church alone.

"Is there anything special I should know to prepare myself? I haven't been to church since I was in diapers." She gave us that flagrant smile of hers, the one she always donned when she thought she'd said something clever.

"No. Nothing special. I think you'll enjoy the service."

"Okay then, I'll see you at ten fifteen." Taking a quick glance at the table and seeing the sack of doughnuts and our coffee cups still sitting there, she gave her head a shake. "I've been gone more than two hours. What *have* you three been up to since I left?"

Sally, Reva, and I sent quick glances toward one another. We'd been so engrossed in our discussion about the bazaar we'd worked right through the lunch hour without even noticing. Of course, we *had* pigged out on doughnuts and the fresh fruit Barbie had brought, so our tummies certainly hadn't been deprived of nourishment.

Not waiting for an answer, Barbie picked up my open notebook and glanced at the cover. "Plans for the Cooperville Community Church Bazaar," she read aloud as we all squirmed in our seats. I knew Sally and Reva were thinking the same thing I was. Being new to the neighborhood, I knew Queen Barbie would want to get involved.

I reached for the book, but Barbie stepped back and began flipping the pages. "You're the head honcho on this project, Valentine? How exciting! I'll be able to give you lots of advice. When I was living in Atlanta—"

Atlanta? Now I knew where that Southern accent came from.

"—I was the chairwoman of the most successful fund-raising event the Atlanta Symphony had ever had."

When she paused, sat down at the table, and made herself comfortable, I knew we were in for a full replay, and I was right.

"I put together this marvelous masquerade ball with a Victorian theme, much like you see in the movies. The women wore lavish ball gowns, and the men were in elegant tuxedos. Everyone wore the most gaudy, showy masks you can imagine." She fanned out her fingers like a peacock's tail. "Some with feathers, some covered with sequins or jewels, some even had fur. You know the kind of masks I mean, where the men wear those little elastic strings around the back of their heads to hold their masks on, but the women's masks are mounted on those stick things that they hold in their hands. I tell you it was something to behold. I even gave prizes for the most unusual mask."

Sally sat spellbound, her eyes glued on Queen Barbie.

Reva just stared.

I rolled my eyes, hoping the others wouldn't notice, though I admit I, too, was impressed.

"At midnight, I awarded prizes for the most beautifully gowned woman and the most handsomely dressed man." Now it was Barbie who rolled her eyes. "Though in all honesty, *I* was the best dressed woman there but, of course, as chairperson of the ball, I wasn't eligible to win."

Still spellbound, Sally asked, "What did you wear?"

Rising, Barbie stood tall, her chin lifted high. "I had on the most exquisite floor-length peacock blue satin gown you've ever seen. One shoulder and arm were covered by a jewel-trimmed long sleeve—" She dramatically ran a fingertip from her shoulder to her wrist. "The other shoulder was completely bare."

A little, "Oh," escaped Sally's lips as she stared at the woman. "It sounds so elegant."

"And uncomfortable. Whatever did you do for a bra?" Reva asked.

Only good old practical Reva would have thought to ask such a question.

Barbie gave a slightly disgusted look but recouped quickly, tacking on her dazzling smile again. It was obvious she was enjoying *performing* for us, her captive audience of three. "A strapless bra, of course. Haven't you ever worn one?"

Reva shook her head. "Never needed one. My shirts and dresses all have two sleeves."

Chalk one up for Reva.

"Anyway," Barbie continued, ignoring Reva's comment, "it had one of those tightly fitted waists with the little point extending down over the navel area into the extremely full skirt—so full, I had to wear one of those hoops under it. If my dress had been red velvet, I would have looked exactly like Scarlet O'Hara," she said proudly, striking a pose.

Sally, the woman I called friend, sat staring at Barbie with admiration, her eyes riveted on this woman who had caused me so much trouble in the past. Yet, I had to admit, there was something different about the woman now, something a little less cavalier. I could sense it in the pauses, the almost sadness that filled her eyes at times, even when she was bragging.

"Everyone said I was the real belle of the ball!" Our storyteller fluffed up her blond halo with the tips of her fingers. "I should have gotten that prize. I looked spectacular!"

"What was the prize?" my naive Sally asked, her hands still cupping her chin.

"It was a gorgeous bronze casting of an Atlanta peach blossom, complete with intricately shaped leaves, with the words *Atlanta's Queen of the Ball* engraved onto it in a beautiful script. The queen's name was added to it later. I would have given anything to have had it to put on my mantel." Barbie stood in a daze, her hand extended, palm up, as if she were holding that imagined bronze casting in her hand.

For a ridiculously long moment, no one spoke.

Finally, Sally asked, "Did you win the next year?"

Apparently Sally's question brought her back to the present, because with a flip of her shoulders Barbie sat back down. "No. I married husband number three, and we moved away."

Sally let out a groan. "It's too bad you had to move. I'll bet you would have won that next year."

Barbie gave her head a sassy tilt and Sally a smug smile. "I'll just bet I would."

Did I say Sally was naïve? Poor girl probably believed every word Barbie was saying. Me? I doubted she was even the chairperson, let alone worthy of being named Queen of the Ball, but what did I know? I've never even been to Atlanta.

Not jealous, are you?

I quickly looked about the room, but other than Barbie and my two friends, no one else was there. Had that question come from the recesses of my heart? Or was God actually speaking to me? I gave my head a shake to clear my thoughts. Whether He was talking to me or it was simply my conscience, I knew the green-eyed monster had struck again, and I was his willing victim.

Barbie clapped her hands together. "Well, you girls might have all day to drink coffee and chitchat, but I have places to go and people to see. Like that yummy real estate agent of mine. That guy is a real man. Nothing sissy about him. We're going to have dinner tonight at that little barbecue place down by the river then take a moonlight ride on his new Honda Gold Wing."

84

And get bugs on your teeth and cramps in your legs,
I wanted to add, but didn't.

She gave us a wicked wink then added, "Maybe after
our romantic little ride, he'll invite me to his home to
see his etchings."

Etchings? Oh, my.

"Doesn't that sound like fun? Riding out under the
stars with my arms wrapped around his waist, my head
resting on his broad shoulders?"

"Yeah, fun," I uttered in an almost groan, remembering how my husband had gone through his midlife
motorcycle crisis and I'd refused to ride on that scary
thing with him. He ended up taking that long trip to the
Grand Canyon with one of his buddies instead of me,
and I stayed home worrying about him. Now I wished
I would have gone.

I took one look at that capacious head of hair, fresh
from a trip to the beauty shop, and wondered how in
the world she would ever get that mass tucked up
under a helmet. But, knowing her, she'd be able to do
it and still look as magnificent as ever.

She fixed me with a ridiculing stare and let loose a
most unladylike snort. "Surely, *you* have a boyfriend,
don't you, Valentine?"

I not only felt Barbie's inquisitive look, but also
Reva's and Sally's. Though those two had been on me
for some time to attend the singles' night praise service
with them, I had refused. I just wasn't ready for the singles' scene yet. I wasn't sure I ever would be. "No, no
boyfriend," I answered simply, realizing I owed her no

more information than that.

"What? An attractive woman like you? I'd think those goody-goody men at your church would be ringing that phone of yours off the hook. You'd better be careful, Valentine, or the world is going to pass you by." A wicked smile burst forth on her lips. "But don't you worry, sugar. I have plenty of men to share. Say the word and I'll have you out on the dating scene in no time."

Me? On the dating scene? I thought not, and, even if I wanted to date—which I didn't—I certainly wouldn't be interested in one of Barbie's men. Barbie's Babes, I liked. But her men? I doubted they would be my style, and more importantly—Christians. "Thanks, but no thanks. At this point in my life, I'm still not ready to date."

"Let me know if you change your mind." Barbie spun on her stilettos, gave us her trademark "Toodles," and was out the door.

"You gotta admit she adds some pizzazz to the neighborhood," Sally finally said, her gaze still anchored on my back door.

I breathed a sigh. "That she does."

CHAPTER 7

Barbie met me at her front door the next morning, looking bright-eyed and more beautiful than any woman our age should have looked, in a classy red couture suit that accentuated her trim figure. A delicate red silk rose was tucked into her hair—which appeared no worse for wear after her motorcycle ride—and she wore red strappy stiletto heels which looked like something that belonged in a torture chamber. How did she walk in those things?

"I was afraid," I said as she pulled the door shut behind her, "you might be too tired to go to church this morning after your big date."

Tossing her head back with a laugh, she pressed the tip of one ridiculously long false fingernail that sported polish in the same color as her suit, to her chest, and her perfectly waxed brows lifted in a flawless arc. "Me? Why should I be tired? He did all the work. I just wrapped my arms about his slim waist and enjoyed the ride, so close to him even our heartbeats joined in time." Then tilting her head to one side, amusement quirking at her lips, she gave another laugh. "Sugar, I'm gonna hook you up with a man that'll set your feet to dancing again. I already have one in mind for you. He's a top-notch—"

"No, thanks, Barbie. I'm just not ready yet." I moved down the steps toward my minivan. "I may never be ready," I called over my shoulder as I climbed in and settled myself behind the steering wheel.

She opened the passenger door and slid in as gracefully as a model doing a car commercial on TV. Then, patronizingly, she placed her hand on my arm. "Now, sugar, you shouldn't talk like that. You're still young. It's a sin to hide yourself inside that lovely home of yours. You need to get out . . . circulate . . . go places, do things. But not alone, or even with those friends of yours. You need male companionship. There's nothing like it."

I put the key in the ignition and gave it a turn, shifted into drive, and we were on our way. "I'm not hiding, Barbie. I like staying home. Besides, I don't stay home all the time. I go to church on Sundays and Wednesdays. I attend a women's Bible study Tuesday mornings." *Um,* I asked myself, *where else beside the grocery store, Wal-Mart, the health club, and the shopping mall do I go?*

"Bor—ing," she drawled out in singsong response. "Boring, boring, boring. Sitting and watching your nails dry is more exciting than that. We need to get you out into the real world where things are happening."

I watched as she tilted my windshield's rearview mirror in her direction, dabbed on another supply of bright red lipstick then rolled up her lips to check her teeth for any leftover residue. Other than being even thinner with a few tiny traces of crow's feet and an almost unnoticeable wrinkle across her forehead, she looked very much as I remembered her all those years ago, right down to the red-red polish she always wore on her fingernails. I glanced at my hands as they circled the steering wheel. When had they started to look like my mother's?

"There's a whole exciting world out there, Valentine, and gentlemen who are more than willing to show it to you."

88

"Show me the world and a few more things I have no interest in seeing?" I asked. "I wouldn't want to waste their time or mine. Even if I were ever ready to date, all those horror stories I see on the news about women who have been taken advantage of by men they thought they could trust scared the wits out of me. I'd even heard that they penetrated church groups for the sole purpose of scamming money from widows and single women. No matter how lonely I might get without Carter, I refuse to let it happen to me."

"You make all men sound like criminals, Valentine. There's some really great ones out there. Ones who are happy to show you a good time, with no strings attached."

I couldn't resist asking. "Have you ever had a man try to—take advantage of you?"

She sent me a condescending grin. "In what way did you have in mind, sugar?"

After a quick glance her way, I focused my eyes on the road. "You know. Wine and dine you, then expect some sort of—" I gulped, not sure what word to use here. "Payment—when he takes you home." Talking about personal things like this was never easy, even with my closest friends, yet here I was talking about them with Barbie.

"You mean does he expect a good-night kiss, or that I'll go to bed with him?"

I felt my eyes bug out as I gasped. I hadn't expected quite that blunt a response, but she'd asked exactly what I wanted to know. "I—I guess that's what I mean.

But—" I hastened to add, "you really don't need to tell me. It's none of my business." I felt the blood rushing to my cheeks. "I should never have asked."

"Well, I do declare, Valentine. I think you're blushing."

Grrr. I hated it when I did that. My mom had blushed easily, too, so I came by it naturally.

"I don't mind answering, but I have to admit—coming from you—your question surprises me."

I fumbled for words. "I only—I mean—well, you know I'm a fairly new—"

"Yes, I know. It hasn't been long since you lost Carter, and you're afraid to even think about dating. Isn't that it?"

Keeping my eyes on the road, I nodded.

"Sometimes men treat me to a marvelous evening then expect me to put out when they take me home, but I've learned how to handle it. Usually, what a man is really like is pretty obvious right from the start. The nice ones take their time and give me a pleasant, enjoyable evening. The ones I have to worry about are the ones who are usually in a hurry. Nice ones hold your hand to assist you, especially if you're wearing the kind of shoes I usually wear." She lifted one leg, displaying a stiletto sandal. "They open doors for you and treat you like a lady. The others? They're all over you like prepasted wallpaper from the time they show up at the door. Those are the ones you have to worry about."

When I didn't respond, she flashed me a grin. "I've never been a wrestler and I don't want to be one now.

No romps in the hay for this girl. I'm a fun date, and at times I may give them the wrong idea by my dress and my mannerisms, but if they want more than fun, they'll have to go somewhere else. This gal ain't shellin' out no mo'."

I was suddenly filled with a new respect for Barbie.

Until she added, "But when the right man comes along, all my rules and resolve go right out the window. He'll be more than welcome to have his way with me."

"Do you think your real estate man is the right man?" I ventured to ask.

"No, he's a great guy but he's only a salesman. Now if he were the owner of the real estate company—maybe. Though he's quite handsome and a marvelous date, he's simply a diversion until I find my next sugar daddy."

Oh, my! I wanted to ask for her definition of a sugar daddy, to see if it matched up with what I thought a sugar daddy was, but I kept my question to myself. Not only had we already engaged in a discussion I'd never expected to have, we'd arrived at the church parking lot.

With me leading the way, we moved up the steps and into the foyer of Cooperville Community Church where we were immediately met by Sally, Reva, and Wendy. Barbie gave both Sally and Reva a hug then turned to Wendy, who extended her hand and introduced herself before I even had a chance. I would have thought Sally and Reva were already members of the

Red Hat club and Barbie was their queen by the way they fawned over her, telling her how beautiful she looked in her red suit, how gorgeous her hair was, and how wonderful it was to have her there. I wanted to think they were doing it to make her feel welcome so she'd want to come back again, but their greetings and words were too sticky for that. Just plain dripping with honey, if they asked me.

Of course, Barbie took all those compliments in stride and wallowed in them before turning the tables and complimenting them in return. I would have thought she was the first person to ever give them a compliment, the way they blushed and thanked her profusely. Even Wendy, who had never uttered a word other than a simple "Hello," looked impressed. Barbie had even managed to manipulate them with her flattery. *Forgive me, God, for saying it, but it's true.*

"You want to sit up front with us?" Sally asked, latching onto Barbie's hand. "We always sit on the front row. Edna's already there holding our seats."

Barbie gasped. "The front row? Mercy, no! I'd much prefer something nearer the back. I have to ease into this church thing slowly. All of this is foreign to me."

I took charge. Barbie was *my* guest. Hadn't I gone to the Red Hat meeting with her so she'd come to church with me? "You girls go ahead and sit up front." I gave Sally a nudge toward the sanctuary. "We'll see you later."

Sally started to protest, but I narrowed my eyes and gave her a slight frown. She got my message and, taking hold of Wendy's arm, moved forward. Reva followed. Suddenly, I felt like a schoolgirl again, claiming my territory and protecting my clique from any would-be intruders.

Once they were gone, Barbie scanned the big foyer. "Where do the single men sit?"

What a question. "Wherever they want to, I guess."

"Then you'll have to point them out to me," she said with a giggle. "Sometimes it's hard to get a good view of that third finger on their left hand, and I sure wouldn't want to intrude on some little wifey and her dear hubby. Unless the man was extra special and worth it."

I gave her a frown. "I wish you wouldn't talk that way."

"Don't be silly. One can't have too many men friends."

I led her through the crowd of milling church members, hoping she'd agree to sit a little closer to the front than she'd intended.

"Oh, Valentine, I'm so glad to see you." The handsome usher standing by the open double doors reached out for my hand as we moved toward him. "I've been meaning to call you. You and I need to get together."

Grinning, Barbie leaned in close to me and in an amused voice whispered, "Trying to keep this gorgeous stud away from me? I thought you said you never dated."

I rolled my eyes, which I seemed to be doing a lot lately, now that Barbie had made herself a part of my life. "Good morning, Robert. I'd be happy to meet with you anytime it's convenient for you. Just give me a call."

I gestured toward Barbie who was nearly salivating with eagerness to meet this man. "Robert, I'd like you to meet an old friend—" Old friend? Now I sounded like Barbie. "Barbie Baxter. We went to high school together." I suddenly realized I didn't know what last name Barbie was using after being married to three husbands.

Robert extended his hand. "Hello, Mrs. Baxter. I'm Robert Chase. It's nice to have you here this morning. Are you new to our city?"

Barbie leaned close to him, probably to make sure he'd catch a whiff of the expensive perfume she was wearing. "It's *Mizzzz* Baxter," she said, in a low, drawn-out voice.

Umm. I guessed since she didn't correct him, she was using her maiden name. *That's interesting.* Though Robert didn't seem to notice, I did, when she craned her neck to get a glance of the third finger of his left hand.

"I've been gone for quite some time. I came back to Nashville about a year ago." Giving him a flirty smile, she paused and batted those long false eyelashes at him. "I've had an apartment on the far east side of town while I've been looking for just the right home for myself, and now I've found it. Can you believe it— it's right next door to my friend Valentine!"

Robert smiled back and seemed impressed. "How

very nice for both of you ladies. I'm sure the two of you are happy to be together again after all these years."

Without missing a beat, the same nauseously sweet smile adorning her lips, Barbie replied, still batting her eyes, "We certainly are!"

"Are you just visiting this morning, or will you be attending our church regularly?" Robert asked. As a dedicated church usher, it was the question he usually asked first-timers. "I think you'll find Cooperville Community Church a friendly place. The music here is awesome, and our pastor really preaches from the Bible."

"I just may come here all the time, if everyone is as nice as you." Barbie fairly cooed the words. "Maybe you and your missus can come and visit me sometime."

Grrr!

Robert's smile disappeared as I knew it would. "I'm afraid that's not possible. I lost my wife several years ago, but thank you for the invitation."

He handed us each a bulletin then lightly cradled Barbie's elbow, no doubt to move her on to keep the aisles clear. "Enjoy the service."

After giving him a glorious smile that could have lit up the foyer without the aid of lights, she leaned toward me and whispered, "I think he likes me already. Did you see the way he looked at me?" and headed through the door. It was only when she heard Robert call to me, "I'll phone you, Valentine," that she turned back and gave me a glaring frown.

The orchestra was already playing the prelude by the time we found empty places in a pew nearly halfway toward the front.

Obviously upset, she leaned toward me and, covering her mouth with one hand, whispered, "Why didn't you tell me you two were dating, instead of giving me that story about not being ready to date yet? Were you afraid I'd take him away from you?"

I hated it when people talked to each other during the service, but I couldn't let her ridiculous accusation go without responding. "Robert Chase is a church board member. He is acting as the liaison between the board and me for the church bazaar we're planning. That's all. The man and I have never dated and have no plans to do so."

Her brows rose. Her eyes brightened. Her smile took on a life of its own. "Oh? Then I guess he's fair game, right?"

"Yeah," I said, releasing a deep sigh, "I guess he is."

After treating me to a smug little leer, she gave my arm a pinch. "Good, 'cause I like his looks. I just might decide to join this church. Wouldn't that be fun? You and me being next-door neighbors and attending the same church? I might even work on that silly little bazaar of yours."

Perish the thought.

I have to admit, other than taking continual glances at those seated around us, no doubt in search of men who were sitting alone or not wearing a wedding ring, Barbie did pretty well during the service. I caught her flinching when the worship team leader had us sing the same chorus over several times, but I was pleasantly surprised when she actually sang the first verse of "Amazing Grace" without even looking at the words that were projected on the screen. Maybe there was hope for her yet.

If you'll have patience with her and show her My love.

There it was! That voice again.

But, why, I said in my heart. *Why me? Why not someone else? You know the friction that has always been there between the two of us.*

He didn't answer, but I knew He was the One who had been speaking to me. "Okay," I said after taking time to think my words over carefully, and before locking myself into something I'd regret later. "I'll try, but I'm not going to make any rash promises. You know my weaknesses and my tender spots and, unfortunately, so does Barbie. She knows just which buttons to push to bring out the worst in me."

"Is he married?"

Abruptly brought out of my thoughts by Barbie's gentle nudge, I turned to face her. "Who?" I whispered back.

Grinning as though she were privy to a secret, she daintily pointed one manicured finger toward a man three rows in front of us. "Him. The good-looking one in the navy suit."

Not wanting to add any more whispers, I simply gave my head a nod.

Barbie squiggled up her face and shrugged her shoulders then focused her eyes on another man seated across the aisle. I doubted she was listening to a word of the pastor's message.

Just before the hands on my watch doubled themselves on the twelve, Barbie pulled her mirror and lipstick from her purse and right there in church applied another generous coat to her already glossy red lips. Minutes later, the service was over.

I didn't think we were ever going to reach the big foyer. Nearly everyone around us stopped to greet me and extend a welcome to Barbie, to which she gushed an eye-batting, "Thank you."

When we did reach the double doors, Barbie nearly knocked me down getting to Robert Chase who was standing at his post, shaking hands and telling everyone to have a good day as they left the sanctuary.

"I really enjoyed the service," Barbie told him, clinging to his hand as tightly as a miser to his last penny. "But I was wondering. Does this church have an active singles' group? I know so very few people here in Nashville. I thought it might be a good way to get acquainted with some really nice folks."

She should have said *single men*. That was what she meant.

Robert tactfully eased his hand from her grip before opening one of the church bulletins and pointing to a notation on the second page. "I think you'll find all the information you need right there."

Without being able to read minds, I knew that answer

wasn't going to satisfy our Barbie.

Lifting a brow and giving him a coy smile, she asked, "Do you attend the singles' meetings?"

He gave his head a shake. "Me? No, I'm afraid not, but many people do, and seem to enjoy it. Perhaps you would, too. It'd be worth a try. I think there's a phone number listed there you can call for more information."

"Thank you, I just may do that." Apparently undaunted by getting the answer she hadn't wanted to receive, she gave him that fabulous toothy smile of hers and surged on. "I'll see you next Sunday, Mr. Chase. Have a good week."

"So you're really coming back next Sunday?" I asked as the two of us headed across the parking lot toward my car.

She released a girlish giggle. "I sure am. That Robert Chase is one fine lookin' man, and I'll just bet he treats his women like ladies."

"He's not rich," I told her.

She gave me a wink. "Money isn't everything, sugar. Especially when you have plenty of money of your own, thanks to generous ex-husbands. Haven't you ever heard of a *gigolo*?"

I responded with a quick intake of breath. "Robert would never be any woman's gigolo, not if that word means what I think it does."

A playful slap landed on my arm. "*Gigolo* is just a figure of speech, Valentine. In addition to the meaning you're obviously referring to, it also means male companion, hired escort. I looked it up in the dictionary once just to make sure. You're much too serious. I just meant good, honest, respectable men are hard to find. Sometimes, if a man has all the other attributes you're looking for, and you have enough money for the both of you, you have to overlook his poor financial standing. Especially if he's single and good-looking like Robert. I wouldn't mind paying that man's way, at least until I got tired of him. Besides, I like his smile. He looks like he could enjoy a good time, and I'd sure like to be the woman to give it to him."

Still in shock over her comment, even if *gigolo* did mean male escort or companion, I clicked the button on the remote on my key ring, climbed into my minivan, and fastened my seat belt. "I'm not too sure your idea of a good time is the same as Robert's," I told Barbie as she settled herself in the seat next to me.

She fanned her hand at me. "Oh, pshaw, Valentine. A man is a man. They're all alike. Flatter them, give them a few flirty smiles and a little attention, and they'll follow you anywhere. I'll just betcha I could have that man eating out of my hand in a month."

With a shrug, I turned the key in the ignition and moved in line with the other cars waiting to exit the parking lot. "I'm not a betting woman," I said, keeping my eyes trained on the car in front of me, "but that's one bet I'd be tempted to take."

Though I didn't turn to look at her, I could feel her mocking gaze as she said with the determination of a marathon runner nearing the finish line, "You just wait and see, Valentine honey. Bet me or not, in thirty days, that man is gonna be mine!"

I had to laugh at her overconfidence. Not even Barbie with all her beauty could accomplish what she was proposing. "Oh? And how do you intend to make that happen?"

"You just wait and see, Valentine. Just wait and see."

Why did those words scare me?

CHAPTER 8

The phone rang at eight o'clock sharp the next morning. It was Robert Chase.

"I have some business to take care of out near your house today, and I wondered if you'd let me pick you up and take you to lunch at Marco's, that Mexican restaurant near your place. There are a few things about the upcoming bazaar I'd like to go over with you."

"Sure." I *was* eager to get his opinion on a couple of ideas I was considering incorporating into our plans. "Lunch would be nice. What time?"

"I'll pick you up about one o'clock. The restaurant probably won't be as crowded by then, and we can talk as long as we want."

"One will be fine. I'll see you then." *Dumb,* I thought as I hung up the phone. *I could have driven myself. Why didn't I just tell him I'd meet him there?* I shrugged. *Oh, well, too late now. One o'clock. That'll give me plenty of time to meet with the girls, take a quick shower, and get ready.*

Though Reva, Sally, and Wendy arrived right on time, Barbie was a no-show. After filling our coffee cups and uncovering the tray of sticky homemade cinnamon rolls Wendy had brought, we settled down to do some catching up on family happenings before plowing headlong into bazaar business.

"How's David doing?" I ventured, hoping for miracles for Reva's son.

"Same old—same old. He and his grandmother had a real knock-down, drag-out when she came over yesterday. Those two yell at each other like two kids fighting over a toy. I feel like I'm living in a zoo and I'm the zookeeper. Only difference is I don't have cages where I can separate the two." Reva closed her eyes and bit at her lip. "I'm worried about him. Every night when I hear him close his door, I breathe a sigh of relief and thank the Lord he's home safely and we've made it through another day." She rubbed at her eyes with the back of her hand, pain etched on her face.

Wendy placed a gentle, spotted hand on her wrist. "Don't give up hope, dear one. Miracles do happen."

Always an encourager, Wendy seemed to know the right thing to say. I wished I was more like her.

Sally swallowed hard. "I need miracles with Jessica, too. She's furious because I finally took her cell phone away from her. She threatened to run away from home again. She knows those words upset me." Sally lowered her face and cupped it in her hands. "I've never

102

seen such hate in her eyes."

"The other kids still doing okay?" I asked, confident Charlotte and Michael had been the bright spots in Sally's otherwise stressful life.

A smile came to her tearstained face. "They're doing just great. I don't know what I'd do without them."

The four of us sat silently for a moment then Wendy bowed her head and prayed the sweetest, most caring prayer I've ever heard on Sally's behalf. It had to have reached God's heart and touched it. When we lifted our heads, I could see that Sally's eyes were rimmed in red. Wendy touched her hand lightly, and Sally smiled. "I'll be okay now."

I moved to the coffeepot and refilled everyone's cups.

"Where's Edna today?" Reva asked.

Sally shrugged. "I haven't heard from her."

"Me, either," Wendy said. "I'm sure she's just busy."

We let the subject drop; then I said, "We need to start talking about the bazaar."

Everyone nodded in agreement. While Reva picked up the tray of rolls and passed them around the table again, I opened the notebook to the index tab marked COMMITTEES. "I'd like each of you to report on whatever progress you've made. Reva, why don't you go first," I told her, knowing she was usually the most efficient one among us.

Reva straightened in her chair then, in a businesslike manner, squared her shoulders, lifted her chin, and reported on her committee's plans for building the booths and making the signs.

Next, Sally gave her report, saying she had contacted a number of the women on her list of crafters and already had twenty-one signed up, with more saying they were sure they would commit.

Wendy, bless her heart, had twenty-six willing prayer warriors committed and in action, praying for us as we put the bazaar together and for the success of the bazaar itself.

After congratulating them on their accomplishments, considering the little time they'd had to get started, and promising to call Bitsy later on in the day about handling the bazaar publicity and to check on her and her pregnancy, I enthusiastically informed them of the things I'd been working on.

Once our reports had all been given and we had discussed the many other things we could do to make the bazaar a rousing success, Sally clapped her hands together gleefully. "Working on this bazaar is really exciting. I needed something worthwhile like this in my life, and a bazaar is exactly what our church needs. The response to my calls have been amazing. I've had a chance to visit with old friends and make many new ones." She reached for another cinnamon roll and absentmindedly picked off two pecans. "It's amazing how you think you know someone so well but, when talking to them about things like crafts and other interests they may have, you find out there is a whole other side to them you never knew."

"You're right about that," Reva chimed in. "Some of

the women I've called have better tools than I have. I figured I'd have to go begging to the men of the church, as much as I hated to do it, asking them to loan us their electric drills, skill saws, and such, but these women have first-class tools of their own and know how to use them. Because of their knowledge and experience, instead of assembling our booth backdrops and sides from PVC pipe and sheeting, which wouldn't be nearly as stable as we'd like, we've decided to build our own backdrops out of two-by-fours and plywood. If we do it right, we should be able to build and paint them, assemble them, use them, then tear them down and keep them in that storage building in my backyard until next year."

I stared at Reva. It sounded like a monumental job to me. Much bigger than we'd originally planned. "Are you sure you want to build them? Wouldn't it be easier to go with the PVC pipe?"

"It'll take more work and cost quite a few more dollars but, in the long run, it'll be more attractive and a whole lot safer, especially if our bazaar is to be an annual thing. We're even thinking about covering a few of the booth backs with Pegboard. That'd be a great way to display smaller items, but that part is still in the planning stage. Any other comments?"

When no one responded, Wendy led in prayer and we adjourned.

"You know," Sally said with a giggle as she looked around my kitchen. "You should have a sign hanging on your wall, saying in big, bold letters: COOPERVILLE

Community Church Bazaar Headquarters."

Reva nodded. "Good idea, Sal. Maybe we could add: Divine service rendered here daily—over coffee and doughnuts."

I had to laugh. "I like it," I told Reva. "You can paint that sign and hang it in my kitchen whenever you're ready."

"So, how did it go with Barbie and church yesterday?" Sally asked as the three of them rose and shoved their chairs back against the table. "She sure looked fabulous in that red suit and those spiky heels."

"Actually, she did pretty well." I couldn't mask a grin as I continued, "Though she did ask me to point out the single men."

"She's really something. With her beauty and her confidence, I'll bet she could catch any man she wanted," Sally said.

It reminded me of Barbie's words about going after Robert Chase, and I couldn't help but shudder. "Maybe."

"What do you mean—maybe?" Sally said.

"Come on, Sally. Any man? I can think of a number of men I doubt would succumb to her charms," Reva added.

"That may be true, but I'll bet they'd be mighty tempted. Face it. She's really a pretty woman."

I tried not to glare at Sally, but I couldn't help it. "Beauty is only skin deep, Sal," I said. "I think most men, especially the ones who attend our church, are smart enough to realize that." I glanced at the clock. It was nearly noon.

"Sorry, girls," I said, herding them across my kitchen. "I hate to run you off, but someone is picking me up for lunch at one and I have to get ready. We'll talk more tomorrow."

"Male or female?" Sally asked, her eyes shining with mischief.

"Male, if you must know, but it's a business meeting."

Reva raised a brow, her eyes twinkling. "What kind of business?"

Sweet Wendy grabbed onto both Reva's and Sally's arms and dragged them toward the door. "Now, girls, leave Valentine alone. Who she is having lunch with is none of our concern."

I knew curiosity was killing them. "Wendy's right, it *is* none of your concern but, if you must know, it's Robert Chase. We're going to discuss the bazaar."

Sally's jaw dropped. "Robert Chase is taking you to lunch?"

"Yes, is that a problem?"

"I didn't think you were ready to date yet," Sally said.

"Date? What's the matter with you, Sally?" Why did everyone assume having lunch with a male friend was a date? "This isn't a date. It's a business meeting."

Sally huffed, one hand going to her hip as she stood in the open doorway. "You may not think of it as a date, but it could be the start of something. Isn't that the way many relationships begin? With a simple business lunch?"

"Sally's right. It's time you started thinking about getting out and circulating, Valentine." Even Reva joined in. "You're a lovely, sensitive, alluring woman with a whole life ahead of you. Carter's gone on, Val. So has Eric. So has my Manny." Reva lowered her gaze and twiddled with her fingers. "As much as we'd like them to, our husbands aren't coming back."

"This is *not* a date," I stated firmly. "Now go. I have to get ready."

After giving me a quick peck on the cheek, Reva and Sally obediently filed out, but Wendy paused at the door, her frail hand cupping my shoulder. "You'd better listen to your friends, Valentine. Take it from this old lady, growing old alone is no fun."

I couldn't help but meditate on her words as I closed the door and leaned against it. I had everything I would ever need, thanks to Carter, but I *was* alone. I thought of all the long dreary nights that I had lain in bed and rested my hand on his empty pillow, crying and wishing I could feel his arms about me, his warm breath on my cheek, and yes, even hear his snoring.

I closed my eyes, visualizing my darling Carter's face and the five-o'clock shadow that had adorned his smiling countenance every evening. How I'd loved being his wife. How I'd loved being married. A part of a twosome. Someone's partner in life.

I'm only fifty-two.

Do I really want to be alone the years I have left?

Robert arrived at my door promptly at one, dressed in a pale blue polo shirt and a pair of tan Dockers. I suddenly realized I'd never seen him dressed casual before. In fact, I'd never seen him away from the church. There he'd always been dressed in either a suit or a sport coat and trousers, and always in a starched shirt and tie. He'd looked quite handsome garbed that way, but he looked good this way, too.

"You're looking nice today," he said as I stepped out onto my porch. "I'm sorry to have called you at the last minute, I really didn't give you much time, but I have a client not far from here who asked me to take a look at his yard. They've just moved into a new house, and he wants me to do the landscaping."

I'd forgotten when Robert had moved to Nashville two years ago, he'd purchased the old Miller Garden and Landscaping business. "No problem. I've been wanting to talk to you, too. The timing worked out perfect for me."

"Hope you don't mind riding in my truck. I decided to bring a few flowering shrubs to show my new client."

I glanced at the shiny new white Avalanche parked in my driveway and smiled. "I don't mind in the least."

"Valentine! Yoo hoo, Valentine!"

I knew in an instant it was Barbie.

Both Robert and I turned toward the voice as she made her way across the lawn. She was dressed in a pair of tight white silk trousers topped with a royal blue filmy silk blouse blazoned down one side with a colorful parrot and, you guessed it, white stiletto-heeled sandals that showed her shapely legs and her red-red toenails to their best advantage. Did the woman ever look like an average woman?

Practically ignoring me, Barbie placed her hand on Robert's bare arm and smiled up at him with a smile so sweet I thought I was going to upchuck.

"Hello, Mr. Chase—Robert." She gave her head a coy tilt, her hand still on his arm. "I didn't know you were going to be here. I wanted to catch Valentine before she left so I could explain why I hadn't made it to her house for coffee."

Finally, turning to me, she stuck out her free hand, her pinky finger extended. "When I got out of bed this morning, I realized I'd lost one of my artificial fingernails. I called my manicurist immediately for the quickest appointment I could get." She held the finger toward Robert who looked at it with an expression that said he couldn't understand what the problem was. Actually, neither could I. What had been the rush?

"Knowing how inconvenient this was for me, she told me to come right in and she'd fix it. I can't tell you how relieved I was. So, without thinking to call you and let you know I wouldn't be here, I just headed for the beauty salon as fast as my car would carry me." She lifted the finger toward me then to Robert again. "See. It's all fixed!"

I tried to inch past her toward the truck, wanting to get out of there as quickly as I could, as Barbie's vow to *get* Robert filled my mind. If she was going to *get* him, as she called it, I determined she was going to have to do it somewhere other than on my front lawn.

Flattening a hand to her chest demurely, much as I imagined Scarlet O'Hara would have done, she asked, looking from one of us to the other, "Oh, I'm sorry. Have I interrupted something? Were you two going somewhere?"

"I'm taking Valentine to lunch," Robert volunteered. "We have some things to discuss."

"Oh? How nice." Turning quickly, she pointed one of those manicured nails toward his truck. "Is that yours? It looks brand new."

He nodded proudly. "It is new. I bought it for my business. I'm in landscaping."

Her eyes brightened, and I could almost hear the bells clanging in her blond-haloed head. "Landscaping? Really? What a coincidence. I'm looking for a landscaper."

He glanced back toward her house. "I'd be happy to take a look at your yard and see what you have in mind."

You'd flip if you knew what Barbie has in mind, and it has little to do with landscaping, I wished I could have said.

She batted her baby browns again. "Could you maybe come over this afternoon, after you and Valentine get back from your lunch? I'm really anxious to get started. I want this place to look like something out of *Home and Garden* magazine, and I'll just bet you're the man to do it."

He gave me a quick glance. "I'm not exactly sure what time we'll be back, but I guess I could."

"Oh, that'll be so wonderful." She backed away. "I'll be waiting. You two have a good lunch."

He nodded then took my arm and led me to the passenger's side of his truck and assisted me in, much like Carter used to do, and soon we were backing out of the driveway, leaving Barbie standing in the middle of my yard.

Having lunch with Robert went much better than I'd expected. I'd thought I'd feel awkward sitting across the table from another man, but his impeccable manners and his thoughtfulness made it easy. After all, we were only there for a business meeting. Nothing more.

We lunched on chicken enchiladas, had some sort of cinnamon concoction for dessert, then got down to business, with Robert nodding his approval at every idea I suggested about the bazaar.

"It seems you have everything under control, Valentine," he said in an easy way that made me feel I really was doing a good job. "I don't want you to get the idea the church board is questioning any decisions you make, but I want you to call me anytime you have questions, comments, need encouragement, anything. I'm afraid you're going to have to put up with me until this project is over."

"I'm sure putting up with you will be no problem." There were others on the board who would not have been as laid-back to work with, as considerate, and certainly not as winsome. I felt really good as we headed back to my house. Excellent food, enjoyable company, and a good business meeting. What more could I ask?

Then I remembered Barbie and her sudden interest in having her yard landscaped.

When we reached my house, after telling me to keep up the good work, Robert escorted me to the door, then said good-bye and walked on over to Barbie's house. I changed into some everyday clothes then sat down at the desk in the kitchen, preparing to go over the few notes I'd taken at the restaurant, but I couldn't get those two off my mind. Feeling like a voyeur, I moved to the room that had been Carter's study and parted the drapery. Through the sheers I could see Barbie and Robert standing in her backyard, her face aglow with excitement, her arms flailing around like a humming-bird's wings as she yakked away at him.

Finally, standing on tiptoe and cupping his face between her hands, she said something I couldn't make out. Whatever could she have said to him? Curiosity was killing me. *Come on,* I told myself, *they're two adults. What they do or say is none of my business as long as it doesn't affect me.*

I pushed my face closer to the sheers, but all I could see was Robert shaking her hand then turning to leave. I felt somewhat responsible for whatever might happen to him. After all, wasn't I the one who introduced them? If it hadn't been for me dragging her to church, she may never have even met him. Suddenly, an idea occurred to me. Maybe I could find another woman for Robert! Do a bit of matchmaking. If he were interested in another woman and became serious with her, that would put Barbie out of the picture. Yes, that was it. I'd make a list of all the single women in the church who would be a good match for him, then I'd somehow arrange for him to spend time with the ones I thought were the best pick. *What about you?* the thought came to me. I brushed it aside, not willing to explore the notion, not with Carter's memory so close to me. Still, I couldn't let him be hurt by Barbie.

I watched until his truck was out of sight then returned to the kitchen and dialed Bitsy Foster's phone number. She answered on the first ring and was surprised to hear that I wanted *her* to co-chair the publicity committee for our bazaar.

"But there are so many others who are far more capable than I am," she protested.

"You'll do fine," I assured her, "and don't forget you'll be co-chairing with Trudy Simon. She'll work with you then take over anything you haven't quite finished when your baby comes. The main thing is to get out news releases to as many radio and TV stations as possible, the newspapers both here in Nashville and the surrounding areas, and maybe arrange for a couple of interviews. That's about it, unless you can come up with some other ways to get the word out."

"I'd really like to do it, Valentine. It'll help me get acquainted. I haven't been in Nashville long and I barely know anyone. That's why I started coming to your church. With my husband in Iraq and the baby coming soon, I knew I needed to meet new friends but just didn't know how to find them."

"Cooperville Community Church is an excellent

place to meet new friends," I told her, feeling bad that I hadn't called her before. How lonely she must have been with her husband gone. "You and Trudy can ask some of the other women to help you, too. You two don't need to do the entire job yourselves."

"Then, yes! If you think I can do it, I'd love to work on publicity with Trudy."

Now that that part was settled, I told her, "Three or four of us get together at my house for coffee every morning. Why don't you join us tomorrow, and we can talk more about it?"

"Really? You want me to come to your house? Cool. What time should I be there?"

The enthusiasm in her voice sent me into double guilt, and I vowed I'd make a real effort to befriend Bitsy in any way I could. "Around ten. Would that work for you?"

She assured me it would, thanked me for asking her to serve as co-chairwoman of the publicity committee, and then said good-bye.

Sweet girl. I'm sure Sally, Reva, and Wendy will work at making her feel a part of our group. Edna, too.

I'd barely hung up the phone when Barbie tapped on the back door. Grimacing inside, I moved toward the door. I felt, just by knowing she had designs on Robert, that I was part of her conspiracy.

"That Robert Chase is one of the sweetest men I have ever met." Barbie fairly bubbled as she pushed her way past me and headed for the coffeepot, which I'd already washed and put back in its place. Finding the pot empty, she abandoned the idea and leaned against the counter, crossing her slender ankles and smiling as happily as if she'd just been declared a finalist in the Miss Universe Pageant. "It was so nice of you to introduce me to him, Valentine. I can't thank you enough."

As if I'd had a choice.

"The two of us really hit it off. Robert is going to plan out my entire yard himself. You should hear the amazing ideas he has. I'm so excited. None of this would have happened if it hadn't been for you."

What could I say? Though I supposed she wanted her landscaping done, I'd never dreamed Robert would be the one doing it. Plus, the woman had boasted she could *get* him in thirty days. The idea of Barbie spending that much time with him terrified me. I was the one who had introduced them! There were no two ways about it. It was my duty, as a concerned friend, to try to match him up with someone else—to protect him from her.

"And guess what? He's coming to dinner tomorrow night!" Barbie said.

Though I had no idea why, that green-eyed monster reared its ugly head again. *This is ridiculous,* I told myself, my eyes pinned on the gorgeous blond standing in my kitchen. *You have no interest in Robert, other than that of a friend. Why should you care if he is going to landscape her yard or they're having dinner together? They're consenting adults.*

"One problem, though. For some silly reason, he would only come if other people were going to be there. Some stupid morals thing with him, I guess."

Ah ha! That sounded more like the Robert Chase I'd heard about.

"So, I told him you were planning to come, too. You will come, won't you, Valentine?"

Inwardly, I had to laugh. I'll bet this was the first time Barbie had ever invited a grown man to dinner and he insisted on having a chaperone. "I guess I could come," I told her, trying to sound casual. The truth was I was glad she was inviting me, otherwise, I would have been sitting in Carter's den peeking through the sheers, hoping to catch a glimpse of them through one of her windows.

"I explained to him that my decorator hasn't even begun to redo the inside of my house yet, but he didn't seem to mind."

"Men aren't usually as concerned about those things as we women are."

She walked to my desk, picked up my phone book, and handed it to me. "Point out the name of the best caterer you know. I want this meal to be perfect."

I eyed her as I took the book from her hands. "I supposed *you* were doing the cooking."

Her false eyelashes parted as her eyes rounded in surprise. "Me? Cook? Whatever for? I don't know how to cook. That's why they have delis and caterers."

Why didn't her answer surprise me? I flipped the pages until I came to the catering section, then pointed my finger at the "Dinners, Dips, and Desserts" catering listing. "Carter and I always hired these people for our business dinners. Their food is excellent, but I'm not sure you'll be able to book something with them at this late date. Most caterers insist on at least several days' advance notice, even for small dinners." I handed the book back to her.

Removing a ballpoint pen from the ceramic container I kept on my desk, she jotted the number down on my scratch pad and stuffed it into her pocket. "Robert is supposed to arrive at seven. Maybe you could come about six thirty and help me with a few last-minute details." She turned as she pushed open the storm door, adding, "Oh, and you might make some excuse about having to leave early when dinner is over. I'd really like to have some time alone with that gorgeous creature." Dipping her head a bit, she batted her eyes then giggled like a teenager looking forward to her first real date. "You know—to get better acquainted. If I'm going to make him mine, I'll have to spend time with him, make him feel special. Wow him with my feminine charms."

I simply nodded. Since I'd never been involved in a campaign to catch a man other than Carter, I certainly did not want to be involved in this one. I wondered how Robert would feel if he knew she'd referred to him as a gorgeous creature. At least that was better than stud muffin, the title she'd hung on Carter as well as her handsome real estate salesman.

"I probably won't see you again until tomorrow evening," she went on. "My new cleaning lady is coming in the morning. You know how those people can steal you blind if you're not there to keep an eye on them. And I'm getting a massage in the afternoon, but I do plan to be home by the time the caterer arrives."

"*If* you can get a caterer on such short notice," I added.

She gave me an impish wink. "If the caterer is a man, I know I can talk him into it, even if I have to resort to tears. Men are real pushovers for a damsel in distress."

I'll just bet you can talk a man into anything.

Since Reva and Sally had offered to pick up Bitsy, the three of them arrived at my house at the same time the next morning. Bitsy looked so cute in her sky blue, smocked maternity dress and blue flip-flops. Her long, straight blond hair hung clear to her waist and swished from side to side as she walked, and she had huge dimples. She looked more like a teenaged baby-sitter than she did a barely twenty-year-old expectant mom-to-be.

"Do you hear from your husband often?" I asked, knowing how difficult it must have been for her with him so far away at a time like this.

Sally motioned her toward a chair at the table then handed her a napkin.

Bitsy treated each of us to a generous smile. "Yes, ma'am, thanks to e-mail and instant messaging, I hear from him several times a week. We even send pictures back and forth." She cupped her hand over her rounded tummy. "He's excited about the baby. He hopes to be here when it's born, but he doesn't think they'll let him come."

"But surely your mother and some of your family can come and be with you."

Her smile disappeared and she shook her head. "No, ma'am. My mother lives clear out in California and is too ill to travel, and my daddy left us years ago. I don't have any brothers or sisters, and Kevin's parents aren't able to travel. They can't make it either."

Sally took hold of Bitsy's hand. "So unless your husband makes it home, you'll be all alone?"

"I have a friend, another Army wife, who has volunteered to be my Lamaze coach. She'll be with me."

I couldn't stand it any longer. I scooted my chair closer to the girl and slipped my arm about her shoulders, giving her a gentle squeeze. "We're your friends now, Bitsy. Anytime you need anything, day or night, give one of us a call and we'll come running. I mean that sincerely."

Bitsy drew back in surprise. "That's very kind of you but I couldn't—"

"Oh, yes, you could," I told her, smiling and tightening my hold on her. "We're all sisters in Christ." From the look on Bitsy's face I could tell something else was on her mind.

"I believe in prayer, but sometimes God doesn't do what I ask Him. Do you think He will answer if I ask Him to bring my husband home safely?"

I hadn't expected a question like that. In some ways, though Bitsy wasn't a widow like the three of us, she *was* enduring a painful separation from her husband without the assurance he would be coming back.

For a long moment, I found myself searching for words. Finally, I uttered, "I don't honestly know, Bitsy. But I do know we can ask Him to protect Kevin and keep him safe from any harm that might come to him while he and the other boys are over there serving our country. As earthly mortals, we don't know the things God has planned for us, but we have to have faith. We have to trust Him and know that whatever happens, it's all a part of His master plan."

"He's also a comforter, Bitsy." I'd never heard Reva's strong voice sound more gentle or more kind. "When things happen to us that hurt us or upset us in any way," she continued, "like a loving parent, God is able to hold us in His arms and take away our pain. I don't know how people make it through some of their trials without having Him in their lives. I know I couldn't."

"Me, either." Bitsy pursed her lips thoughtfully. "I've been asking Him to give us a healthy, happy baby. I sure hope He answers that prayer."

I looked at these women, women who had become such an important part of my life. We were not only friends, we were one another's support system. How great that we were all there for each other. Like I told Bitsy—true sisters in Christ.

CHAPTER 9

I must have changed clothes ten times before I finally settled on my pale blue floral silk top with its matching broomstick skirt. I knew Barbie would be dressed to the hilt and, while I had no reason to compete with her, I did want to look my best. But when it came to her stiletto heels, she definitely had no competition. I was sticking to my mini-wedge-heeled sandals.

Up or down? I asked myself as I twisted my head from side to side and gazed at my reflection in the mirror. Deciding wearing my hair up gave me a little more class than wearing it down, I wound it into a French twist, adding the pair of white puka shell earrings and a matching necklace that Carter had bought for me on one of his business trips to California. Then I checked my lipstick once more and headed across the lawn to Barbie's house. I'd considered wearing my new perfume, but I knew Barbie would have enough on for both of us.

"God," I said aloud, casting my eyes upward, "if You want me to talk to Barbie about You, you're going to have to make it happen, 'cause, to be honest, pleasing You is the only reason I'm befriending this overbearing woman."

The front door stood open when I arrived, and there she was, draped across a magnificent white chaise lounge in all her glory. With a fragile lily tucked into her halo of hair, a low-cut blouse, and a spectacular long flowing skirt with slits up the sides that revealed her long slender legs, she looked like something out of the movie *Cleopatra*. When she waved her hand at me, I stepped inside. The purple walls and purple and sage green carpet were still there, nearly worn out and as hideous as ever, but with the drapes open and the late-afternoon sun filtering in through the windows, casting a wide beam of light across the chaise lounge, the room didn't look half bad.

"I'm so glad you came early, Valentine." Smoothing her hand over the exquisite silk skirt, she asked, "Does this look all right? Is it too dressy for a casual at-home dinner?"

I wanted to say, "You look awful! That thing makes you look fat," but I couldn't. She looked incredible. So instead, I told the truth. "You look beautiful. That outfit is perfect for an at-home dinner." Why did I suddenly feel dowdy and underdressed? I gave her a smile. "You wanted me to come early so I could help. What can I do?"

"Nothing right now. I wasn't sure how much the caterers would do, but they set the table and every-thing. All that has to be done is to pull the casserole from the oven and take the salads from the refrigerator. I thought maybe you could do those things for me once Robert gets here. Oh," she reminded quickly, "and don't tell him I didn't prepare the food. I want him to think I'm domestic. I even tossed a fancy apron across a kitchen chair for effect."

Domestic? Ha! That was a laugh. I'd call Barbie any-thing but domestic.

"Do you really want to go through with this? Making a play for Robert Chase? I mean, I'll take your word for it that you could have him eating out of your hand in thirty days," I said, even though I doubted she could make it happen. "You don't have to go to such lengths. I'm sure there are many Nashville men that seem more your style than Robert. He's kind of a plain-vanilla type guy. I visualize you with more of a caviar-and-stuffed-mushroom kind of man. You do realize Robert digs in the dirt for a living, don't you?"

She laughed as though I'd just told a big joke. "Valentine Denay. I do believe you're jealous. Do you have a secret crush on Robert that you're not telling me about?"

"Of course not," I shot back, feeling a flush rise to my cheeks. "But I can't understand why you're going to all this trouble. True, Robert owns his own business. And true, he's single, but he's not on the make. He seems perfectly happy the way he is. Why do you want to rock his boat? You know, even if you could catch him, you wouldn't be happy staying with him. You'd be bored to tears."

She grinned and gave me a wink. "Sugar, you do have a bit of a spark left after all! I was beginning to wonder. This is more like the Valentine who did all she could to keep me away from Carter. Good for you, girl! Maybe there's hope for you after all."

Hope for me? Wasn't that almost word-for-word

what I'd said about her?

"Carter has been gone a long time. What you need," she said, giving me a wink, "is another man in that uneventful, nondescript life of yours."

In some ways, I knew she was right. My life, other than the things I did at and for the church, *was* uneventful and nondescript. I had no real purpose. Nothing to look forward to. I thought of a whippy comeback, and had it right on the tip of my tongue just waiting to be released, but before it could come out, Robert appeared at the door.

With a childlike smirk toward me, Barbie rose and quickly made her way to welcome him, her stiletto heels clicking loudly on the foyer's marble floor.

"Come in," she said sweetly, taking on that exaggerated Southern drawl of hers, "you're right on time."

"Good evening, Ms. Baxter. It's nice to see you again."

I had to laugh at the formal greeting. *Ms. Baxter?* Apparently Barbie hadn't gotten as far with him as she'd led me to believe.

He stepped into the foyer, looking freshly shaven and more handsome than ever in a soft Hawaiian silk shirt printed in beige tones and trousers in a subdued tan. "It's nice to see you again, Valentine," he said, walking toward me, leaving Barbie standing at the door. "I ran into Bitsy Foster at the bookstore this afternoon. She had nice things to say about you." He glanced around the room then selected a chair across from me and sat down, still smiling. "I'm really glad you asked her to serve as publicity co-chairwoman. She's excited about it, and spending time with you and Trudy will be good for her. I understand both her and her husband's parents are miles from here."

Barbie brazenly sat down on the arm of Robert's chair, exposing a long bare leg through the slit in her skirt. "Would you like a glass of white wine before we go in to dinner?" she asked.

He held up his hand. "None for me, thanks. I'm not a wine drinker."

"Perhaps something stronger then?"

Again, his hand went up. "No, thank you. I'm not a drinker at all, but I will have coffee later, if it isn't too much trouble."

Barbie turned toward me then hiked her head toward the kitchen. "Weren't you about to set the food on the table, *Valentine?*" Her tone was about as subtle as a tanker truck rolling down the highway at eighty miles an hour.

"I'll get right on it."

As I left the room, I heard Barbie say, "You must call me Barbie, Robert. You and I are friends now."

Friends? Not for long, if she has her way. I've got to find another woman for him.

Once I had the food on the table, I placed the rolls in the microwave and hit the On button, then announced dinner was ready. Of course, Barbie made a grand entrance into the dining room, with one hand daintily holding out her skirt allowing the filmy fabric to softly billow out behind her as they walked, the other hand anchored firmly onto Robert's arm.

Once we were seated and our napkins placed in our laps, Barbie reached for the entrée.

Robert gave her a quick glance, then cleared his throat. "Would you like me to pray for this meal you've prepared?"

I nearly choked. Number one, because of the easy way he'd asked, I knew he was assuming she was a Christian. And number two, because he also assumed *she'd* prepared the food!

For a nanosecond, she gave him a blank stare, then, in typical Barbie fashion, she batted those lashes of hers and sweetly said, "Thank you, Robert. I was just about to ask you."

Barbie was the perfect hostess, but still accepting Robert's compliments about the food as though she'd prepared it herself. He guided most of the dinner conversation, talking about the various plants and trees she might consider using in her yard. When that subject had been exhausted and our catered meal consumed, we took our cups of coffee into the great room, seating ourselves on the pink and green floral upholstered sofas she was using until her new ones were delivered.

Robert gazed through the floor-to-ceiling windows that lined an entire wall. "Once we get the landscaping finished, this is going to be a beautiful view."

Barbie, who'd seated herself beside him on one of the comfy sofas—surprise, surprise—scooted a bit closer to him. "I just think you're a genius, Robert. I love the plans you have for my yard."

Charm fairly oozed from the woman.

While Robert talked about lighted fountains and other options for her consideration, Barbie kept giving me weird nods of her head. I thought she had a crick in her neck until the nods turned into piercing glares. Suddenly I remembered her request that I make an excuse and leave early. I debated whether I should do it or not. It hardly seemed fair, leaving unsuspecting Robert alone with her, especially after he'd told her he would only come tonight if someone else was going to be here, too. But there seemed to be no other way than to excuse myself and leave. He was a big boy. If he didn't want to stay, he didn't have to.

I was ready to hold out my wrist and make an obvious glance at my watch when Robert, looking directly at me, placed his cup on the coffee table and stood. "I hope I haven't taken too much time out of the evening you ladies had planned."

We had planned? I gave him a curious stare. "We didn't have—"

"What Valentine means is"—Barbie rammed in, leaping to her feet and wedging herself between us— "we can watch that video another time. It really wasn't that important. Just a girls-night-in thing."

Video? What video?

"It was nice of you to let me intrude. What gentleman could resist an invitation to spend the evening with two lovely ladies such as yourselves? Certainly not me." He extended his hand toward Barbie. "Thank you for a great dinner and good company. You're a terrific cook."

Cook? Ha!

"I think we've covered everything we needed to about your landscaping, so I'll be going."

Barbie grabbed onto his wrist. "Valentine told me *she* had to leave early, but there's no reason for you to go."

He tried to back away, but she continued to hold onto him. "Thank you, but I have an early morning tomorrow, and I still have some paperwork to do yet tonight. I'll call you once I get the sketches of my proposed landscaping plan completed, and you can come by the greenhouse and take a look at them. I know you're anxious for my crew to get started on your project."

"Surely you can stay long enough for another cup of coffee." Barbie stuck out her lower lip and looked crestfallen.

"Thank you, but I really must be going." Robert nodded his head toward me. "If you're ready to leave, Valentine, I'll walk you to your house."

I knew the two of us leaving together would upset her, but it seemed rude to refuse his offer.

Both Robert and I bid Barbie a good night; then, like a real gentleman would, Robert took hold of my arm, and we started our short walk across her lawn to my house, leaving Barbie standing in her open doorway watching us. I could only imagine what was going on in that conniving head of hers.

Robert lifted his free hand and pointed toward the sky. "Look at that moon. Isn't that a beauty?"

"Uh huh, a real beauty." I gazed at it dreamily. It was the kind of moon that had been in the sky the night Carter proposed to me.

"I'd like to talk to you about something," he said.

"Something about the bazaar?"

He frowned. "No, about Ms. Baxter. To be honest, I'm nervous about being around her. I've never met anyone quite like her. If she hadn't told me you two had already made plans to spend the evening at her house, I wouldn't have accepted her invitation. I've noticed she can be a bit overbearing. Is she always this friendly with everyone she meets?"

"I can't honestly say." Truth was, up until a few days ago, I hadn't seen her in years. Maybe deep down she'd changed. I figured I'd best keep my mouth shut and let him find the answer to that question for himself. "It's been years since I've seen her, and we really haven't spent much time together since she moved in next door to me." Should I have added, "But you'd better watch out because she's out to get you"?

"I'm glad she's attending our church."

"Me, too." And I really was glad. The more I was around Barbie, the more I knew we had been put together so I could be a witness and a help to her. Barbie needed God and, though I would have preferred He'd chosen someone else, He had placed the two of us together. I was sure of it.

"I have something else I wanted to ask you."

After pulling my house key from my purse, I stepped up onto my porch and turned to him, noticing how the streaks of moonlight filtering through the trees brought out the silver in the graying areas at his temples. "Yes? What?"

He paused before answering, his gaze fixed on my face. "I'm hosting a barbecue for my employees tomorrow night. Most of them are either married or bringing a date, even the young high school and college boys I hire in the summertime. I feel really awkward being the only one there without a partner." He reached out and took my hand. "I know it's short notice and I'm asking a lot, but I'm wondering if I could talk you into coming with me?"

CHAPTER 10

You're kidding. You actually said 'Yes'?" Sally asked.

I felt a blush rise to my cheeks as my friends and I sat at my table the next morning. "Come on, Sally, it's not that big a deal. It's only a barbecue. I'm simply doing the guy a favor." What I should have done was encourage him to ask one of the other ladies from our church. Some matchmaker I was.

She walked a complete circle around me, checking me over from head to toe, one finger tapping her chin. "Let's see. What should you wear? Blue jeans? A plaid shirt? Cowboy boots?"

Reva shook her head. "Naw. That sounds like something I'd wear. Our Valentine is a lady. I think she

131

needs something more feminine. How about that long tiered denim skirt she bought a couple of years ago?"

Sally bobbed her head. "Good idea. That'll work. That skirt and cowboy boots, but not with a plaid shirt. I think she should wear that white ruffled peasant-type blouse I saw hanging in her closet."

"Good idea," Edna agreed.

I waved my hand in their faces. "Hey, girls! Don't talk about me like I'm not here."

"I think she should wear her hair in a ponytail," Sally went on as if she hadn't heard a word I'd said. "Maybe tie it up with a red bandana. That'd be cute."

"Or maybe use the curling iron and let her hair fall loose around her shoulders," Bitsy added.

I loved them for their concern about my appearance, but they were making entirely too big a thing out of this. "Look," I said, keeping my voice in a low controlled tone. "I'm only going as a favor for a friend. That's it. Nothing more. Don't read something into this that isn't there. I barely know the man."

"He seems really nice," Reva contributed. "Great smile, too."

"He owns his own business," Sally remarked. "That shows he's responsible."

"He's a Christian," Reva added. "That's definitely important."

"And a man of prayer." Even Wendy chimed in, smiling. "A man who prays is a man you can count on."

Edna nodded. "Absolutely."

132

I stared at the five of them. "You girls are impossible. What are you? His fan club?"

Levelheaded Reva sat down beside me. "And he's a widower. You two have a lot in common, Valentine. No one is saying you should marry the guy—"

"Although it might be a good idea." Sally scooted into the chair next to me. "I know you're lonely."

Bitsy gave my shoulder a pat. "Take it from me, being lonely is awful."

"Look, you guys, I *am* going to the barbecue. I've already told Robert I would. And I'll wear the white blouse, denim skirt, and cowboy boots. I may even curl my hair and wear it down, but I won't be dressing up to catch a man. I'll be dressing up because I respect Robert and wouldn't want to do anything to dishonor him. As head of his company, I'm sure he'll be clothed appropriately and so will I." I placed my folded hands on the table with a thud. "Subject closed. Now let's get busy. We still have a lot of work to do on the bazaar."

I'd thought getting ready for a barbecue would be simple.

It wasn't.

Sally and Reva showed up to help me, which only added to the problem.

With those two watching my every move, I was a nervous wreck. *Come on, Valentine, you're a grown woman,* I said to myself. *As you told your friends, this isn't a date. You're simply helping out a friend. Stop being so jumpy about it.*

133

That self-lecture helped, but I was still nervous. Nervous enough that I accidentally touched my forehead with the hot curling iron. It hurt so badly I would have cried if my friends hadn't been standing there gawking at me. Thanks to the big red mark it made, I had to cover my forehead with bangs rather than wear my hair slicked back as I'd planned.

Reva let out a low whistle as I slipped my feet into the boots and scanned myself in the full-length mirror. "Lookin' good, girlfriend. He's gonna think you're a real cutie."

I gave her a scowl. "I'm not out to impress him. We're just friends."

But I did think the denim skirt and white peasant blouse had been a good idea. I liked the cowboy boots, too, but they were killing my feet. It had been years since I'd worn them. Oh, well, it was only for a few hours. Surely I could survive that long.

"Enjoy yourself, Valentine," Sally told me, her expression serious. "You've been through a lot. You deserve a little happiness. Carter would want you to be happy."

Reva nodded. "She's right, you know. Carter is gone, but *you* still have many years ahead of you. Perhaps this fine Christian man has been sent into your life for a purpose. Keep your mind open, Valentine, and keep your heart open."

Touched by her words and her gentle spirit, I clasped her hand in mine and gazed into her eyes. Tough, strong, independent Reva had a heart of gold. "I will,"

I promised. "Just pray for me that whatever I do will always be God's will."

"You know I will."

With Sally's encouragement, I transferred the contents of my day-to-day purse into the small, red leather, hand-tooled clutch bag she'd brought for me to use, and we all hurried downstairs to wait for Robert. A quick glance at the clock reminded me he wasn't due for another fifteen minutes, but when the doorbell rang I assumed he was early and began shouting orders.

"Okay, you guys—" I grabbed onto Sally and Reva and shoved them toward my kitchen. "Stay out of sight and keep quiet. I don't want him to know it took three of us to get me ready for his barbecue. And don't come out until you're sure we're gone, and lock the door behind you when you leave."

Sally firmly planted her feet in my hallway. "But we—"

"Out. Now!"

Once I was sure they were safely sequestered in my kitchen, I picked up my bag and hurried to open the door.

"Help! That handsome Realtor of mine is taking me out to dinner, and I can't get my necklace fastened."

Oh, no.

It was Barbie.

"You're dating him again? I thought you were after Robert."

She gave me a flip of her hand. "I *am* after Robert. My Realtor is only a diversion until I can get Robert to come around."

I could only imagine how upset she'd be when she found out Robert had asked me to his barbecue, so I decided not to mention it, hoping the two in the kitchen would stay there and not come barging in and blabber everything they knew. Especially Sally. Though she never meant any harm, naive little Sally was notorious for saying things she shouldn't, when she shouldn't.

Necklace in hand, Barbie looked me over from my ponytail to my cowboy boots. "That's some getup. Where are you going? To a masquerade party?"

I gave her a shrug, hoping it appeared nonchalant. "No, a barbecue." I reached for the necklace. "Turn around and let me fasten it."

"You should've told me you were going to a barbecue. I have this really cute concho belt and a to-die-for squash-blossom necklace that would look smashing with that skirt. Want me to go get them for you?"

I hated her to think I was rushing her off, but I really wanted her to leave before Robert arrived. "Thanks, but it's just a simple little barbecue. I don't want to be overdressed."

"Well, you know you're always welcome to borrow anything you need." She gave me a friendly smile that almost made me feel guilty for not telling her I was waiting for Robert.

"Thanks for fastening my necklace."

"You're welcome. Have a good time with your Realtor."

"I will. You have a good time—" She paused on my

bottom step and turned to look at me. "You're not going alone, are you? Oh, look!" She pointed toward the street. "Isn't that Robert's truck pulling into your driveway?"

I should have known the truth would come out, one way or another. "Yes, he's going to the barbecue, too." Well, a condensed version of the truth anyway.

Robert, wearing a black Stetson pulled low on his brow, stopped the Avalanche then swung his long legs out of the cab, setting a pair of highly polished black leather cowboy boots on the pavement. "Hello, Valentine. Barbie." I'd half expected him to say, "Howdy!"

"Good evening, Robert," Barbie sang out while batting her long lashes. "You sure look handsome in that cowboy outfit. Makes me wish I was going to that little barbecue. Is this a church function?"

He moved to stand beside me. "No. Actually, I'm having it for my employees, and Valentine was kind enough to accept my invitation to go with me."

Barbie gasped as though she'd had the wind knocked out of her. "You're taking Valentine?"

I flinched when Robert took my hand in his. This was the first time another man had held my hand in a personal way.

"Sure am, and we'd better get a move on. It wouldn't be good for the host to be late."

One closed fist flew to anchor itself on her hip. "Why didn't you tell *me* about your barbecue?"

"Didn't see any reason to," he answered simply. "It's a business function."

I figured we better get out of there. Fast. "I'm ready if you are," I told Robert, giving his hand a gentle squeeze.

He tipped his hat her way. "Nice to see you again, Barbie. Looks like you're all dressed up to go somewhere, too. Have a good evening."

I guess she wanted to leave him on a pleasant note 'cause she mustered up one of her stickiest smiles and gave her head a sideways tilt. "You, too. Maybe next time you can take me to your barbecue."

Not if I can help it! I thought.

He smiled back. "Maybe."

The barbecue turned out to be more fun than I could have imagined. Robert had transformed one of his buildings into what looked like an old barn, complete with red and white checkered tablecloths and bales of straw placed here and there for extra seating. He even had stuffed scarecrows with straw and tied them to the support posts. Big pots of pink geraniums were tucked into every open space. The barbecued ribs and chicken, though messy, were fantastic, but Robert had taken care of that, too, by providing huge terrycloth bibs for all of his guests. He'd even hired a three-piece band to play old timey, foot-tapping tunes. All in all, it was a marvelous evening.

"I can't tell you how much I appreciated your going with me," he told me as we strolled hand in hand from his truck to my door. "You were the perfect hostess the way you jumped in and helped out when the servers needed an additional hand to dip the food."

"I enjoyed doing it."

"You know," he said, taking hold of my shoulders and turning me to face him, "I'm not ready to officially date again, and I'm sure you're not either, but I had a really great time with you tonight."

"I had a great time, too."

"Do you suppose—" He paused and took both my hands in his.

I wasn't over Carter yet. Why did my heart feel a sudden flutter?

"Do you suppose you and I could just spend some time together as friends? I love to go to concerts, music theatre, and ball games, but I hate to go alone, and I get tired of being with men all the time. I'd like some female companionship now and then."

"So long as we keep it on a platonic basis."

"Good. Then let's plan on attending a concert next week. I've heard a great Christian artist is going to be in town."

Was I making a mistake? I hoped not, but I had to admit Robert was easy to be with. In many ways he was different than Carter, but every bit the gentlemen. I liked that.

"I'll call for tickets tomorrow."

"Only if you let me pay for my own."

Gently taking my house key from my hand and inserting it in the lock, he gave it a twist and pushed the door open. "Sorry, I could never let a lady pay for her ticket. If you're going to be buddies with me, you'll have to let me pay. Your part will be to fix me a home-cooked meal occasionally."

"The pleasure would be all mine."

He tipped his hat and backed off my porch. "Thanks again for going with me, Valentine. It made this evening extra special."

I said good night and closed the door, locking it securely behind me. I'd had my first evening out with a man since losing Carter, and it hadn't been half bad.

Am I desecrating your memory, Carter? I asked later, lifting my face heavenward as I sat on the side of my bed, hoping my dear husband could hear me. *By spending time with Robert? I don't mean to. I love you. You were my everything. I'll always love you, but I'm so lonely without you.*

The framed picture of him on my nightstand smiled at me. Through tears, I smiled back, turned out the light, prayed, and went to sleep.

Barbie arrived about a quarter of ten the next morning, full of questions and accusations.

"You knew I liked Robert. Why didn't you suggest he take me to the barbecue instead of you?"

"You already had a date."

She pointed an accusing finger at me. "Just as I thought. It *was* a date!"

"You're not listening, Barbie. I said *you* already had a date. I said nothing about my evening with Robert being a date. You told me you were going out with your Realtor. At his request, I merely accompanied Robert to his barbecue so he wouldn't have to go alone. That's all."

She scooted into the chair next to me, the scowl on her face changing into an expression that reminded me of a little girl who'd just had her favorite doll snatched away from her. "You had a perfect husband, Valentine. All three of my husbands were louses. It's just not fair. Now I've finally found the one man I think I could trust—the one man who would treat me like a lady and give me the kind of unselfish love I've always wanted—and he's paying attention to you instead of me. Usually, men fawn all over me. I just don't know what I'm doing wrong."

"I don't think it's that you're doing anything wrong. It's just that you and Robert are worlds apart. Robert's relationship with God and his set of values are of the utmost importance to him. I doubt he'd ever be the least bit interested in a woman who didn't love God and share his values."

"Despite what you think, Valentine, I'm not a bad person. Just because I've been married three times doesn't make me an infidel."

The last thing I wanted was to make her angry. "In God's sight, marriage is sacred. When, at the marriage ceremony, we vow to love someone until death do us part, He expects us to keep that vow. I've no doubt Robert meant those words when he said them to his wife."

"I would have kept those vows, too, if any one of those men would have been what I thought they were, but they weren't. All three of them were mean and had a selfish streak a mile wide. I find it hard to believe

God, if there is a God, would have wanted me to stay with any one of them and be unhappy."

I wasn't about to touch the subject of her ex-husbands with her. And it was hard to keep from going into detail about why I was sure there was a God, although I definitely intended to take up that subject with her later on—just not now. I reached for her hand and gave it a gentle stroke. "I'm sure Robert likes you, Barbie, but it probably doesn't set well with him that you've been married three times and none of them worked out." I felt bad after I said it, but it was the truth.

She puckered up her face. "But they were bad husbands. Doesn't that count for anything? It wasn't my fault they were hard to live with." Her expression softened a bit. "Valentine, you have no idea what it's like to have your husband leave you for a younger woman, like my last husband did. I've never been so hurt and so humiliated."

She was right. I didn't have a clue as to what it was like. I was beginning to actually feel sorry for her, until she added, "I never understood why Carter married you instead of me, Valentine. I would have made him a much better wife." It was all I could do to keep from grabbing hold of her necklace and choking her with it, but fortunately Reva and Sally arrived and our conversation came to an abrupt end.

What, I wondered, would Barbie say if she knew Robert had invited me to attend a concert with him?

Though I wondered, I wasn't about to be the one to tell her.

She gave me a flip of her hand. "I'd like to stay and visit but my French decorator, Donatienne Cholmondeley, is due any minute." With barely a hello to my friends, she gave us a dismissive wave and headed home.

"What was that all about?" Reva asked as we all moved into my kitchen. "She looked like she'd been kissin' pigs."

"She thinks I'm trying to take Robert away from her."

Sally set her purse on the cabinet with a kerplunk. "What? How could *you* take him away from her if she doesn't even have him?"

Pushing an errant lock of hair from my forehead, I shrugged. "Beats me. There's not much about Barbie I understand."

Reva pulled three mugs from the cabinet and began filling them with coffee. "Though she puts on that flighty look-at-me-I'm-better-than-the-rest-of-you air, I'd guess she's one unhappy female."

"She is," I confirmed. "From what she's told me, her last husband about did her in. Leaving her for a younger woman must have been the worst blow her ego ever had."

Sally blew into her cup then took a sip of hot coffee. "When I first met Barbie—I hate to admit—I was jealous of her. Now I feel sorry for her. What a miserable life she must lead. Doesn't she know she doesn't have to impress everyone she meets? It's like she's onstage all the time. An actress in a play. No wonder she's always so strung out!"

"You're right, Sal." Reva pushed her cup aside and perched both elbows on the table. "*I* was even envious of her at first. I'd lost Manny. David was giving me all sorts of trouble. My testy mother-in-law was constantly picking at me. Yet, here she was, with everything going for her. Now, like Sally, I feel sorry for her. The three of us may not have our husbands to turn to, but we have our Father in heaven."

Sally nodded. "God is the only one who can clean up that girl's act."

I looked at the two women seated across the table from me. We three had shared so much, and we were important to one another. I knew I could trust these women with anything. And though Wendy, Edna, and Bitsy weren't here with us, I knew I could trust them, too. Friends. True friends. There was nothing like them.

I took a soothing sip of coffee then cradled the cup between my hands. "You're right, Sally. He has been speaking to me about Barbie, and though I admit I wasn't thrilled about it, I know He wants me to be kind to her and treat her with understanding. Barbie and I have never gotten along in the past. I resented her and didn't like her when we were teenagers and, sometimes, I don't like her now. But God has placed her in my life, right next door to me. I'd say that's pretty good evidence He wants me to share my faith with her."

Sally snickered. "I guess he wants Reva and me, and

144

even Wendy, Edna, and Bitsy, to share our faith, too, since we're your friends and are here nearly every day."

Reva nodded. "Yep. Strength in numbers."

I reached out my hands, and we joined in a prayer circle. With one accord, we prayed for Barbie.

But before we could say *Amen,* Reva's cell phone rang.

David had been arrested.

After news like that, Reva was in no condition to drive, so we took my minivan. Poor Reva, who was a usually master at hiding her emotions, cried like a baby all the way to the police station. I couldn't say I blamed her. I would have done the same thing. "I've failed my boy. I've failed Manny," she kept saying between sobs.

We tried to tell her she hadn't, but she was in no frame of mind to hear us.

David was being held in a room off the lobby. Sally and I waited outside the door while Reva went in to visit him. It was nearly an hour before she joined us again. "My son is in a lot of trouble. He's been charged with stealing. I should tell his grandmother about this before she finds out from someone else. As much as I'd like, since she already thinks I'm a bad mother, I can't keep it from her. Would you both go with me?"

"Of course we will." I wrapped an arm around each of them, and we headed toward my car.

Mrs. Billingham met us at the door. "Don't you three have anything better to do than drink coffee and gab all day? When I was your age, I was home doing laundry, baking bread, and waxing floors. I kept my house spot-less."

We moved through the door single file and regrouped in her living room. It was all I could do to keep from telling that cantankerous old woman to hold her tongue.

Apparently choosing to ignore the undeserved tirade, Reva took the old woman's hand and led her to the sofa, seating herself beside her. "I have something to tell you, Mother Billingham. David has been arrested for stealing. We just left the police station."

Her mother-in-law gave her a nasty smirk. "It's your fault, Reva. You're much too permissive with that boy. If my Manny had been here this wouldn't have happened."

I had to step in and defend Reva. "That's not fair!" I told her in no uncertain terms. "There's no better mother than your daughter-in-law."

Mrs. Billingham glared at me. "As I recall, Mrs. Denay, you never had children of your own. What makes you an authority on child rearing?"

The old pain echoed. Who was I to say anything?

Sally came to my rescue. "Valentine may not have had children of her own, but she's been like a second mother to our children."

Mrs. Billingham huffed. "Your children? Didn't I hear your daughter is giving you as much trouble as David is his mother?"

Now I had to defend Sally. "Having to raise a child as a widow is not an easy task but, like Reva, Sally is

146

doing her best and trusting God to answer prayer."

"Prayer? How blind can you women be? There is no God. He's only a figment of simple minds. If you're expecting a miracle from Him, you're going to have a long wait. My Manny was an intelligent man until he met Reva, then he turned into a Bible-believing robot just like her."

I pressed my lips together so hard it almost hurt, to keep pent-up angry words from escaping them. The nerve of that woman. But then I reminded myself Mrs. Billingham had recently lost her own mate, and I began to see her in a different light. Oh, not that becoming a widow gave her permission for such insolent behavior. It didn't. But I remember how grumpy I felt those first few months after I lost Carter. Losing him took all the joy out of life.

Sally bent toward Reva's mother-in-law. Lightly touching her hand, she spoke to her in a soft, controlled voice. "Reva loves you because *you* gave birth to Manny, her beloved husband. And God loves you, Mrs. Billingham. You can say what you want about Him, but that doesn't make Him any less real. I hope someday you'll understand, feel your need for Him, and call upon Him for forgiveness. He's ready to listen to us anytime."

The woman fairly exploded. "Forgiveness? What have I got to be forgiven for?"

Reva gestured toward the door. "Maybe you two had better go."

I pulled her aside and whispered, "Are you going to

be all right? I hate to leave you with that dreadful woman."

She shrugged. "I'll be fine. I'm used to her rantings. Besides, I'm too concerned about David to pay her much attention."

I cast a quick glance over my shoulder as Sally and I stepped out onto the porch. I felt as though I was deserting a friend in need.

"I wonder how soon they'll be coming after Jessica?" Sally said.

I turned quickly to face her. With everything going on in Reva's life, I'd nearly forgotten about the MP3 player in Jessica's possession. "Surely you don't think she stole it."

Sally cast her eyes downward. "I don't know what to think. It'd kill me to see the police haul her off to jail."

Robert called about nine that evening. "The pastor told me about David. I'm planning to go see him first thing in the morning, if they'll let me in."

"I know Reva would appreciate it. She's tried so hard to be both mother and father to that boy. I'm afraid without his father around, he's trying to find out who he is by any means possible."

"Pastor told me he lost his job at the car wash?"

I shifted the phone to my other ear. "Yes, he and one of the other kids put a scratch in some guy's Lexus."

"I'd like to spend some time with the boy. I wonder if David would be interested in working on one of my landscaping crews?"

His question surprised me. "You'd actually be

willing to hire him? Knowing he'd not only been fired from his job but was accused of stealing?"

"He wouldn't be the first troubled kid I've hired. Unlike my own son—"

"You have a son? I didn't know that. You never spoke about having children."

The pause on the other end alarmed me. Had I said something wrong?

"He died serving his country. His unit was one of the first to enter Baghdad."

A stabbing pain pierced my heart. "I'm so sorry. I—I didn't know."

"He was a great kid but, like most boys, he pulled a few shenanigans. The worst one was running the high school football coach's jockey shorts up the flag pole." He let loose a full-fledged snicker. "He got detention for that one and was benched for the next two games. Of course, he was also the school hero for doing it." Robert sighed and a silence descended. "We spent many happy hours together. Fishing, camping, going to ball games. I can't tell you how much I miss him. He died not long after his mother did. I'm really glad she didn't have to go through his loss. That was the only real blessing to come out of that horrible experience."

My heart ached for him. I'd thought I'd never recover after losing Carter, and here he'd lost both his wife *and* his son. "Oh, Robert, how terrible for you. I—I had no idea you'd been through so much."

"That's why the church's new youth center is so important to me. My son had planned to go to a Christian university after he'd served his term in Iraq. His goal was to become a youth minister."

I was speechless. What could I say to a man who has just told me something as heart wrenching as that?

"Well, I won't keep you," Robert broke the silence. "You've had a busy day. Please convey my good wishes to Reva and tell her to keep praying. Prayer changes things."

After mumbling a feeble, "I'll tell her," I said good-bye and hung up, with an even greater respect for Robert Chase than I'd had before that phone call.

I dialed Reva's number. "How're things going? Any word from David?"

"They're keeping him in a holding room overnight, which might put some fear into him. They'll release him sometime tomorrow."

"That's good. Robert said he was going by to see him first thing in the morning. He even talked about offering David a job." I heard a quick intake of breath on the other end of the line.

"Do you think he was serious? Maybe the judge *would* be more lenient with my son if he had a job lined up. That's really nice of Robert, especially under the circumstances. I'm glad you two have become friends."

"So am I. I'm surprised at how much we have in common, and he makes me laugh. I feel comfortable with him. He's taking me to a concert next week."

"A real date this time? No last minute fill-in like the last time?"

"I guess you could call it a real date, though he and I don't think of it that way. I just hope Barbie doesn't find out about it. She'll come unglued since she's already accused me of trying to take him away from her."

Reva let out a snort. "She actually thinks he's interested in her?"

"I guess so."

"She'd better forget about him. That woman, with all her beauty and so-called charms, can't even begin to compete with you."

"Reva! This is not a competition. Robert and I are simply friends who enjoy each other's company. Nothing more, and that's exactly what I'm telling Barbie. If she chooses to believe otherwise, that's her problem."

"I have a feeling she'll make it your problem, too. Other than when she was young and after Carter, you're probably the first real competition she's had for a man."

I laughed. "Spoken like a true biased friend, but let's forget about that for now. It's not important. What is important is you and David. Have faith. Okay?"

"I'm trying but, right now, my prayers for David seem to go unanswered."

"I know what you're saying. I felt that way when I lost Carter. But, slowly and surely, I'm learning again to trust God and His wisdom. I just wish I could see the whole picture."

"Me, too. Maybe that would help me deal better with David."

"I love you, Reva. You're a great mom and an even greater friend. Don't you forget it."

"Thanks. Your confidence in me helps. Good night."

"Good night."

So much was happening to the people I loved, my mind kept going in circles like it did so many nights when I couldn't sleep. I reached my hand toward the other side of the bed and splayed my fingers across the empty pillow, Carter's pillow. How I missed him. How I longed to feel his arms around me, holding me close, telling me how much he loved me. Tears, tears that flowed frequently in the darkness of the constant parade of lonely nights I have been doomed to face since Carter's death, ran down my cheeks, dropping silently onto my pillow as I thought about my beloved husband.

Will the hurt ever go away?

Will I ever feel like more than half a person?

I doubled my fist and rammed it into the pillow— hard. "God, why did you have to take my husband? I hate being a widow!"

CHAPTER 11

As the sun peeked around the edges of the Venetian blind the next morning, even though I'd had little sleep, I decided I might as well get out of bed. The way things had been going in my life, there was no telling what might happen next.

After a refreshing shower, I slipped into my favorite jeans and pulled on a bright cherry red T-shirt, hoping the brilliant burst of color would activate my energy. I hadn't exercised in days so, deciding with everything going on in my friends' lives they wouldn't be coming to my house for coffee, I grabbed a water bottle from the fridge, shoved my cell phone into my pocket in case one of them called, and slipped on my sunglasses. I was ready for a nice relaxing walk.

It was a typical late-spring day. The sun was shining, the birds were singing, and colorful flowers were bobbing their heads in countless well-cared-for flowerbeds in my neighbors' yards. It wasn't that I was avoiding Barbie, but this morning I'd conveniently decided to walk in the opposite direction of her house. I certainly didn't want another confrontation with her over Robert.

I'd reached the corner and was about ready to cross the street when a car pulled up in front of me and stopped.

A yellow Mercedes convertible with the top down. Barbie.

"Whatever are you doing this far from home? Did your car break down?"

I looked up the street and, noting no cars were coming, stepped off the curb and approached Barbie's car, bracing my hands on the passenger door. "No, my car's fine. I'm just out for a walk. It's a beautiful morning, and I figured I needed the exercise."

She patted the seat beside her. "Hop in. I want your

opinion on the color they're painting my walls."

I shook my head. "Maybe later. I really need to walk. Besides, you don't need my opinion. You have a professional decorator. A French one, no less."

She lowered her sunglasses and peered at me over the rims. "Even though she's highly qualified and supposed to know what she's doing, I'm just not sure I can live with the colors she's selected. I'd really appreciate it if you'd take a look."

What could I say? Begrudgingly, I tugged open the door and crawled in beside her. So much for getting exercise.

"Surely you have a treadmill, Valentine." She threw the gearshift into drive and gave me a victorious smile, as though she'd talked me into doing something I really didn't want to do.

Come to think of it, that's exactly what she had done.

Mentally working at tamping down my disgust with myself for giving in so easily, I shrugged. "No, I don't have a treadmill, but I have been thinking about getting one. I love to walk outdoors when the weather is beautiful, like today, but a treadmill would be nice when it rains and during the cold winter months."

"As far as I'm concerned, a treadmill is a must. I walk two miles on mine every morning. I can't imagine any woman who wants to maintain her beauty and her figure not having one."

I flinched when she made a left turn without flipping on her turn signal. "I like to look nice, but I'm not as concerned about those things as I am about good health and keeping my heart in shape," I said.

"Would you believe at one time I was fifty pounds overweight?"

My head spun around as if it were on a pivot. "You? Fifty pounds overweight? No, I can't believe it. You're even thinner now than you were when we were in high school!"

"Well, I did. After my last divorce was final I went on the king of all eating binges. I lived on fried chicken, mashed potatoes and gravy, chips and dips, consumed gallons of ice cream, devoured cookies and cakes. Anything I could find to eat, I ate." She gave me a toothy grin. "If I'd painted Goodyear on my thighs, people would have mistaken me for that famous blimp."

I gazed at Barbie, trying to visualize her slim body with that much weight on it. It certainly didn't have an extra ounce of fat on it now.

"I finally came to my senses and realized I'd never catch a man that way, so I checked myself into one of those expensive California fat farms and spent the next three months eating bird food, exercising, meeting with doctors, and listening to lectures." She said it as proudly as if she were telling me about a relaxing trip to an exotic resort.

"By the end of those three months, I'd dropped thirty-five pounds."

"Then you lost the additional fifteen on your own? That's marvelous." I was impressed. "What will power that must have taken."

After guiding her car into her driveway and turning off the ignition, she reached into her purse and pulled out a prescription bottle. "Most of my will power is right here in this little bottle."

I stared at the brown plastic container. "I don't understand."

"I take three of these a day, and *voilà!* No hunger pains!"

I couldn't help frowning. "Are they safe?"

She chortled. "They'd better be, with the kind of money I'm paying for these jewels. The only way I can get them is from the doctors at the fat farm." Pushing open her door, she actually giggled. "They're what got me through those three months. I couldn't have made it without them then, and I sure couldn't maintain my current weight without them now." Balancing the pill bottle in her flattened palm, she held up her hand. "These babies are pure magic."

I stared at the bottle in amazement. "What's in those pills?"

She gave me a toss of her hand. "Who cares? As long as they work."

Warning flares went up in my mind. How many times had I heard on the news about a diet pill or a weight loss scheme being pulled off the market because it wasn't safe? I'd even seen interviews with people who had experienced severe health problems because of some lose-it-fast diet plans that included pills of some sort.

I leaped out of her convertible and rushed to catch up

with her as she headed for her front porch. "Oh, Barbie, I hope you're being careful. There are so many horror stories about—"

She turned quickly, holding up her hand between us. "Not another word, Valentine. I trust those doctors completely. It was a mistake to tell you about my weight problems. I should have known you'd over-react."

With a haughty tilt of her head, she punched the code into the keyless entry pad and opened the door.

I quickly stepped in and shut the door behind us. "I'm concerned about you, Barbie, that's all."

"Well, you needn't be. I'm a grown woman and a smart one at that. Let's just drop the subject. I invited you here to look at my walls, not give me the third degree."

I sucked in a couple of deep breaths and swallowed at the words I wanted to say. I *was* concerned about her—genuinely, deeply concerned. Those first few days when she came to my house, I'd thought she was nothing but fluff and a ton of folly, a true Barbie doll, living a fairytale life with none of the problems most of us mere mortals faced. How wrong I was. "I'll drop the subject if you want me to, but that doesn't mean I won't pray for you. Those pills of yours scare me to death!"

"You can pray all you want, as long as you don't try to lecture me." After stepping into her museum-sized living room, she pointed toward her newly painted walls. "I want your honest opinion. What do you think of this color?"

For the first time since entering the foyer, my mind and my thoughts still caught up with my concern for Barbie, I fully glanced at the room.

"Lime green?" I nearly screamed out at the repulsive color. I felt as if I were standing in the center of one of those nasty upset-stomach commercials. "Whatever was your decorator thinking?"

"It's not lime green. It's Tahitian Foam from the Sea. Donatienne Cholmondeley told me she had the color mixed up especially for me and then made the paint company promise to throw away the formula so no one else could ever have the same color."

"Who'd want it?" I let my lower lip roll down. "Remind me never to go to Tahiti if that's the way their sea looks. Surely you didn't suggest this color."

Plopping down on one of her still-covered-with-plastic sofas, she gave her head a sad shake. "No, I didn't suggest it, although I did give her carte blanche. I never thought she'd use something like this. You don't like it, do you?"

I sat down beside her, my eyes still focused on those awful, nauseating walls. "You do want my honest opinion?"

She nodded.

"I hate it. Just looking at it makes me want to heave."

"She said it was the new *in* color in the world of design, and by having my walls painted this color my home would be on the cutting edge of interior fashion design."

"And you believed her?" The words slipped out

before I could stop them.

"I didn't know what to believe, Valentine. I was lucky to get her. She's a highly sought-after interior decorator, but I hate it, too. That's why I wanted your opinion. I thought maybe it was just me. And those walls are just the beginning." She pulled a carpet sample from beneath one of the sofas. "She's planning to use this on the floors."

I blinked my eyes, thinking surely they were playing tricks on me. "Rust?"

"She called it Island Sand at Sunset."

I couldn't resist. "To go with Tahitian Foam from the Sea, right?"

"Yes. But there's more." Rising again, she pulled back the plastic cover from the sofa where she'd been seated.

"Pink?"

Barbie threw back her head with a laugh. "Passionate Mingle!"

"Passionate Mingle? You've got to be kidding. Did she make up those names, thinking they'd be more impressive than lime green, rust, and pink?"

She shrugged. "I don't know. Do you think she did? They do sound more impressive."

"Let's take a look." I grabbed up the carpet sample and flipped it over to the back side, read the label and, nearly bursting inside, pointed to the manufacturer's description.

"Rust? It says rust right on the label?" With close to a belly laugh, Barbie dropped back onto the sofa,

159

flailing her hands in the air. "That woman *did* make up those words."

"Want to check out the sofa?" I asked, in a fit of laughter myself.

She stood quickly, her eyes shining with glee. "Yes, let's!"

It took both of us to turn the heavy sofa onto its back. "You want to do the honors?" I asked, gesturing toward the manufacturer's tag stapled to the frame.

Barbie grinned then bent to read the tag. "Ninety percent Egyptian cotton, ten percent silk. Trim, eighty percent rayon, twenty percent, silk. Color—" With a flourish of her hand, she yelled, "Ta da! Pink!"

After a good laugh, I had an idea. "Did the painters leave the paint cans in your garage? It'd be interesting to see what color was printed on the lids."

Grinning, she crooked a finger at me, and we both made our way down the hall toward the door that led to the garage. It took us a few minutes of rummaging through paint drop cloths, soaking brushes, ladders, and such, but we finally located two empty cans in a trash container the painters had brought with them.

"It's your house. You look," I told her, even though curiosity was getting the better of me.

Moving forward dramatically, she held her nose with the fingers of one hand, then slowly lifted the other hand high before plunging it deep into the container and pulling out one of the filthy dirty cans. Some sort of sticky putty stuff was stuck all over it. For an anxious moment, I was afraid she was going to toss it back without a look. But she bravely held on. "It says right here in big bold letters—" Smiling a huge smile at me, she paused.

"Okay. Out with it." I raised my brows. "It says what?"

"Lime green!"

From the way we grabbed each other, throwing back our heads and laughing hysterically, an observer would have thought we were teenagers again, instead of grown women.

"The gall of that woman." Barbie finally said, dropping the can back into the trash and brushing at her hands. "She actually read me the riot act when I referred to those walls as lime green. What a faker."

Off in the distance we faintly heard what sounded like Westminster chimes.

"The doorbell. That's got to be Donatienne. I'd called and asked her to stop by."

I hurried to catch up with her as she rushed out of the garage and back into the house. I had to admit, her designer's appearance was impressive. She wore some sort of ethnic bead-trimmed shirt over a pair of white pants, with her jet-black hair pulled severely back into an oversized chignon at the nape of her neck. Her flawlessly applied makeup made her appear deeply tanned, but it was her eyes that drew my attention. Outlined with a deep black liner, they appeared quite large and almond shaped, almost like a cat's. Shadowed with a deep plum-colored eye shadow, she looked like something out of a travel magazine. In some ways, as I gazed at her, she looked familiar, but I'd never used a decorator. How would I know her?

Lifting her head regally, she did a slow three-sixty about the room, her eyes scanning each of the four walls with a look of satisfaction. "Nice!" she finally said as the two of us stood there like the bumpkins she probably thought we were. "Tahitian Foam from the Sea. The perfect color for this room. I was a genius to come up with this mystical color."

From the look on Barbie's face when she heard that statement, I thought she was going to explode.

"I can't believe you'd lie to me like that. You're fired!" she literally screamed at the woman. "Tahitian Foam from the Sea? You mean lime green, don't you? Plain, old, garden variety lime green? How dare you try to trick me like that? You must have thought me a real fool. Combining lime green, rust, and pink and calling your crazy combination the cutting edge of interior decorating might work with some of your gullible clients, but not this one! Maybe you could live with those colors, but I can't and won't. I refuse to be the laughingstock of my friends because I was dumb enough to turn my decorating job over to you."

Suddenly, it hit me. I *did* know this woman who called herself by such an exotic name! Myrtle? Myrtle—something.

"Myrtle Peabody!" I cried out in total shock. "You're Donatienne Cholmondeley? When did you change your name?"

All color drained from her face. "I don't know what

162

you're talking about. You must have me confused with someone else."

Barbie let out a gasp. "You know her?"

"Of course, I know her. She was in my junior high cooking class."

Barbie glared at her. "You told me you had lived most of your life in France."

Turning her head aside, the decorator narrowed her eyes and became indignant. "This is ridiculous. I've never seen this person before."

I grabbed onto her left hand and gave it a slight twist, revealing a long, shiny scar across the width of her palm. "You got that scar when you picked up a hot dish without using a hot pad! You were in terrible pain. Remember how you cried? We all felt sorry for you."

"If she went to school with us, why don't I remember her?" Barbie asked, sizing her decorator up.

"She moved away at the end of that semester. You hadn't moved into our school district yet," I explained.

Barbie huffed. "Myrtle Peabody to Donatienne Cholmondeley? That's quite a leap!"

Lifting her chin, Myrtle gave us a mightier-than-thou look. "Just because I changed my name doesn't make me any less a decorator. I have credentials from The American Institute of Design, I'm a professional member of the American Society of Interior Designers, and I'm certified by the National Council for Interior Design."

With that kind of arrogance, I couldn't resist challenging her. "Lime green you call Tahitian Foam from the Sea. Rust you call Island Sand at Sunset, and pink you call Passionate Mingle? Isn't that a bit strange? Especially when the lids on the paint cans very clearly stated lime green? Surely you don't deny what you used on those walls is anything but plain lime green, commercially prepared and produced by the thousands at a plant somewhere."

She visibly bristled. "I give my clients what they want. They don't want green, rust, and pink. They want exotic names. Something created exclusively for them. There's nothing wrong with that. When people are paying big dollars to have a certified decorator decorate their home, they expect the unusual, something no one else has. I give it to them. What I do makes them happy."

"Well, this girl is anything *but* happy!" Barbie planted her Manolo Blahniks firmly on the floor and crossed her arms over her chest. "Unusual, I like. Exotic, I like. You could put potted palms all over my house and I'd be happy, but I want to live in a house that doesn't scream out at me. As far as I'm concerned, you can take your Tahitian Foam from the Sea, your Island Sand at Sunset, and your Passionate Mingle, and shove them you know where."

"Barbie!" Though she used words that set my teeth on edge, I had to agree with her. I could never live with that combination of colors.

Reaching into her purse, Barbie pulled out her checkbook, hurriedly wrote a check then handed it to the woman. "Here, Donatienne Cholmondeley or

Myrtle Peabody or whatever your name is. This pays you in full for your services."

Frowning and giving Barbie a look of confused bewilderment, she begrudgingly accepted the check. "This is for one dollar!" she railed angrily.

Barbie jutted out her chin. "And that's all you're going to get out of me. I've already given you more than I should. Now, take it and go."

Donatienne Cholmondeley gave her a look that would have made the strongest weakhearted. "You'll hear from my lawyer about this."

"If I do, you'll hear from mine. I wouldn't recommend suing me, Myrtle. Believe me, others have tried and failed. I'm an old hand at lawsuits."

The frazzled woman grabbed her handbag from the table, spun around on her heels, and literally raced to the door, slamming it behind her.

Barbie threw back her head with an exaggerated laugh. "I can't tell you how glad I am to be rid of her. What a fake." She gave me a high five. "You and I make a great team."

Barbie and me? A team? That was a first, but, actually, the thought felt pretty good. "You're rid of her, but you still have a house that needs decorating. What are you going to do about that?"

Seeming unconcerned with her dilemma, she giggled as if she didn't have a care in the world. "I already have someone in mind to help me with the decorating. Someone I think will be perfect."

I raised a brow. "Really? Who?"

"You!"

I scraped myself up from the floor. Me help Barbie decorate her home? I thought not. "I'm no decorator!"

"I know, but you have good taste. Look at what you've done with your house. Victorian tinged with eclectic is not my style, but you've done an incredible job of pulling everything together. With your eye for color and my eye for the unusual and the exotic, I think the two of us could really pull this decorating thing off! We might even want to band together and do it commercially." She fanned her hand in an arc. "I can see it now. Barbie and Valentine Designers. Decorating with flair."

"Commercially? Me and you? You've got to be kidding."

She gave my arm a playful pinch. "Come on, Valentine, it'll be fun. Say you'll do it. Maybe we can even enlist Robert's help."

Oh, that'd just be peachy keen. The three of us picking out paint, carpet, drapery, and bric-a-brac together. That would be a sight to behold. "Sorry. Right now, my life is focused on making the Cooperville Community Church bazaar a success, and I know this is Robert's busy season."

Barbie did a turnabout and put on a pouty face. "But I need you, Valentine. Barbie's Red Hat Babes are meeting at my house in four weeks. You wouldn't want them to see my new home looking like this, would you? With lime green paint on my walls and this ugly worn out purple and sage green carpet on my floors?

I'm their queen! People expect the queen's house to look like a palace."

Why did I always seem to be bailing Barbie out of one problem or another? If it wasn't going with her to her Red Hat meeting, or fastening her necklace, or having dinner at her house so Robert would agree to come, it was something else. All the years I'd known her, she'd always been a taker. She was nothing but a partially grown-up, selfish kid. If I weren't so busy right now, I'd enjoy helping with her home, just not now.

"I'm sorry, Barbie. I can't do it. There just aren't enough hours in the day. You're talented. I'm sure you'll do fine without me."

Crossing her arms, she gaped at me.

"But you always find time for Sally and Reva. I thought I was your friend, but you always put me in last place in everything."

"I haven't put you in any place. The problems Reva and Sally are facing are very real problems. Problems that are bound to affect the future of their families. Those two need all the help they can get."

"I need help, too. My problems are real."

"It's not the same thing." I gestured around the room. "Your problems can be solved with a paintbrush and a shopping trip. Sally's and Reva's problems are life issues. I can't turn my back on them in their hour of need."

"But you can turn it on me in my hour of need?"

"Oh, grow up. Contrary to what you may think, the

world doesn't revolve around you." I'd had it with her. Normally, I never would have talked that way to anyone. And here I was talking that way to Barbie, the one person I'd been trying to influence for Christ. What was the matter with me?

"I have other friends, you know. I'm not dependent on you," she shot back defensively, her eyes filled with fire.

"I know you have other friends. I met some of them at your meeting. Perhaps one of them could help you."

With a shake of her head, she crossed the room to the foyer, opened the front door then spun around toward me, her face red with anger. "Thank you for coming, Valentine. Now you'd better run along to your friends—your *real* friends. I can get along fine without you. I should never have let you talk me into firing my decorator, but don't worry about me. Barbie Baxter always lands on her feet and I will again this time."

Me talk her into it? I couldn't believe she'd accused me of such a thing. "You're saying I talked you into getting rid of Myrtle? I had nothing to do with it. As I recall, you were already unhappy with her before I even came along. Didn't you beg me to come and see if I hated your lime green walls as much as you did?"

"I might have learned to live with that Tahitian Foam from the Sea color if you hadn't made such a big deal about its name. After all, Donatienne Cholmondeley is a certified interior decorator with a fine reputation. I'm sure she knows far more about decorating than you'll ever know."

The condescending tone of her voice really upset me. "I do need to check on Sally and Reva," I told her through gritted teeth, "and I'm sure you'll want to put in a call to Myrtle, to apologize for *my* behavior. Maybe, if you apologize real nice, you can convince her I coerced you into firing her." I pushed past her and moved out the door and across her lawn without even a backward glance. All I wanted was to get out of there and back to my house.

If God wanted someone to share their faith with Barbie, it looked like He was going to have to find someone else.

CHAPTER 12

What a day this had been and it was only half over. My plans were to devote the entire afternoon to the bazaar. I couldn't let anything stand in the way of its success. I knuckled down at my desk and spent the whole afternoon going over the proposed budget and checking the various bills that had already come in, making phone calls, and a myriad of other tasks that were a part of it. At five, I closed the ledger and leaned back in my chair with satisfaction. Despite the difficulties my friends were facing, things were right on schedule.

"They let me in to see David," Robert told me when he phoned a few minutes later. "At first, the boy was standoffish. I tried to explain I was a friend of his mother's and I wanted to be his friend, too, but he wasn't interested. I won't bore you with the details but once David realized I was there to help him and I offered him a job, he loosened up and actually began to talk civilly to me. I could tell he was scared, although he wouldn't admit it. I spoke to the detective. He said David told him, in addition to the other things he'd stolen from the discount house, he'd given an MP3 player to Sally's daughter and one to another friend. Since this is his first offense, they'll probably let him go right away, but he'll have to appear before a judge in a few days. I talked to the detective about David working for me. He thought having a job lined up would definitely work in his favor with the judge."

Robert was going out on a limb for a boy he barely knew? It reminded me of something Carter would've done.

"I got the feeling he was pretty excited about working for me. I think most young men like the idea of working outside with their hands. I explained it's hard work and the pay is just slightly above minimum wage, but that didn't seem to matter. I warned him I give people one chance. If they blow it, they're gone. I can't afford to have my crews doing shoddy work for my clients."

"You barely know Reva's son."

"True, but I like to think I'm a pretty good judge of character. I know what it's like to lose your dad at such a young age. I lost my dad when I was ten. I can relate to David. I understand what that boy is going through—the sorrow, the confusion, and the stability a father can bring, especially a Christian father. I can't take his father's place, no one can, but I'd like a chance to make a difference in his life."

My admiration for Robert hit the top of the charts. As busy as he was running his business and serving on the church board, he was still willing to devote his time and energies to a boy he barely knew. And here I was grumbling about Barbie. "Not many men would have reached out to David like you have."

"That kid is at a real crossroads in his life. I want to help him get headed in the right direction."

As we ended our conversation, I stared at the closed ledger. With Reva and Sally having so much on their plates, maybe I should consider replacing them as the chairwomen of their committees, especially if Jessica was arrested, too. But who could take their place? I had already appointed the most responsible women in the church as head of the other committees. If no one on her committee felt like taking over, maybe I could get one of the men to take over Reva's position. Someone with building experience. But who could take Sally's place? *Hopefully Jessica is as innocent as she claims, and it won't be necessary to replace Sally.*

I glanced at the calendar on my desk. We weren't anywhere near the panic zone yet. I decided to give things a few more days to work themselves out; then I'd worry about it.

The next few days went by without further incident. Sally, Reva, Bitsy, Wendy, and I, along with several other committee members, worked nonstop on the bazaar. I was thrilled with some of the ideas my committee chairwomen had come up with. This bazaar was going to be even better than I'd hoped it would be.

"You'll have to come by the church and see our progress," Reva told me. It was good to see her smiling again. "We've already built a prototype of our first booth, to make sure it was going to work out well and, if I have to admit it, it's lookin' good!" She gave me a thumbs up. "That new woman—Carlotta—she can really swing a mean hammer. I'm sure glad she decided to help us. If the rest of the booths go as smoothly as this one, we should have them finished in no time."

"Good job, Reva. Tell your committee we really appreciate their efforts."

I turned to Wendy. "Are those women on Reva's committee really as talented as she says they are, or is it your prayer team that's making those booths go together this easily?"

Wendy sent a mischievous smile toward Reva. "Let's keep peace in the church family and say it's a combination of both. After all, God *is* the One who is in control of this project, isn't He? We are doing this for Him."

Leave it to our tactful Wendy to say the right thing.

"My committee has a prayer request."

We all turned toward Bitsy.

"Trudy and the women on our committee are doing an admirable job getting the word out about the bazaar,

172

but we need to start thinking about who will be doing the radio and TV interviews we've arranged. No one on our committee is brave enough to be interviewed. We need to pray for a spokesperson. Someone who is comfortable in front of a video camera and can make people want to come to our bazaar."

Everyone's attention turned toward me. I held my hands up defensively. "Oh, no. Not me. I'm the general chairwoman, not a TV spokesperson. You'll have to find someone else. How about Sally? She's a people person."

Sally gave her head a vigorous shake. "No way! I do fine face-to-face and on the telephone, but in front of a camera? Knowing there are thousands watching? I'd freeze up."

"Then how about Reva?"

Reva frowned at me. "Not me. My life is in constant turmoil. I never know when a problem is going to flare up. Besides, I'd be scared speechless with that camera pointed at me. Nope, you'll have to find someone else."

One by one, every person there turned down the opportunity to appear on behalf of our bazaar, and none had any worthwhile suggestions.

"How about the pastor?" someone finally asked. "He's used to talking in front of people."

"I thought this was going to be an all-woman thing," Reva reminded us. "I think a woman appearing on those interview-type shows would do a better job. You know, she'll be talking about crafts and food and sale booths. It's definitely a job for a woman."

All eyes turned back to me.

Pointing a finger at me, Sally grinned. "Looks like it's up to you, Valentine. Unless you can think of someone else who is as outgoing and brave as you are, and wouldn't mind appearing on TV."

Before I could again refuse, my back door opened.

"When I saw all the cars in the driveway, I figured you girls were having one of your little bazaar meetings, and I just thought of a way I could help," Barbie said, smiling enthusiastically and nodding toward each lady present. Me included, as if everything was perfect between us. "I'm great at decorating. Why don't I head up a committee to decorate the church for the bazaar. You know, hang up dozens of colorful balloons, bright strips of crepe paper, strings of blinking lights. Maybe we can make it a Mardi Gras theme!"

I wanted to roll my eyes at her ridiculous suggestions, but I didn't. "I don't think a Mardi Gras theme would be appropriate, Barbie. Besides, we want our booths and our food service to be the center of attention. I'm afraid balloons, crepe paper, and blinking lights might distract from the real purpose of the bazaar."

Placing her hand on her hip, she rolled down that pouty lip. "You're being way too stuffy, Valentine. Think of all the fun a Mardi Gras theme would add to the atmosphere. I'll bet the people would love it. Maybe we could sell strings of those colorful Mardi Gras beads to make extra money!"

Knowing it was pointless to argue with her—she'd always come up with an answer to counter my reasoning—I decided to do the only thing I could think of. Stall her. "Why don't we think about this and talk about it later, okay?"

Undaunted, she continued on, "I have another idea. I used to be married to Skip Morrison, the network news television anchorman, and my last husband was a big wheel executive at the network, so I know my way around television. Maybe I could help you line up some interviews with the local TV and radio stations so you could publicize the bazaar."

The other women in the room smiled at one another as though our answer to prayer had just walked through the door. I felt as if another nightmare was about to begin.

One of the women, her eyes shining with excitement and looking directly at Barbie asked, "Have you ever done any television—"

"Time is getting away from us," I broke in quickly, knowing exactly what she was going to say. "Why don't we table this discussion about publicity until later on, after we've had time to think about it and do a bit more research." Before anyone had time to respond, I adjourned our meeting.

"Why don't we use her? I think she'd make an excellent spokesperson," one of the ladies said to me on her way out. "She's very attractive, and I'll bet she's articulate. What do you think, Valentine?"

I pasted on a smile and attempted to hide my true

feelings as best I could. "Let's pray about it, okay? We have plenty of time to make that decision."

Thankfully, she nodded and moved on out the door. But I knew that wasn't going to be the end of it. The seed had been planted in everyone's mind. Only Sally, Reva, and I knew the real Barbie. Maybe, when the ladies found out Barbie had been married three times and was actively seeking a fourth husband, they'd change their minds. But, much more importantly, she didn't share our faith. No matter how beautiful and articulate she was, she may not have been our best choice.

One by one the committee chairwomen left. Even Sally and Reva left me alone with Barbie.

"I do want to help with your little bazaar, Valentine." Barbie pulled her compact from her purse and stared at her image. "You simply have to find something for me to do. I'm not going to leave you alone until you come up with a job for me."

I searched my brain for something nondescript, something she couldn't mess up. "Ah, you said you were good at hostessing. I do need someone to greet people at the door as they enter the bazaar. You know, tell them how glad we are they came and make them feel welcome. Maybe you could do that." That'd certainly be better than letting her go on television as the church's spokesperson.

Closing her compact with a snap, Barbie brightened and gave me a toothy grin. "What a great idea! I guess this means I'm a part of your committee, doesn't it?"

176

I nodded. "Yes, I guess it does."

"Oh, good. Now I can officially attend your little meetings." She gave her head a thoughtful tilt. "Let's see, what shall I wear? I'll have to buy new outfits, of course. Something bright and cheery. Maybe red. Red is always good. That's it. I'll wear red the first day, and a rosy pink the second day. Those are my best colors."

I had to bite my tongue to keep from telling her this bazaar wasn't about her and what expensive outfits she wore. "Wear whatever you like. I know you'll look good."

Sidling up next to me, her smile left her face. "I know you want to apologize to me, Valentine. I thought I'd make it easy for you by coming over to your house." She leaned against my counter and crossed her arms over her chest. "Go ahead. I'm listening."

If I'd been a champagne bottle, I'd have popped my cork. The nerve of that woman! "You have got to be kidding," I said in a not-too-kind way, my eyes narrowed, my brows furrowed, and my heart beating a mile a minute. "*You* should be the one apologizing, not me!"

Giving her head a haughty tilt, she sauntered her way across my kitchen and seated herself at my table. "Come on, Valentine. We both know you were the one who drove my decorator away. Then when I humbled myself by asking, you weren't even nice enough to help me with my home."

My chin dropping nearly to my collarbone, I stared

at her in amazement. "*I* drove her away? If I remember correctly, *you* were the one who wrote her a check for one dollar and sent her packing."

"Only because you drove me to do it."

I dropped myself in the chair next to her, my chin jutting out for emphasis. "I didn't drive you to do anything. I simply agreed with you that Myrtle was not the premier decorator you'd thought she was."

"If you hadn't agreed with me, maybe I wouldn't have fired her and I'd have my house in the process of being decorated, instead of just sitting there with nothing happening. I tell you, Valentine, it's depressing living in a house in upheaval. It's driving me crazy!"

That part I could agree with. I couldn't stand living in a mess like that. "Have you tried to find another decorator?"

"Yes, but the good ones are all booked up."

"Have you tried to get Myrtle, or whatever her name is, back again?"

"I've considered it."

Okay, I admit it. She was beginning to get to me with her woe-is-me sob story. "Maybe you could get her to come back, only this time you could insist that you be the one to make the final decisions. That way, you'd end up with what you wanted, instead of what she wanted."

"It's a thought."

We sat there in dead silence. I didn't know what else to say, and I certainly wasn't about to apologize for something I hadn't done just to appease her.

Finally, taking on a slightly contrite expression, she rose and walked slowly to the door then turned back to face me. "If I can't get Myrtle back or find another decorator who can get the job done in time, will you at least help me pick out the paint colors and the colors for the carpet and furniture?"

Before I could answer, my phone rang. I excused myself and picked it up.

"Hi. This is Robert. I know the concert starts at eight, but I thought it'd be nice if we could have dinner first. Would it be okay if I picked you up a little before six instead of seven?"

I glanced at my watch. That would only give me an hour to get ready. "Sure, dinner would be nice. I'll be looking for you a little before six."

When I hung up the phone, I found Barbie with one hand perched on her hip, glaring at me. "That was Robert? You have another date with Robert?"

Knowing my answer could start World War Three, I simply nodded.

"Well, that beats all. Just when I thought you were going to apologize and be my friend again, you pull something like this."

Grrr! Why did she always show up at the most inappropriate times? Then have the nerve to act as if she had claims on Robert? Determined to hold back the snappy retort that was just aching to be said, I slowly counted to ten.

"If you'd quit chasing him, he might have more time for me."

Fortunately for both of us, I'd only reached six.

"You say you're not ready to start dating, yet you shamelessly lead that man on. It's just not fair!"

Nine. Ten! "That is the stupidest remark I've ever heard. I've never *led* any man on!"

"Oh? What about Carter? Do you honestly think he would have pursued you if you hadn't led him on? I'll just bet you even let him—"

I flung my finger into her face. "Don't you dare make such a derogatory remark about my and Carter's relationship when we were courting. Carter and I respected each other. We would never—cross the line!" I was so upset at her implication I thought I would explode.

Obviously unfazed by the angry tone of my voice, she simply shrugged. "Oh, don't get your bowels in an uproar. What you and Carter did in his parked car is of no concern to me, but I know what I would have done with him."

I rushed across the room, pushed her aside, and grabbed open my door, swinging it wide. "Out!" I shouted angrily, pointing my finger again. "Now! Before I say something we'll both regret."

Still seeming unfazed, she gave me a flip of her hand. "You're way too touchy, Valentine." Moving out the door at her own speed, when she reached the bottom step she turned and smiled up at me with that sticky sweet fake smile of hers that drove me wild. "You'd better get a handle on that temper of yours. I doubt your God would like it."

I had no comeback. No retort. Nothing.

What she said was true.

Speechless, I watched as she crossed my lawn and headed for her in-the-middle-of-being-decorated house, with its ugly purple and sage green carpet and its lime green walls. I wanted to cry. I'd never thought of myself as an angry person. Quite the contrary. But today, I'd let her false accusations get the best of me. I'd responded in a way that even she, who didn't believe in God, could see was not pleasing to Him.

Though the clock on my kitchen wall reminded me I had only fifty minutes left to get ready for my evening with Robert, I fell to my knees and prayed, asking for forgiveness.

"What's wrong?" Robert asked me later as we sat opposite each other at the trendy restaurant, enjoying our delicious steak dinners. "You seem a bit glum this evening. Where's that pretty smile?"

I wasn't about to tell him he had been the main source of Barbie's and my unpleasant confrontation, so I just shrugged. "Sorry. This was just one of those days."

He reached across the table and cupped his hand over mine. "Anything I can do to help?"

Just being with this pleasant man, and knowing he was concerned enough to offer to help, lifted my spirits. I gave him one of my best smiles. "You already have."

He smiled back, giving my hand a gentle squeeze. "Then put on a happy face, set aside whatever was troubling you, and let's enjoy our evening, okay?"

"I've been thinking, Robert," I said slowly, choosing my words carefully. "There are several really nice, attractive, friendly widows in my women's Bible study class. Maybe instead of taking me to dinner and concerts, you should ask one of them. I know you'd like them."

His brow creased. "You don't like going places with me?"

"I—I love going places with you but—"

"But you want to match me up with someone else?"

"I—it's just that you've talked about remarrying, and I'm just not sure if—"

"I think I'm capable of deciding which women I want to spend time with and which ones I don't. I've chosen you." Raising one brow, he gave my hand a pat. "Now, no more attempts at matchmaking, okay?"

There it was. That blush I could never hold back. "Okay," I said, feeling somewhat stupid for even mentioning it to him. That didn't mean I wasn't going to continue to look for a good woman for him. This man was too precious to let Barbie get her hooks into him.

The concert lifted my spirits. "This evening has been just what I needed," I told Robert, feeling somewhat awkward as we stood at my door. I couldn't recall how to end an evening with a male companion. It'd been so long since I'd dated. "Would you like to come in for a cup of coffee?" I finally managed to say.

To my amazement, he bent and kissed my cheek.

182

"Thanks, but no. I'd better get on home. Early day tomorrow. We're starting Barbie's job."

I didn't know which flabbergasted me most. The unexpected kiss or his announcement that tomorrow he would be beginning work at Barbie's house. It was actually going to happen. I thanked him once again and said a simple good night.

The good time I'd had with Robert was suddenly forgotten as I lay in bed thinking about Barbie and the things we'd said to each other. Though I had been furious with her implications, I knew regardless of what she'd said, I'd had no right to speak to her in that way.

I was out of bed early the next morning with the full intention of making things right with her as soon as possible. I waited until eight o'clock before heading toward her house. But before I even reached my bottom step, three trucks rolled into her driveway. The first was Robert's truck. The second, an expanded cab model loaded with workmen who piled out almost before the engine was turned off. The bed of the third truck was filled with all sorts of equipment, and attached to it was a trailer carrying a backhoe. It looked like Barbie's yard was in for a serious overhaul.

I paused for a moment, trying to decide if I should go on over or wait until later, when Barbie was alone, to apologize to her. But before I could come to a decision Robert called out my name and motioned for me to come over to where he was standing talking to one of the men.

"Good morning," he said brightly as I joined them. "I wanted to introduce you to my foreman. Valentine Denay, this is Jake Gorman. Jake is not only my foreman, he's my accountability partner." He chuckled. "He's the one who keeps me on the straight and narrow."

"Big job, too," the man said, extending his hand. "Nice to meet you, Mrs. Denay. Robert speaks highly of you."

"You're early!" an all too familiar voice called out.

The three of us turned as Barbie came bustling out her door, the sun shining through her filmy orange printed caftan as it furled out behind her, her orange lipsticked mouth forming a brilliant smile. Totally ignoring Jake Gorman's and my presence, she grabbed onto Robert's hand and attempted to drag him toward her house. "You must come and have coffee and a roll with me before you begin your day."

He stood his ground, leaving her looking frustrated and embarrassed. "Sorry. As much as I'd like to, I can't. I have a crew to get busy." He nodded toward Jake. "Jake's my foreman. He and I will be working together on your project. Why don't you show him which trees you want saved while I have a word with Valentine?"

After a quick, piercing glare at me, and a flirtatious wink to Robert, she drawled out, "Don't you let these men take too long, sugar. You know how anxious I am to get this job finished." Then turning her head so he couldn't see her face, she gave me a scathing look that could have frozen homemade ice cream. Then she turned and latched onto Jake's sleeve and led him into her backyard.

Apparently not noticing the strain going on between the two of us, Robert turned to me with a broad smile. "I spoke with the judge early this morning. Turns out he's an old classmate of my wife's. I explained about David losing his father at such a young age and how hard Reva has been trying to be both mother and father to him. Then I told him I had offered David a job and he had accepted. Because I promised I would keep an eye on the boy, the judge has agreed to put his hearing off for a few weeks, to give David a chance to settle down and evaluate the seriousness of his offense. If, at that time, he is doing well and getting along okay on his job, since it's his first offense, if agreeable with the discount store's manager, he may let him off with only a severe scolding."

I couldn't contain my happiness. I wanted to reach out and hug him. "Oh, Robert, what good news. Reva's been so worried about her son."

"I couldn't wait to tell you. I know how concerned you've been about both David *and* Reva. You're a good friend."

My glow turned to gloom. He wouldn't have given me that nice compliment if he'd known what a lousy friend I'd been to Barbie.

"Yoo hoo! Robert!" Barbie called out from her backyard. "Are you and Valentine about finished with your chat? Jake needs you to help him do some measuring."

"Be right there." Robert gave my shoulder a squeeze. "Gotta get to work."

I watched him go, thinking what a blessing it was that he had decided to come to Nashville and to Cooperville Community Church after his wife died. As I turned and headed across the lawn to my house, a car pulled into Barbie's driveway. A convertible with the top down, one very much like Barbie's, only this one was flame red, and who should crawl out all decked out in a beaded purple top and purple slacks, a brilliant red scarf tied around her head? Myrtle Donatienne Cholmondeley Peabody, and she was all smiles.

I had to laugh, despite the ridiculousness of the situation. Throwing my arms open wide, I lifted my face heavenward. *God, what have I done to deserve this? I was just beginning to adjust to living without Carter when Barbie came into my life and turned everything upside down. I hate to admit it, but I've been a tiny bit jealous of her.*

I paused and gave that last sentence a second thought.

Okay, I've been a lot jealous of her, but I'm trying to get victory over it, honest I am. It's just that she's so pushy. Just look how she's throwing herself at Robert. I know it's none of my business, but he's such a fine man, and he doesn't know her like I do.

I glanced toward Barbie's house and hearing no fireworks going off inside decided to forget all about her, her decorator, her designs on Robert, the work going on over there, and concentrate on the job that had been given me.

The Cooperville Community Church Bazaar.

I didn't see Barbie all day Saturday, and Sunday she wasn't at church. I felt terrible. Maybe if I hadn't spouted off at her she would have been there. My big mouth had probably driven her even further away. Though I sat in my regular place in the pew and sang the praise songs with a smile on my face, inwardly I was miserable. I'd been purposely put in her path, and I'd acted like a spoiled, pampered child.

Determined to go through with my apology, I went to her house early Monday morning, rang her doorbell, and waited. No answer. I even tried going around the house and knocking on the back door. Still, no answer.

The landscaping crew arrived a few minutes later, but Robert wasn't with them.

Around ten, three men dressed in painter's clothes arrived, unloaded several boxes which I assumed contained cans of the new paint color, and went inside. They must have had a key. I couldn't imagine her leaving the door unlocked. Maybe she was off with Myrtle, shopping for the new carpet and drapery fabric, I told myself as I walked away from the window. Oh, well, I can apologize tomorrow.

But she didn't answer Tuesday or Wednesday morning, which didn't make sense. She'd been in such a hurry to get things done, why wasn't she there?

I stopped by the church late in the afternoon to see how things were progressing. The basement was humming with the sounds of electric saws and drills as I entered. The way Reva had designed those booths, to easily go together and come apart, was remarkable. Her committee worked together as a team, doing everything assembly-line fashion and smiling at one another in the process.

"Things going any better at home?" I asked after talking her into taking a quick break for the glass of iced tea I'd made for us in the church kitchen.

With a smile, Reva patted my hand. "I can't tell you how grateful I am that Robert stepped in to help my son like he did. He really looks up to that man."

The joy in her voice nearly brought tears to my eyes. We talked a bit more; then I said good-bye and headed toward Sally's. With everything that had been going on, we'd all been too busy for just plain girl talk. Besides, I needed to touch base with her about a few things for the bazaar.

Before I even stepped up onto her porch, I could hear yelling. Jessica was screaming at her mother, something about a red shirt, and Sally was screaming back. I hesitated, not sure this was a good time to turn up on their doorstep uninvited. But, I was there and, after all, Sally was my best friend, so I put my fears aside and knocked.

Sally answered immediately. Without even a quick *hello,* she motioned me inside and went right back to ranting at her daughter. "How many times have I told you, Jessica? You can't wash a red shirt with white items?" She held up a pink shirt that almost looked to be tie-dyed. "I paid thirty dollars for this white shirt because you wanted it and look at it now! It wouldn't be so bad if this was the first time you'd pulled this trick, but you've done it before."

To Jessica's credit, or maybe it was because I was standing there, the girl remained quiet, gazing at the shirt and looking contrite.

Sally settled herself onto the sofa, still ignoring my presence. "I love you, Jessica, but I don't like you. You do the stupidest things. Have you no pride? No modesty? Look at you. That top is way too tight. Your belly button is showing above that too-short skirt, your face is made up like a clown's, and I won't even go into what I think about that green streak in your hair and that row of earrings lining the rim of your ear."

"But all the girls—"

Sally's finger flew out in an exaggerated point. "Don't even go there. I don't care what all the girls are doing. You're not all the girls. You're my daughter, and I've just about had it with you, young lady."

Jessica drew back at Sally's words. I held my breath. I didn't have a daughter, but if I did have one I wasn't sure this would be the way I would handle things. I stood there, feeling almost invisible and totally out of place. I had no right to be privy to this mother-daughter discussion. "I'll come back another time," I said in a whisper, moving toward the door.

"No, you stay right there." Sally's statement was more a command. "Jessica and I are through with our conversation for now. She's due next door to baby-sit with our neighbor's children." As she gave the girl a dismissive wave, Jessica, looking relieved, nearly bolted out of the door.

"You're being a bit hard on her, don't you think?" I asked, hoping I wasn't treading where I shouldn't.

Sally's eyes blazed. "Hard on her? Through her carelessness, she ruined a thirty-dollar blouse and you say I'm hard on her?" She sank onto the sofa, folded her arms across her chest and let out a deep sigh. "Okay, I have a temper, and sometimes I make comments without thinking them through first, but that girl and the stupid things she does makes me angry. Not everyone can control themselves like you do. Someday, someone is going to make you angry and then you'll understand."

I sat down beside her. "Someone already has," I confessed.

Sally turned toward me.

"Barbie," I said.

"Oh, no. What did she do now?"

"You want the entire list or the condensed version?"

Throwing back her head, Sally chortled. "Our sensible, even-tempered, always-in-control Valentine is angry with someone? Barbie, no less? I find that hard to believe."

"Yeah, me." I felt like a complete fool. "And, believe me, it was ugly. Just be glad you weren't there to see it. I behaved pretty badly." I nudged her elbow playfully. "Nearly as bad as you just were with Jessica."

"I guess I was hard on her."

I wrapped my arms about her and drew her close. "I can't speak from experience, but it seems to me what

190

that girl needs right now is love. Unconditional, dependable love from you, her mother. Most of us are a lot more responsive to love than we are to anger."

Sally nibbled at her lower lip. "The raving and ranting sure hasn't worked. Maybe I'll give that unconditional love thing a try. It's worth a shot."

I smiled at her. "I love you, Sally."

As soon as I got home I rushed over to Barbie's house. It was becoming an obsession with me—I had to apologize. Robert's landscape crew was busily working, tearing up the old turf and planting trees and bushes around the perimeter, and the painter's truck was still in her driveway. I walked up onto the porch and rang the bell. When the door opened, instead of Barbie greeting me, it was one of the painters.

"Is Ms. Baxter at home?" I asked, peering around him, eager to see what color they were putting on the walls and wondering why she'd ever let a painter answer the doorbell.

"No. She hasn't been here since we got here on Monday."

"Do you know where she is?"

He shook his head. "No, ma'am. Some lady with a weird name just told us where to paint and what color to use. We haven't met the lady of the house."

I thanked him then walked toward home, my shoes sinking into the new, thick lush green turf Robert's crew had laid down that very day.

Strange.

This was really strange.
Where was Barbie?

$\mathscr{C}$HAPTER 13

Robert called that night, all excited about the way David had so readily taken to the landscape business. "I told him if he did a good job, I might even help him with his college tuition. I do that sometimes for the boys I think have potential."

I added another point to the list of things I admired about Robert Chase. That list was getting longer by the day. The growing attraction I had for him almost frightened me.

"He's a fine boy, just mixed up, and hurting from being without a dad. By the way, how's Barbie doing? My foreman had to duck out yesterday afternoon, and I've been really busy on another big job and haven't had a chance to touch base with her and see if she's happy with the way her landscaping is coming. I'm sure she's expecting me to take a personal interest."

"You haven't seen her?"

"No, why? Has she been complaining to you because I haven't been around?"

"I haven't seen her since last Friday. I stopped by her house this morning, but the painters said they hadn't seen her either. She was so excited about the redoing of her house and yard, I figured she'd be right there every minute, supervising the job. I thought for sure she'd get in touch with you."

"Have you asked her decorator? I'll bet she knows where she is."

"No, but maybe I'll do that. I have her number." I definitely didn't want to tell him about the disagreement and outright argument Barbie and I had over the interior decorator.

"Keep me posted. We're going to start building the gazebo in a few days. I'll need to make sure we're putting it exactly where she wants it, so if you talk to her ask her to give me a call."

"I will."

"Isn't it about time you and I got together again? How about dinner and a movie next weekend? Maybe Friday night. I'm tired of spending all my time with a bunch of boring guys."

His comment made me laugh. I could picture his handsome face on the other end of the line. "Sounds great, only why don't you let me cook dinner this time? That *was* part of our agreement, wasn't it?"

"You cook. I'll eat. Only make it simple, okay?"

"How about hot dogs cooked out on the grill?" I asked facetiously. "That simple enough?"

"Hey, that sounds good to me. I love hot dogs."

"I was only kidding, Robert."

"I wasn't. Hot dogs cooked on an outdoor grill is exactly what I want. I've haven't had them in ages."

"Okay, hot dogs it is. How about renting a movie and staying at home for the entire evening? You work hard all week, you deserve an evening just to relax."

"Fantastic idea. I'll be there at six, unless you want me to come early and start the grill for you."

"I know how to start the grill, but you can come early and start it if you like. I'll see you Friday night." I smiled as I hung up the phone. Robert wasn't the only one who needed a relaxing evening. I needed one—badly. And I needed male companionship every bit as much as he needed the female kind.

I needed male companionship? A sudden panic rose. What was I thinking? I wasn't ready for this.

He'd said he was ready to take on a permanent relationship and, as much as I enjoyed his company and got goose bumps when he smiled at me or took my hand, I just wasn't sure I was ready to fall in love again. I might never be ready, and I was certain I'd never marry anyone just for companionship.

I stared at the phone, then quickly before I changed my mind, I dialed Marsha Keller's number. Marsha was an attractive woman, a widow in her early fifties like me, and an avid gardener. I knew Robert told me not to attempt any matchmaking but Marsha and Robert would have a lot in common, and I'd heard she'd started dating again.

"Marsha," I said, trying to sound casual when actually my heart was pounding and my voice quavering. If I really wanted to find another woman for Robert, why did I feel like this? "Remember that bird statue I have in my garden? The one you admired when you came to visit me? I've decided to replace it with a different statue, and I wondered if you'd like to have it?"

Well, it wasn't exactly a lie. I did plan to replace it— eventually—with something a bit larger. Just not now.

"I love that statue. Are you sure you want to get rid of it?" She sounded so excited on the other end, I almost felt guilty.

"Yes, and I'd like you to have it. Maybe you could come over Friday evening to pick it up. Any time after seven would be fine."

"I'll be there," she said brightly. "Thanks, Valentine. I have the perfect spot for it."

After I hung up the phone, I began to wonder how I was going to explain to Robert that I'd invited Marsha to come by that evening when I knew he'd be here. Well, it was too late to worry about that now. I'd already invited her. Maybe they wouldn't even hit it off. Then again. Maybe they would. Was that what I really wanted?

I checked Barbie's house both Thursday and Friday and there was still no sign of her. Something had to be wrong. It wasn't like her to leave with so much going on at her house. I checked with the ladies at morning coffee—but none of them had heard anything either.

"She's a big girl," Reva assured me.

"She's probably at some Red Hat function she forgot to tell you about, like a retreat or something," Sally said. "You could call one of them."

"I don't have their numbers."

Truth was, Barbie didn't owe me any explanations as to her whereabouts. I was probably getting nervous about nothing. Still, three times Friday afternoon, I dialed the interior decorator's number and three times I hung up. I just couldn't get up my courage to talk to her after the angry way Barbie and I had parted. Maybe she knew why none of us had seen Barbie since last Friday, maybe she didn't. But I'd never know if I didn't talk to her. The fourth time I dialed her number I didn't hang up. Of course, I got her answering machine. I waited until the beep sounded then hurriedly flipped my phone closed, promising myself I'd call her tomorrow.

By five thirty, I had a bowl of freshly made potato salad in the refrigerator, a pot of smoky baked beans in the oven, and the picnic table in my backyard set with my new yellow and white daisy dishes. As I stood at my kitchen sink cleaning the big bowl of fresh strawberries I planned to serve for dessert, I gazed out my window, experiencing feelings of sadness. Carter had loved to cook hot dogs, steaks, and veggies on that grill. Then we sat at that table and ate and laughed and talked, and simply enjoyed each other's company. What wonderful memories. I'd cherish them forever. But Carter was gone. We'd never do those things together again.

I brushed aside a tear as I placed the bowl of lush red strawberries in the refrigerator. I told myself, *You shouldn't be moping like this. Life goes on and you know Carter would want you to make the best of it.*

But, with someone else? I argued back. *Would he want someone else taking his place?*

Robert rang my doorbell before I had time to settle

the argument with myself. Determined not to let my confusion ruin our evening, I tacked on the biggest smile I could muster and opened the door.

"Hope you like white roses," Robert said, grinning and holding out a gigantic bouquet.

I stared at the lovely array of flowers. Huge white cabbage roses with some sort of shiny greenery tucked into it. "I—I love roses. They're my favorites! I've never seen such big roses. Each one is so perfect." I lifted them and let their velvety softness touch my face. "What a delightful fragrance. Oh, Robert, I love them. Thank you for being so thoughtful." I motioned him to follow and moved into my kitchen to locate a vase worthy of their beauty and get them into water as soon as possible.

"Lovely roses for a lovely lady. Growing exotic roses is kind of a hobby of mine. I keep an area roped off in one of my greenhouses where I grow my personal collection. I like to experiment with crossbreeding, trying to enlarge the size, change the colors—that sort of thing. Those white roses are the result of some of my work. I was hoping you'd like them." He nodded approvingly at the tall crystal vase I'd selected then briskly rubbed his hands together. "Ready for me to start the grill?"

I nodded then watched as he moved out onto the deck and lifted the lid of my grill. Though I was intrigued with thoughts of Robert, it wasn't that I was forgetting Carter. It was just that Carter had been Carter, and Robert was Robert. Though similar in many ways, Robert was different than Carter. Less serious. More outgoing. Funny. He made me laugh. I found myself enjoying our time together immensely.

"Great potato salad," Robert told me, taking his third helping, which I considered a real compliment. "And what great baked beans. My wife made great baked beans, too. They tasted very much like these. Must be the bacon."

"Bacon and lots of brown sugar." I gave him a smile. "You did a terrific job on the hot dogs. I can't believe I actually ate two of them. I never eat two hot dogs!" For some unknown reason, the hot dogs were the best I'd eaten in years, or was it the company?

He lifted a forkful of potato salad and sat staring at it. I wondered if something was wrong. Had I accidentally left a piece of eggshell in it? Maybe added too much mayonnaise?

"Valentine," he said slowly, his gaze still pinned on the potato salad, "I'd like to get married again."

I gagged on the big gulp of iced tea I'd just taken, spewing the liquid onto my favorite pale green knit shirt.

With a worried look, Robert grabbed up his napkin and handed it to me. "Are you all right?"

Rapidly blinking my eyes a few times, I swallowed hard. "I think so. Yes, I'm fine. I just—well—"

He gave me a sheepish grin. "I didn't mean that the way it came out. What I meant was . . . it's been so nice sharing supper and the evening with you . . . I just thought . . . I would like . . . someday . . . if I found the

198

right woman . . . one who could put up with me like my Lydia did . . . I'd like to marry again. I wasn't cut out to live alone."

I sucked in another breath of air and tried to gather my wits about me. "Ah—I don't like living alone either. I mean—I can understand where you're coming from . . . and I'm not saying I won't marry again—someday—but, like you, I'd have to find the right person. In fact . . . unless God sent me a bolt of lightning on a cloudless day as a message, I probably wouldn't know the right man if he were standing in front of me." Then I flushed red as I realized what I'd just implied.

"Well, it's nothing for us to worry about." He smiled good-naturedly, but I could tell by the glint in his eyes that he hadn't missed my faux pas. "You and I are just two lonely people who love the Lord and enjoy each other's company." He reached across the table and took my hand. "Thanks for agreeing to share your time with me, Valentine, and for being my friend. My guy friends are great, but there's something special about being with a woman, especially a Christian woman. I want you to know I'm here for you anytime you need me. No strings attached."

I loved the sweet innocence of his remarks. Right from the beginning, I've felt comfortable with Robert. Safe. Secure. Respected. Reaching slowly across the table, I allowed my hand to cup his then gave it a gentle squeeze. "And I'm here for you, too." I paused with a coy smile. "No strings attached."

He threw back his head with a hearty laugh. "You're one in a million, Valentine Denay. I'm so glad we found each other."

"I'm glad, too." I felt myself blush again. "You're a good man, Robert, and so was my Carter. It's too bad you two never had a chance to meet. You would have liked each other and probably would have become best friends."

I gulped hard as I heard a car pull into my driveway and then my doorbell ring.

Robert frowned then smiled. "Who could that be? Barbie maybe?"

"I'll be right back." Pushing back my chair, I hurriedly headed to answer it. It was Marsha. After exchanging greetings, I led her through the house and into the backyard. "Look who's here, Robert," I said, trying to sound casual and doing a very poor job of it. "Marsha Keller."

"I didn't realize you had company," Marsha said. "I hope I'm not interrupting." Marsha looked at Robert then back to me. "You did tell me to come anytime tonight after seven, didn't you, Valentine?"

Robert smiled, as if he had known she was coming, and gestured toward an empty space at the picnic table. "We're glad you're here, Marsha. How about having a nice dish of strawberries with us?"

She sent me a questioning look. "I appreciate the offer but if it's okay with you, I'll just take the statue and go on home."

Robert moved quickly toward her, taking hold of her

arm. "No, you must stay and have strawberries with us. We're going to watch a movie later. Why don't you stay and watch it with us? We'd love your company."

What *was* he doing? I expected he'd be upset. Instead, he seemed pleased that she was here.

"Well—if you're sure—"

He literally pushed her into the chair. "We're not only sure, we insist, don't we, Valentine?" he asked me with a raised brow. I was sure I detected a smirk.

"Ah, yes, sure. We do insist."

Robert chatted on endlessly with Marsha about gardening and landscaping as we enjoyed our dessert. Well, *they* enjoyed their dessert. I was miserable. What had I done? What if Marsha and Robert really hit it off? What if—?

"Of course, I'll come and take a look at your wisteria, Marsha," Robert was saying. "How about tomorrow?"

"You wouldn't mind?"

"It'll be no trouble at all."

I wanted to scream, "Get away from him, he's mine!" when he gazed up at her and patted her hand, but I didn't. *You're stupid,* I told myself. *Trying to match Robert up with someone else is one of the dumbest ideas you've ever had, and you've had some real dumb ones in your time. There aren't many men like Robert, and you're trying to pawn him off on someone else. You should have your head examined.*

He turned to me with as innocent a face as I'd ever seen on a man. "Valentine, why don't you go on into the house and set up the DVD player while Marsha and I gather up the dishes?"

What could I say but, "Okay"?

By the time they came inside, laughing and talking like *they* were the ones on the *date*, I had the movie cued up and was waiting impatiently on the sofa. What could have taken them so long?

Robert motioned to the empty seat on the sofa next to me. "Why don't you sit in the middle, Marsha, next to Valentine?"

He didn't want to sit next to me? If he was trying to make me jealous, he was doing a good job of it. I hit the play button on the remote and the movie started. The movie must have been good, at least those two seemed to enjoy it. Me? I couldn't keep my mind on it. I was too busy casting sideways glances at Robert.

"Good movie," he said when it ended. "The kind I like. Lots of action, a little romance, and no bad words."

"That's the kind I like, too," Marsha fairly cooed, looking up at him and batting her long eyelashes. Well, maybe I was imagining the part about the cooing and batting, but she was paying more attention to him than I liked. "I'd better be going," she told us, rising and heading for the door.

Robert glanced at his watch then gestured toward the statue he'd placed on the floor in the hall. "Me, too. I'll carry that out for you and walk you to your car."

"Would you?"

Grrr! The woman was actually flirting with him!

What had I started? I was beginning to feel like Yente from *Fiddler on the Roof* and not enjoying the role.

Scooping up the statue, he took hold of her arm and ushered her toward my front hall. "Thanks for the supper, Valentine," he called over his shoulder, almost as an afterthought before closing the door behind them.

I sank back onto the sofa.

My heart felt crushed.

Aching and still feeling blah, I arose early Saturday morning and dialed Myrtle's number, only to be greeted by her answering machine again. "This is Interior Designer Donatienne Cholmondeley. I'd like to take your call, but I am attending the International Association of Interior Designers Convention in New York City and will be gone the entire week. Please leave a message when you hear the beep and I'll get back to you with the latest and greatest innovations in interior design. Remember, when designed by Donatienne Cholmondeley, your home is always on the cutting edge and will be envied by all your friends."

So much for that idea. I glanced across the space between my house and Barbie's. The only signs of anyone being there were the two vehicles parked in her driveway. A truck that belonged to the painters, and one of Robert's trucks loaded to the hilt with the treated lumber for the gazebo. Neither Barbie nor her convertible were in sight.

Thinking perhaps she'd arrived back home unnoticed and parked her car in the garage while Robert, Marsha, and I had been watching the movie, I crossed the lawn and rang her doorbell. The same painter opened the door with the same answer to my question. "No, ma'am, the lady of the house is still not at home."

I decided to peek in through one of her garage windows to see if her car was there. I gasped as I cupped my hands about my face to block out the sun and peered in. The yellow convertible *was* there, the top still down, just as it had been the last time I'd seen Barbie drive her car. I wracked my brain for someone else to call. I'd met a number of ladies at her Red Hat meeting, but I couldn't recall any of their last names. Knowing that Barbie was out there—somewhere—and that I didn't know where she was, or if she was okay made my guilt about not apologizing to her that much greater. *God,* I promised, *I don't care if there are a dozen witnesses, the minute I see Barbie I'll apologize. Please keep her safe, wherever she is.*

I barely saw Robert at church Sunday, but he did manage to wave a friendly hello as I drove out of the parking lot. It was almost as if he was avoiding me. I had hoped he'd invite me to have lunch with him, but I guessed he had other plans. Hopefully, not with Marsha! I checked Barbie's house as soon as I got home, but no one answered when I both rang the doorbell and knocked.

The rest of the week was busy as I worked closely with each bazaar committee, making sure everything was on schedule and progressing as planned. I had to say I was impressed. These women were working their hearts out, determined this bazaar would not only be a financial success so the youth center could be built, but also so that many of the neighborhood people and other visitors who would attend might feel our warm hospitality and decide to visit our church. A by-product of this effort of love was the new kinship we all felt by working together toward a common goal. How sweet it was to fellowship and work side-by-side with other church members, some whom I had barely known. Other than my constant concern for Barbie, who had still not shown up, it was a good week. It would have been a much better week though, if I'd heard from Robert.

He finally phoned late Thursday afternoon. "Sorry I haven't called you, Valentine, but I haven't had a spare minute. Things have happened so fast this week, my head is still spinning. Thanks to you and the way you invited Marsha over to pick up that statue, I've found the woman of my dreams. We're getting married a week from Saturday."

He might as well have kicked me in the chest with the heel of his boot! I found myself gasping for air. Robert and Marsha were getting married? And I'm the one who brought them together?

"I hope you'll come to the wedding. It's going to be in Marsha's garden."

He sounded so happy. Me? I felt sick and wanted to throw up. I was miserable. How could I have lost him that quickly? How? Because I'm the idiot who threw him into Marsha's waiting arms! Hadn't he told me he didn't want to live alone and wanted to remarry?

"Aren't you going to congratulate me, Valentine?"

The words wouldn't come.

"Valentine? Are you there?"

"I—I'm here," I finally eked out, choking on each syllable.

"I thought you'd be happy for me. You knew I wanted to get married again."

"I . . . am happy for you."

"Good, then you'll come to the wedding?"

My head was splitting. My heart was aching. And my brain was asking me why I'd done such a stupid thing. "I'll—try."

"Good, because I'm sure Marsha is going to make a beautiful bride. I should have asked her out long ago. I can't thank you enough for bringing us together. If it weren't for your unselfishness in giving her that bird statue, we may never have found each other. You're a good friend, Valentine. I'll see you in church Sunday. Again, thanks for helping me find my perfect woman."

I stood there, stunned as I heard the phone click in my ear. I'd lost Robert! I'd not only lost him, I'd pushed him into another woman's arms. Slowly, I placed the phone back in its cradle. All I wanted to do was go to bed. To close the blinds, climb in under the quilt, pull a pillow over my head, and escape into a sound sleep. I grabbed onto the handrail and was ready to trudge up the stairs to my room when the stupid doorbell rang. I didn't want to see anyone, so I ignored its sound.

It rang a second time, then a third. Apparently, whoever was there wasn't going to quit until I answered.

Maybe it was Barbie! She must have come back from wherever she'd been and was ready to tell me all about her adventure. I hoped so.

$\mathscr{C}$HAPTER 14

I rushed down the stairs to the front door. Without even peeking through the peephole, I pulled the door open. Someone rushed past me.

But it wasn't Barbie.

Arms encircled me and pulled me close as a mouth sought mine in the kind of kiss only Carter had ever given me.

Stunned, I pushed back and stared up into the face of my assailant.

Robert?

He kissed me again. This time, my toes curled up, my hands grew numb, and my lips eagerly sought his.

Wait a minute, I told myself, pushing away from him. *Didn't he tell me he'd found his perfect woman? What's he doing kissing me?*

"You little conniver," he said in a low sexy voice, his lips pulling slightly away from mine. "Did you think you were going to get rid of me that easily?"

I wasn't sure exactly what he meant, what any of this meant.

"Didn't I tell you not to do any matchmaking?"

"Yes—but—" I froze as he kissed me again.

"I hope you've learned your lesson."

Pushing away, I gazed up into his beautiful eyes. "My lesson?"

"Marsha and I aren't engaged, Valentine. Other than taking a look at her wisteria plant, I haven't even seen her again." His arms tightened around me, drawing me even closer. "You're the only woman for me. Can't you see that?"

"But you two were—"

"Friends. Only friends. I *was* trying to make you jealous." With his finger, he lifted my face to meet his. "No more matchmaking. Promise?"

I was so relieved, I nearly melted into a puddle at his feet. I hadn't lost Robert! Not to Marsha. Not to Barbie. Not to anyone. At least, not yet!

He gazed into my eyes. "Now kiss me, and let's quit playing these silly games."

Who was I to refuse?

Robert and I went to a movie Friday evening, a romantic comedy, which he said he enjoyed as much as I did. Afterward, using two straws, we shared a single chocolate milkshake like a couple of giggling teenagers. It seemed my life was settling down some, and the roller-coaster ride of emotions was easing up and falling back into a regular routine. Though I was still lonely for Carter, I felt as though I was finally getting used to widowhood and the idea of dating again. I couldn't keep complaining to God for taking my husband. Carter would never be a constant part of my life again, but life went on, and if I wanted to be a part of it, I had to put my anger aside and go on, too. But it was so hard.

I rose early Saturday morning, intending to spend the entire day doing laundry and cleaning my house. I may be weird, but there was something about leaving all those telltale sweeper lines across the carpet that I truly enjoyed. I'd been so busy with the bazaar, I'd let things go undone for weeks, which was definitely not my habit.

I'd just unplugged the sweeper when my phone rang. It seemed, these days, my life was filled with ringing doorbells or phones. Thinking it was Reva or Sally or one of the other ladies from the bazaar, I hurried to answer it.

"Valentine? This is Barbie," a troubled-sounding voice whispered on the other end. "Could you come to the airport and pick me up?"

I clutched the phone tightly, as if by hanging on I could find all the answers that had plagued me in her absence, most notably the realization that I cared about her well-being. Why hadn't that thought occurred to me before now? But as I listened to her fragile voice over the line I realized that I did care about her. "Barbie? Where have you been? I've been calling and calling you."

"I'll tell you when I see you. Please say you'll come. I'm at baggage claim two."

There was something in her voice that sounded strange, almost frantic. "I'm on my way."

"Thank you, Valentine. I didn't know who else to

209

call. I'll be waiting at baggage claim two. Please come alone." She hung up, leaving me with all sorts of unanswered questions.

Exactly one-half hour later, I pulled the car up in front of the doors to baggage claim two, but I didn't see Barbie. There was only one person standing by the double doors. A woman in an oversized black shirt and black pants, leaning against the wall, her head draped with a black scarf, and she was wearing dark glasses. I pulled up next to the curb and rolled down my window. "Have you seen an attractive blond lady? I was supposed to pick her up at this gate."

The woman hobbled slowly toward my car. It was then I saw her face.

"Barbie! What happened to you?" I screamed as I leaped out my door and hurried to assist her. "You look awful!"

She leaned against me, bracing herself as we walked. "I'll tell you when we get to the car."

I helped her inside, then hurried back to retrieve her carry-on bag from where she'd left it by the door. After placing it in my cargo area, I crawled behind the steering wheel and stared at her. This did not look like the Barbie I knew. This woman's face was a mass of fading bruises. One of her eyes had a slightly bluish-green ring around it, and her lip was swollen and split. "What happened? Did you have an accident? I've been so worried about you."

"I didn't tell anyone where I was going since I'd planned to fly back home the same day." She lowered her head and pulled the scarf closer about her face. "*He* was responsible for it."

"Who?"

"My first husband."

"Dirk?"

She nodded without looking up. "I told you I was afraid of him, but I didn't tell you he'd hit me and shoved me around so many times I couldn't count them during those few months we were married. He had a terrible temper. I never knew when he was going to explode. That was the real reason I divorced him. He terrified me."

I sat spellbound, totally shocked by her words. "He beat you up again? How? Why?"

She pulled the scarf tighter about her face. "Dirk and his daddy are living in Miami now. Pillars of the community, as usual. Though I've never told anyone—due to the gag order I'd agreed to—the reason I got such an outlandish divorce settlement and that big diamond ring was because I'd threatened to make my beatings public, which would have ruined their precious reputations. They knew I had documented proof. The ring and the money were to keep me quiet. They sure didn't want to have their dastardly deeds splashed over the headlines or be the lead story on television news. Now, all these years later, they decided they wanted the diamond ring back. Duke was getting married again and wanted to give his mother's ring to his new bride. When I told them they couldn't have it, that I deserved it for all the things I went through being married to

Dirk, they offered to buy it from me. You wouldn't believe the amount of money they offered me, which I could really use. I figured the ring meant more to them than to me, so I agreed to take it to them. They were to pay me with a cashier's check." She winced as she shifted her position in the seat.

"Shouldn't you be in the hospital or something?" I asked, still concerned about her.

"I've been in the hospital, well, a rehab."

"A rehab?"

"Physical rehab. Not the kind you're thinking. I hadn't been drinking or taking drugs."

I felt my eyes widen. "Dirk actually did this to you?"

"Not directly. When I got to the restaurant where I'd insisted we meet, they were both waiting for me. I didn't trust them, so instead of wearing the ring or carrying it in my purse, I'd strapped it to my thigh. We had a pleasant lunch. They were both really nice to me and seemed interested in what I was doing with my life. Finally, we got around to the real reason for my visit. Dirk handed me the cashier's check and demanded the ring. But when I took a quick look at the amount on the check, it was for less than fifty percent of what they'd promised, so I flat refused to give it to them. At first, Dirk got really upset, but his father calmed him down, saying he could understand why I wouldn't want to give up such a beautiful ring. He felt, if they were going to have to pay me that much for it, they might as well buy his new wife an even bigger diamond ring. His reasoning made sense to me, and I really did want to keep that ring."

"It sounds like at least his father had good sense."

She gave her head a sad shake. "Believe me, it only sounded like it. Dirk apologized, too, which was something he'd never done before, and the three of us actually ended up having a cordial conversation. Finally, I asked the maitre d' to call a taxi to take me back to the airport, but his father insisted they would take me as soon as he made an important phone call. I wasn't so sure it was the wise thing to do, but they were being so nice and everything seemed just fine, so instead of following my instincts, I agreed. Bad decision."

"I don't understand. If they were being nice to you and took you to the airport, what happened to you?" It was all I could do to keep my eyes on the road as I drove.

"Oh, there's more to the story. Finally, after Mr. Banes excused himself and went to the lobby to make his phone call, the three of us crawled into his Lexus and headed for the airport. At least that's where I thought we were going."

I took my eyes off the road long enough to give her a quick glance. "They didn't take you there?"

"No." Her trembling fingers moved to touch her sore lips. "They had it all planned ahead of time, Valentine. That's why his father made that phone call. I'm sure of it."

"I still don't get it."

"They didn't take me to the airport. They took me to some sleazy part of town and forced me to get out, then left me standing there with my carry-on bag by my side, and drove off. I thought they'd done it just to be mean, to show me they were the ones in control."

"They actually left you there?"

"Yes." Clamping her eyes tightly shut, Barbie winced. "I looked around, but there wasn't a business or café, or even a house, where I could find a phone, and I'd forgotten to take my cell phone with me. So I just stood there, trying to figure out what to do, when someone approached from behind and pushed me to the ground and held me there while he went through my purse and my bag. After calling me a few obscene names, he flipped me over and, for the first time, I could see him. He had one of those stocking caps with holes for his eyes over his face." She shuddered just talking about it.

I shuddered, too.

"He slapped me around and told me he was going to kill me if I didn't tell him where that ring was. When I told him I didn't have it, he kicked me and broke my rib. The pain was excruciating. I tell you, Valentine, I've never been so scared. I really believed he'd kill me so I took the ring off the strap on my leg and gave it to him. Once he got it, he was gone. I was hurting so badly, all I could do was lie there and cry."

"Oh, you poor thing."

"Finally, a really dented-up old car came along and drove slowly by me. I was so afraid it was him coming back, but it wasn't. It was a nice old couple. They stopped and offered to take me to the police or hospital, or wherever I wanted to go, so I asked them to take me to the hospital."

"You're really fortunate they stopped. Did the police arrest your ex-husband and his father?"

She shook her head. "For what? Grabbing my arm and swearing at me? Getting upset because I wouldn't hand over a ring?"

"Could Dirk have been the one who beat you up? Maybe he got out of his father's car and came back with the mask on."

She gave her head a slight shake. "No. The man who beat me up was a head taller than Dirk. Remember I told you Dirk's father made that phone call before he left the restaurant? I'm certain they had this all arranged ahead of time, knowing I wouldn't accept the minimal amount they'd planned to offer me. I think Mr. Banes called that man and told him the exact location of where they were going to leave me off. How else would the man have known about the ring unless they'd told him? I doubt it was just happenstance that they dumped me out in that particular spot in that crummy neighborhood and that man just happened to be there at that very moment, just waiting to rob someone. He didn't even take the credit cards or my checkbook out of my purse. Just the cash."

"You did report it to the police?"

"Yes. They came to the hospital, though it was hardly worth the effort. When they interrogated Dirk and his father, they denied knowing anything at all about the ring or promising me any money. They said I was nothing but a troublemaker who was always trying to get something out of them. They claimed that was the reason they'd met me, to tell me in person they were not going to give me any more money. They even denied that they let me off in that awful place, insisting they'd taken me clear to the airport. I had no proof of any of it, except that I'd been beaten. I hadn't even gotten that nice couple's name."

"So? That was the end of it? No one was charged and those two got off scot-free?" I ached for her.

"Yes. Scot-free. The police had nothing to go on." Her hands still shaking, she tugged at her wrinkled trousers. "I can't believe I was stupid enough to meet them, and wouldn't have, if they hadn't offered that exorbitant amount of money for the ring."

When we reached her house, I pulled my minivan into her driveway and hurried around to the other side to assist her. "With everything going on both inside and outside of your house, I was amazed you weren't here. I was about ready to call the police myself."

Barbie grabbed onto my hand and, with great effort and a lot of groaning, lifted herself out of the seat. "Ouch. Just give me a minute."

She leaned against the side of my car, her breath coming in short pants. "I'm so glad he broke only one of my ribs. At first, they thought my spleen had been damaged, too; but, fortunately, it was only bruised. When they were ready to release me, I transferred to the hospital rehab center for a few days, because I had no place else to go and I didn't feel like traveling by myself."

She clamped a clammy hand onto my wrist then, for the first time since getting into my car, looked me directly in the eye. "Thank you for coming after me, Valentine. You were the only one I knew who wouldn't ridicule me for my stupidity in going to Miami like that. I should have known I was walking into trouble. They knew all they had to do was dangle a lot of money in my face and I'd come running."

Carefully slipping my arm around her waist, I eased her forward, slowly putting one foot in front of the other. "Would you like to stay at my house so I can look after you?" I asked, surprising myself.

Her painful expression turned to one of surprise. "You'd do that for me? After the argument we had before I left?"

"At least half of that argument was my fault. That's one of the reasons I was trying to find you. I wanted to apologize. I had no business talking to you the way I did." There, though the words were difficult to say, I knew I had to say them, and it actually felt good.

"We all say things we shouldn't. I've even done it myself."

She had even done it herself? I felt my ire rising. *Calm down,* I told myself. *This woman has been through a lot. Her cockiness is nothing more than a façade. Be kind to her.* Yet I couldn't help but wonder where the contrite Barbie of just a few minutes before had gone.

"So, do you want to stay with me?" I asked again, smiling through gritted teeth.

She gave her head an almost invisible shake. "Right now all I can think about is climbing into my own bed, but you could bring my meals over to me. And some fresh fruit. My refrigerator was nearly empty when I left. And maybe you could do a couple loads of laundry and take my clothes to the cleaners."

So much for the woman who had just confessed to being stupid. This was more like the Barbie I knew. But I vowed to do whatever she asked, no matter how ridiculous.

When she was finally in her pajamas and settled into her bed with a cup of freshly brewed coffee, she reached out and took hold of my hand. I smiled at her.

"You must promise me you won't tell anyone what happened to me."

I gave her an incredulous look. "Isn't it pretty obvious?"

"I don't want anyone to know I suffered a beating. I'm going to tell everyone I fell down a flight of stairs, and I want you to do the same thing. Promise me that's what you'll tell them."

"You want me to lie for you?"

"Call it a lie or whatever you want. Just don't let anyone know what really happened. I'm counting on you to keep your mouth shut, Valentine. The truth is really no one's business."

"I'm sorry, Barbie. I can't lie for you."

With a disgusted look, she rolled her eyes at me. "I suppose that's another one of your silly Christian ethics. All right, don't lie for me, just avoid the truth.

If someone asks you what happened to me, tell them to ask me about it and I'll do the lying."

I hated being put in this position, yet what had happened to her *was* her business. It wasn't up to me to tell anyone. Finally I decided I wouldn't lie for her, but I could steer the topic back to Barbie whenever possible.

For the next week, in addition to all the things I had to do to prepare for the bazaar, I took care of Barbie, carting three meals a day to her house, doing her laundry, helping her dress, making sure she had everything she needed to keep her comfortable while she recuperated. Occasionally, she even thanked me, but most of the time she simply handed me a list of the things she wanted done next.

Robert stopped to see her almost every day, bringing her flowers, doing his best to comfort her, too, although she seemed to be in much more pain when he was around than she was at other times. As I expected, she was working her fall-down-the-stairs lie for everything she could. Though he and I shared smiles and a few private moments together, working on the bazaar, caring for Barbie, and running her errands took most of my time, and making sure her landscaping was going the way she wanted it took most of Robert's. To my surprise, I realized I could hardly wait to see him again.

By the following Monday Barbie was feeling much better and, although her broken rib was still paining her, she was back to her old bragging self. I figured it was time to wean her and let her begin taking care of herself.

She took on a look of desperation when I told her. "So you're deserting me?"

"No, not deserting you, but the bazaar is not quite two weeks off and there is still so much to do. I need to give it my full, undivided attention." I gave her a confident smile. "You'll do fine. I've filled the refrigerator with your favorite fruit, yogurt, and drinking water and, if you get desperate, there are a couple of frozen dinners in the freezer. All you have to do is pop them into the microwave. The instructions are on the package. I'll be happy to drive you anywhere you need to go, but you have to give me a little notice so I can work it into my schedule."

Her expression quickly changing to one of irritation, she lifted her hand and gave me a dismissive wave. "Go on. Do what you have to do. I'll manage without you. I have other friends who have been begging to take care of me."

That was an outright lie! Her Red Hat friends had been calling their queen, leaving dozens of messages, asking her where she was and if she was sick or something, but she hadn't returned a single call. No one had been *begging* to take care of her. I knew, because I'd overheard their messages when she'd played them back.

"I haven't seen them beating a path to your door," I almost said, but I kept the words trapped inside my mouth. They tasted awful!

Plumping up her pillows and smoothing out the sheets, I forced a smile. "I'm sure it would only take one phone call and those nice Red Hat friends of yours would be willing to do anything you asked. Would you like a fresh glass of water before I leave?"

"No, but I would like to talk to Robert about the plant hangers for the gazebo. If you see him, tell him I'd like him to stop by."

Keeping the false smile in place, I nodded. "I'll be happy to tell him. You have my phone number if you need me."

Robert was getting something out of his truck when I closed Barbie's front door and headed across the driveway. "She wants to see you," I told him, hitching my head toward the house. "Something about plant hangers."

He closed the tailgate and stood looking at me, his hands awkwardly digging deep into his pants pockets. "I don't know what to do about her, Valentine. I know this sounds arrogant and dumb, but she makes me nervous. Anything nice I say to her, she reacts to it like she thinks I'm—well, you know—making a move on her. I don't want to hurt her feelings, but there is no way I would ever be interested in Barbie, other than as a friend. At times, that's even hard. I need your advice. What should I do?"

Tell her to bug off! She's lying to you about her so-called accident. Can't you see that? "I know she likes you, Robert. She's made it perfectly clear."

"But I'm not her type at all. Surely she knows that."

"Maybe that's what attracts her to you. Maybe she's tired of her type and wants someone who is nice,

221

steady, even-tempered—" I paused and gave his arm a playful pinch. "Sexy, good-looking, treats a lady in the respectful, gentlemanly way she wants to be treated."

His troubled face took on a grin. "Okay, I can go along with all except for the sexy, good-looking part. Those descriptions don't fit me."

I gave his arm another pinch. "I just threw those two in for good measure—to boost your ego."

He laughed and grabbed hold of my hand. I wasn't sure if he really wanted to hold my hand or was simply keeping me from pinching him again.

"I know that you've been busy with the bazaar and taking care of Barbie, but I've missed you this past week, Valentine. I'm having withdrawal pains. I want to be with you."

"I've missed you, too." He had no idea how much.

He gave my hand a squeeze. "Think you could work me in next weekend? The Community Theatre group is doing *West Side Story*. I'd like to take you. I'll even treat you to a hot fudge sundae afterward."

"I always have time for you, Robert. I'd love to go, but now you'd better go see Barbie." I pulled my hand from his grip and gave him a teasing smile. "She's waiting for you."

My phone was ringing when I walked into my house. Not Barbie already! She was probably wanting to know if I had given Robert her message. I grabbed it up and said a sharp, "Hello."

"Valentine! I'm so glad you're at home. I need help! I've been having pains all night, and they're getting closer. I—I don't know what to do!"

It was Bitsy, and she was crying hysterically. I pulled the receiver tightly against my ear. "Is your friend there with you? Can she take you to the hospital?"

"Both she and her children are sick with the flu." Her deep sob went straight to my heart.

"Do you want me to take you?"

"Would you? I'm so scared, Valentine."

"I'm on my way, sweetie, and I'm praying for you and that baby!" Snatching up my keys from the desk where I had tossed them only minutes before, I raced out the door to my minivan.

Looking forlorn and anxious, she was waiting for me at the curb, her overnight bag in hand. I reined my car to a stop in front of her and pushed open the passenger door. "Have you had any more pains?" I asked excitedly, hoping she wouldn't have that baby in my car.

"Yes, they're getting harder." She waddled her way inside and lowered herself into the seat with a heavy sigh. "I'm so glad you're here."

"I'm glad I'm here, too, sweetie." I revved up the engine, and we took off like a flash. Getting a speeding ticket was the last thing on my mind. In fact, I hoped an officer would stop me so he could escort us to the hospital. "Hang on, Bitsy, we're on our way."

"Ahhhh! Ohhhh! Ouuuu!"

At the sound, I quickly turned my eyes away from the road and found Bitsy's face contorted with a look of horror, one hand flattened on her rounded abdomen, the other grasping the knob on my gearshift with a deathlike grip. "Is the baby coming?" I asked, my heart racing faster than my car.

"I don't—know!" She winced with pain again, her face devoid of color. "But it hurtsssss!"

Not knowing what else to do, I reached out my hand. "Here, squeeze it. Maybe that'll help." Instinctively, I called out, "God, help! Be with Bitsy and this baby. Please! And let us make it to the hospital in time!"

Bitsy sucked in a deep breath then yelled, "Amen!"

I could only imagine how she felt. Her husband overseas. Her mother unable to come. Her Lamaze coach sick with the flu.

Her Lamaze coach! What was she going to do without her Lamaze coach?

Doing a yo-yo routine back and forth from Bitsy to the road ahead of me then back to Bitsy, I pressed the foot pedal even harder.

Within seconds, she straightened up, a relieved look on her face, long strands of blond hair plastered to the sweat on her cheeks and brow. "It's over."

"What's over?" I screamed out hysterically, sending a glance toward her voluminous skirt. "You've had the baby?"

A tiny smile formed on her exhausted face. "No, the pain quit."

"Oh, good." How was I to know? She could have given birth and that baby might have been hidden under that long skirt of hers, for all I knew. I hoped her pain ceasing meant we had a few minutes' reprieve and would make it to the hospital before the next one hit.

All was going well—Bitsy was quiet, and I'd settled down by reminding myself this was a natural process. Women gave birth everyday. There was nothing to panic about.

Then Bitsy let out another yell, only this one wasn't like the one she'd yelled when she'd had a pain.

"What's wrong?" I gave her a panicked sideways glance, my hands white-knuckling the steering wheel.

"My water broke!"

Not sure if that meant the baby was definitely on its way out of the birth canal and I was going to have to help her deliver it, I swung my minivan to the right, pulled up next to the curb, and quickly turned to her, my heart pounding so fast I could feel it in my throat. Bitsy's eyes were wider than I'd ever seen them and the poor girl looked terrified. I was terrified, too. "Bitsy, tell me what's happening!"

"My clothes are soaked, and I'm getting your seat all wet." She began to cry. "It's in my shoes, too, and all over your floor."

"Oh, I thought you were having the baby." Relieved, I reached across and patted her hand. "It's okay, sweetie, don't worry about it. I can sop it up later." I flinched as I remembered how much I had paid just a few days ago to have my minivan washed and detailed. Oh, well, that was nothing. It could be done again. The important thing was that Bitsy was doing okay and we were just blocks from the hospital.

The hospital!

I shoved the gearshift into drive, and we took off again.

I nearly shouted for joy when the hospital finally loomed up before us. As Bitsy uttered a loud cry and doubled up with another pain, I wheeled into the emergency entrance and squealed to a screeching halt, all the time frantically honking my horn.

A uniformed attendant rushed out, followed by a second attendant pushing a wheelchair. I nearly yanked her from the seat, wet clothes and all, and thrust her toward the men who barely lifted a brow. This kind of thing may have been old hat to them, but to me and to Bitsy it was utter chaos.

One of the men gently lowered her into the chair while the other one held it securely in place. "Go ahead and park your car," the shorter one told me calmly. "You'll need to come in and check her in."

"She's having a pain!" I yelled at them, wondering why they hadn't noticed. "And her water broke!"

"She's fine. Don't worry about her."

Bitsy looked at me with her big, round innocent eyes. "You won't leave me, will you, Valentine? I need you with me."

I shook my head. "Of course I won't leave you. I'll park the minivan and stay with you until you're holding your baby in your arms."

Leaping back into my car, I took stock of the wet seat and the damp floor, thankful I'd paid extra to have the seats Scotchguarded.

I whizzed up and down the marked rows of the

parking lot, looking for an empty space, but couldn't find one until I'd reached the far, outer rim. Within minutes I was entering the emergency entrance door. The lady at the desk motioned me toward her. "You're with Mrs. Foster? The doctor is examining her now. As soon as he's finished you can go to her." Then giving me a questioning look, she asked, "Are you her Lamaze coach?"

I wondered if I said no, would that mean I wouldn't be able to stay with Bitsy? I'd promised her I wouldn't leave her and would help her in any way I could so, without giving any thought to what being her Lamaze coach might mean, I smiled and said, "Yes, I am."

She motioned down the hallway. "In that case, you can go right in. She's three doors down. Room 106."

I ran down the hall. I hated the idea of poor Bitsy being alone.

"It's going to be awhile yet," the doctor said, casually turning to look at me as I rushed into the room. "She's not at ten centimeters yet. I'll be back to check on her from time to time. Since you're her Lamaze coach, you know what to do. She may want to move around. Maybe get up and walk a bit. Press the call button if you need anything."

Ten centimeters? I had no idea what that meant. I stared after him as he sauntered out of the room. He was just going to leave her there? Without even a nurse to watch over her?

Bitsy's tired eyes brightened. "You're going to be my Lamaze coach, Valentine?"

I moved up close to the bed and stroked her sweaty brow. Come to think of it, mine was sweaty, too. She was too young to be having a baby. "I told the lady at the desk I was your coach so they'd let me stay with you, but I have no idea what a Lamaze coach does. You'll have to help me."

Bitsy grabbed tightly to my hand, and I could tell by the look on her face that another pain was beginning to grab her in its clutches. "Aren't you supposed to breathe or something?" I asked, feeling totally inadequate.

Squeezing my hand so tightly I was afraid the bones would break, Bitsy gritted her teeth, her face contorted with pain. "I—am—breathing!"

I watched, wishing I could do something to take the pain away. No wonder they call labor, labor. It was awful!

"Thank you, Valentine," she grunted out, her body finally going limp, her eyes clamped shut. "With you here, I'm not afraid anymore."

"Does it hurt really bad?"

"Really bad. I need to go to the bathroom."

She reached out her hand so I could pull her to a sitting position then, with my help, carefully swung her legs over the side and stood.

"Take it easy," I told her in a coacherly way as I assisted her toward the bathroom. It wasn't until we reached the door and she moved ahead of me that I noticed that, due to the gown being open down the back and having to span her oversized tummy, her

228

backside was totally bare! I looked around the room for something to cover her but, finding nothing, I removed my jacket and waited by the bathroom door. When she finally came out, I tied its sleeves around her expanded waist, knotting them in front above the bulge, allowing the body of the jacket to hang over the open area in back until I could come up with something better. It looked strange, but it was the best I could do at the moment. If it were me, I wouldn't want my bare fanny showing through that slit.

Bitsy gave me a bewildered look. "Why'd you do that?"

"I knew you wouldn't want your behind exposed to anyone who might walk down the hall or come into your room. Your gown leaves a little to be desired." I gave the bottom of the jacket a tug, trying to manage a bit more coverage.

"How're we getting along in here?" a nurse asked, entering the room. She stopped short and stared at Bitsy. "Why is she wearing that jacket tied around her waist?"

"That skimpy gown doesn't cover up her—ah, derriere."

The nurse gave me a mocking smile. "I know you mean well, but I have a better solution." She reached into a closet and pulled out another gown.

"Is that one bigger?" I asked. It didn't look any bigger to me.

"No, but trust me. It'll work. We do this sometimes for our more modest mothers."

I watched as she unfolded the gown and tied it on

Bitsy—backwards! Why hadn't I thought of that? With one going one way, and the other gown the other, Bitsy was totally covered.

"There you go. Problem solved." The congenial nurse grinned at us, picked up a chart from the table and left the room.

"Valentine! Here comes another one!"

I rushed to Bitsy and held tightly to her hand as another pain hit. Why couldn't the pain have come when the nurse was here? "Breathe, Bitsy, breathe!"

Bitsy started making strange sounds like *he, he, he, he.* At first, I thought it was hysterical laughter or she was trying to tell me something, but then I realized she was expelling short gasps of breath. I felt so stupid. Was I the only woman in the world who didn't know this Lamaze thing?

When the pain, this one even more intense than the last, finally subsided, I pointed toward the bed. "Maybe you'd better lie down and rest."

She allowed me to assist her then just sat there on the edge looking totally spent. "Are you supposed to do something with pillows?" I asked, reaching for the two pillows I'd spotted earlier on a chair. "I always see them use pillows in the movies."

Wearily, she motioned behind her, her voice weak. She was still trying to catch her breath.

"You want me to prop you up?" I bowed my head and said a quick prayer. *God, help! This sweet, sweet girl is trusting in me, and I have no idea what I'm doing.*

Bitsy nodded. I stacked the pillows and helped her lower herself against them. She'd barely gotten situated when she suddenly drew up her knees.

"Another pain?" I asked, wondering when this was going to end. She was already tired and pale. I was trying to figure out what a real Lamaze coach would do to help her when the doctor came into her room. I'd never been so glad to see anyone in my whole life. A Lamaze coach I wasn't!

I guess he could tell from my worried face that I had no idea what was going on because he gave me a smile and a dismissive wave. "I'll take over from here, but you can stay. I think she'd like to have you here."

I was so thankful to hear those words. I was sure, at this point, Bitsy needed help from someone who knew what they were doing, not me.

I watched as one of life's greatest miracles slowly unfolded right before my eyes—the entrance of another new life into the world, as a tiny girl made her appearance. She was pink and wrinkled, and covered with a coating of some kind, but to me she was the most beautiful baby I'd ever seen. Even her first tiny cry was beautiful. How could anyone witness the miraculous birth of a baby and deny the existence of God?

Within minutes, the doctor placed the baby in Bitsy's arms. I gazed at the delicate, pink-cheeked child. She was so tiny and looked as fragile as a china doll. Our Bitsy had given birth to this miracle of God, and I had been a part of it.

Though I tried to hold them back, tears of joy and wonderment filled my eyes and rolled down my cheeks as Bitsy reached out her baby to me.

I was holding a new life in my arms. What a privilege. I knew I'd never forget that awesome experience as long as I lived. Suddenly, I realized I didn't even know this endearing child's name. Had Bitsy and Kevin decided on names? She hadn't mentioned it.

As if reading my thoughts, Bitsy lifted her weary head and smiled at me. "Kevin and I had thought of Bernard if our baby was a boy, and Bernice if she was a girl, but he told me I could name our baby whatever I wanted."

She reached out her hand to me. Thinking she wanted to hold her baby, I moved up close to the bed. Instead, she gently took hold of my wrist. "I'm naming her Valentine Denay Foster. After you, Valentine. The best friend I've ever had. I want her to grow up and be a godly woman just like you."

It's impossible to explain the surge of joy that rippled through my body at her words. "Oh, Bitsy, I can't tell you what an honor it would be, to have your darling little girl named after me, but I'm not worthy of—"

"You've come to mean nearly as much to me as my own mother, Valentine. Especially after today."

I cradled that baby to my bosom and kissed her pink cheek. Her skin was as soft as one of the petals of Robert's prize roses. "I love you, baby girl, and I'm honored that you'll bear my name." Just the sight of this wonderful child brought an unspeakable thrill to my heart.

Though hating to give her up, I carefully placed the bundle in Bitsy's arms. All I could think about was Kevin. He should have been here. Not me. He would have been ecstatic to witness the birth of his baby. Then I thought of Bitsy. And again I asked, *Why? Why? Why did Kevin have to be in Iraq serving his country at this time, instead of here at the hospital with his wife?* There were so many answers I needed from God.

I dialed Bitsy's mother's phone number for her, but no one answered. Then I phoned the Red Cross as Bitsy asked. A representative assured me they would get right to work on contacting Kevin with the news of their baby's birth. Next, I phoned Bitsy's mother again, but again, no one answered. Disappointed we couldn't reach her mother and badly in need of sleep, Bitsy asked if I would continue to try her mother's number. I promised I would keep trying until I reached her mother with the news.

It was midnight when I reached home, but it was still ten in California, so I dialed the number. This time a woman answered on the first ring.

"Are you Bitsy Foster's mother?" I asked without thinking to identify myself.

"Yes, I am," the voice came back. "Is she all right?"

"She's fine, but she'd be even better if you were here."

"Who is this?"

233

"My name is Valentine Denay. I'm a close friend of your daughter's. She's been trying to reach you and asked me to call and tell you she gave birth to a beautiful baby girl a few hours ago. Six pounds and five ounces. I'm sorry you were too ill to come and be with her. She'll probably call you first thing tomorrow."

There was a long pause on the other end. "I'm not ill, Mrs. Denay. I only told Bitsy that because I didn't have the money to travel, and I knew she would go without food and the things she and that baby would need if she knew."

An idea popped into my head. "How would you like to come to Nashville, spend some time with your daughter, and see her beautiful new baby?"

"I could never afford that."

"My treat. I'd love to do it. That daughter of yours is important to me. Nothing would make me happier than to see the look on her face when you walk in the door. How soon can you leave?" I tingled with excitement at the thought.

"I couldn't let you do that, Mrs. Denay. I'm not used to handouts. I've worked all my life to pay my own way. Is there something I can do for you in return? I'm good at ironing and cleaning houses. That's how I've been supporting myself, but it's barely enough to pay my bills."

From the sound of her voice, I could tell she was a proud woman. "Yes, my house is a mess, and I've always got ironing to do. You can help me while you're here. I'll call and arrange for a prepaid ticket. You can pick it up at the counter when you go to the airport. As soon as I have it worked out, I'll call you back with the details." We talked for a few more minutes; then I hung up and called the airline. Amazingly, they had one seat left on the 7:00 a.m. flight. I booked it, then called Bitsy's mother, gave her the time, and told her I would pick her up at the airport. By noon tomorrow, Bitsy's mother would walk into her hospital room.

I thought once I'd climbed into my own bed I'd be tired enough to drift off right away, but it didn't happen. All I could think about was Bitsy and how alone she was. What a shame neither her husband nor her mother could have been with her when she delivered that darling baby.

I got to the hospital as early as I could the next morning and tiptoed into the room. Bitsy was looking well, rested, and relaxed with the baby snuggled at her breast, sucking away peacefully. Bitsy smiled a hello at me with that angelic face of hers. The scene of mother and child was too beautiful for words, and to think I was a part of it brought tears to my eyes.

Bitsy tenderly touched the blond fluff of hair peeking out from under the blanket. "I wish my mother could see my baby."

"Maybe she will—someday."

I stayed until ten, discreetly glancing at my watch every five minutes. I had to leave. I had no intention of being late to pick up Bitsy's mother.

"I'm sorry," I told Bitsy, shouldering my purse and trying to keep a straight face. "I'm going to have to leave. I have an errand to run, but I'll be back in a couple hours, in plenty of time to take you home. I hope you don't mind, but I've arranged to have a lady stay with you for a few days, to help with the baby. I'd invite you to stay at my house, but I thought you'd rather be in your own home."

"I can't let you do that, Valentine. You've done so much already. The baby and I will be fine."

"Sorry. It's already a done deal. She's going to meet us here at the hospital."

On the way to the airport, I thought of Barbie and wondered how she was getting along without my help. I didn't want her to think I'd forsaken her.

Mrs. Weaver's plane arrived right on time and, since all she had with her was a small carry-on bag, we were out of the airport and to the hospital in a matter of minutes.

"Wait here in the hall until I come for you," I told her, both of us so excited we could hardly stand it. "I told Bitsy I'd arranged for a lady to stay with her for a few days. She's going to be so pleased when she finds out that lady is you."

I tried to appear calm as I walked back into Bitsy's room but, inside, I was a basket case. "Errand's all done," I told her as I bent over the sleeping baby.

"You really didn't have to come back, Valentine. I could have taken a cab home."

I donned a frown. "And deprive me of the joy of escorting my namesake home? No way. Besides, the lady who is going to stay with you should be here any minute. I think I'll walk out in the hall and see if I can find her. Maybe she's lost." I wanted to run into the hall, but I forced myself to walk at a normal gait. When I reached the door, I motioned Bitsy's mother to come in.

"Here she is," I said, about to burst. "The lady who will be staying with you."

Bitsy let out a shriek that I was afraid would send hospital representatives to the room, thinking we had an emergency. "Mom. Oh, Mom. Is that really you? I've been trying your number over and over. I was so worried when you didn't answer."

Her tears flowing, Bitsy reached out her arms, and her mother ran into them, hugging her daughter with all her might. "I love you, Bitsy girl!"

After several minutes of hugging and kissing, Bitsy frowned at her mother. "How did you get here? Are you feeling better?"

Her mother pointed a bony finger at me. "Your friend Valentine. She did it, and I'll be forever grateful to her."

Bitsy started to say something, but I raised my hand to silence her. "We'll talk about the whys and the wherefores later but, right now, you and your mother need to spend time together with that new baby. I'll be back later to take you home." I backed out the door, closing it behind me.

Planning to be back at the hospital by four when Bitsy checked out, I headed for home and a short nap, feeling I deserved it.

By five thirty, I had taken a nap, checked Bitsy and her baby out of the hospital, delivered mother and daughter and grandmother to Bitsy's apartment, and was on my way home, fully intending to check on Barbie. When I got there, I noticed that Robert's Avalanche was parked in her driveway.

I deliberated over whether to ring her bell and risk her anger for interrupting her time with Robert or go on home and have her be mad at me for not checking on her all day.

CHAPTER 15

Thinking perhaps Robert was in need of rescue, I opted to interrupt them. He answered the door when I rang the bell, looking as though he was really glad to see me.

"She's had a setback. She said she was going to the kitchen for a bowl of fruit and got her foot tangled up in her robe. I guess, from the way she described it, she bounced against the wall and was afraid she'd done more damage to her rib."

"Maybe we'd better take her to the emergency room."

"I already have. She phoned me when it happened. They checked her thoroughly and said she'd probably just irritated that rib when she fell against the wall. The X-rays didn't show any new injuries. She's sleeping now."

Now I really felt bad. "She might have tried to call me, but I was with Bitsy. She had her baby. A healthy baby girl."

"Really? That's great. I'll bet she's glad it's over, being alone like she is with her husband gone."

"I wonder if Barbie even tried to reach me? I had my cell phone with me. I'd have taken her if I'd known she had fallen like that."

He shrugged. "I don't know. She said something about you being too busy to check on her."

Grrr. "That wasn't exactly the way it was, Robert."

He took hold of my arm and pulled me inside. "I didn't think it was." After glancing around, he bent and whispered in my ear, "I'm not really sure her story is true. I hate to say it, but I think it was her way of getting me over here. She may not have fallen against the wall like she said she did or, if she did, it may not have been as serious as she led me to believe. She got really bent out of shape when I insisted on taking her to the emergency room. She didn't want to go. She's stuck to me like glue ever since we got back. I haven't been able to get away from her."

"I could stay with her." Glutton for punishment that I was. "That way you can leave."

"I'd hate for you to have to stay. She's a real handful. Let's talk about something more pleasant. Tell me about the new baby."

I happily explained about our rush to the hospital, my feeble attempts at Lamaze coaching, and Bitsy's mother. "You should have seen that girl's face when her mother walked into the room. I wouldn't have cared if that airline ticket would have cost ten times that much, it would have been worth it." I grabbed onto his arm, my smile broadening to the width of my face. "You'll never believe what she named the baby. Valentine Denay Foster!"

Robert pulled me into his arms and gave me a big bear hug, then planted a kiss on each of my cheeks. "I couldn't have thought of a better name for that baby."

"Valentine! Where did you come from? And what's going on here?"

Looking as guilty as two young lovers caught making out, Robert and I pushed apart and stared at the figure glaring at us from the head of the stairs.

The queen was awake and in true royal form.

"Bitsy had her baby. A girl." I wiggled my mouth into a smile. "Six pounds and five ounces."

Not even asking if mother and baby were doing well, Barbie placed a hand over her left rib cage and moaned. "I've had a terrible day. I can't tell you how much I hurt. Did Robert tell you he had to take me to the hospital?"

Robert nodded. "I told her, and I told her they said it didn't look like you'd done any damage when you fell against that wall."

"What do they know? I'm the one who's hurting." She huffed, then straightened her back and rubbed at her side. "Robert, would you please get me a fresh glass of ice water and bring it up to my room?"

He bobbed his head. "Sure, coming right up."

"I wish you'd called me. I would have come."

She stuttered and stammered a bit. "I didn't want to be a bother."

"But you called Robert?"

"He's a nice man. I knew he'd want to help me."

Robert came back with the glass of ice water and started up the stairs. I grabbed onto his arm and stopped him, taking the glass from his hands. "I told Robert to go on home. I'll stay with you."

If looks could kill, I would have been dead and buried.

"But Robert—"

"I'm sure he has plenty of work to catch up on. It'll be no trouble for me to stay."

As Robert backed toward the door, he gave me a grin that said *thank you*. I grinned back. "Don't worry about her. I'll take good care of her. She'll be fine."

"You will come back tomorrow, won't you?" Barbie called out, waving her hand at him, which made me wonder how she could do that without screaming out in pain.

"I'll try." With another grin toward me, he stepped outside and shut the door.

Though I wanted nothing more than to go to my own house, take a shower, and crawl back into bed, I put on a happy face and climbed Barbie's stairs, glass of ice water in hand. "Looks like it's just you and me, kid," I told her, ignoring her intense gaze and attempting to put a Groucho Marx twang to my voice. "Ya wanna talk, or ya want me to pop some popcorn and we'll watch a video? Maybe a chick flick. We've got the entire evening to ourselves."

Without a word she grabbed the glass from my hands, spun around, and marched toward her room, her head held high. All she needed was a jeweled crown, a robe, and a scepter.

"Looks like the decision is up to me," I told the air around me. "The queen has already gone into her royal chambers and slammed the door. Popcorn and a movie sure sound good, if I can stay awake." I headed for the kitchen.

I checked on Barbie several times during the evening, but each time I peeked in her room she was asleep—or faking sleep. I wasn't sure which. Eventually, I hurried over to my house, changed into my pajamas, and rushed back. As I climbed the stairs, I could see light shining out from under her door. I cleared my throat and rattled the knob a bit then pushed the door open a crack. The light was off, and in the dim slanted beam shining in from the hallway I could see her eyes were closed. Stifling a snicker, I crossed the room and settled onto her chaise lounge, pulling its afghan up over me. I was up to her tricks. If Barbie wanted to turn on the light again, or wander about the house during the night, she was going to have to do it with me in the room.

I closed my eyes and prayed for all those I loved, and for Barbie, whom I was trying to love. But unable to sleep myself, I stared at the ceiling. What was this crazy cat-and-mouse game we were playing? We were adults, not kids. Why were we both acting so childishly? Finally, I drifted off to sleep and dreamt of a handsome man on a white horse coming to my rescue, sweeping me up in his arms and carrying me off to his castle. Strangely enough, the man looked like Robert and the horse brought to mind his white Avalanche.

I awoke about seven and found Barbie sitting up in bed staring at me. "Hungry?" I asked, rising and stretching my arms and my aching back. That chaise lounge was never designed to be a bed. "How about a nice omelet?"

"I don't eat eggs," she all but growled.

"Oatmeal?"

"Fattening."

"Orange juice?"

"I don't like the pulp."

"I have some pulp-free orange juice in my refrigerator. Want me to go get it for you?"

"I'll have cranberry juice."

"Okay, cranberry juice. Anything else? Cantaloupe? Or how about some nice stewed prunes?" To go with your disposition? I wanted to add but restrained myself.

"No. Just cranberry juice."

"Coming right up!" I couldn't help but use Robert's words, not that she noticed. Or maybe she did.

By the time I got back up the stairs she was in the bathroom with the door closed. I could hear water running and assumed she was brushing her teeth. "Need any help?"

"No."

I set the glass on her nightstand then made my way to the downstairs bathroom to brush my own teeth. When I climbed the stairs again she was sitting on the side of the bed talking on the phone.

"You can go home, Valentine," she told me, returning the phone to its cradle. "One of my Red Hat friends is coming over to stay with me."

I frowned, surprised that she'd actually called someone. "You sure about this? I can stay if you want me to."

"You've done quite enough for me." She gave me that famous dismissive wave of hers. "Now run along. I'm doing just fine."

"Call if you need anything." *Okay, lady, have it your way. If that's the way you want it, I'll go. But don't say I didn't offer, and don't you go running to Robert with some big story about me deserting you in your hour of need.*

I refilled her water glass, straightened her bed, made sure her phone was where she could reach it, and said good-bye. A few minutes later I walked into my house. The day was mine. All mine.

Why did I feel so guilty?

Anxious to tell Sally and Reva and the other women who had been working on the bazaar with Bitsy about the new baby, I decided to go to the church where I knew they'd all be working. I was already on my way out the door when my cell phone rang. It was Trudy Simon.

"Valentine. I'm glad I caught you. One of the television stations had a guest cancel on them for their live noon news program. They want us to send someone to talk about the bazaar, and you know more about it than anyone. Can you make it? It's a great opportunity for us."

"I guess I could go, but can't someone else do it?"

"No one could do it like you, Valentine, besides, you look great. Please say you'll go."

How do you say *No* after a compliment like that? "Oh, all right, but I'm not going to do all the interviews. Just this one." I scribbled down the details as she gave them to me and said good-bye. There wasn't time to go by the church. I'd have to do it after the interview.

I arrived at the TV station, was led to the set where the noon news took place, and was introduced to a man about my age, Ryan Cane, the newsman who would be interviewing me. "Just sit right there until we're ready; answer my questions, and you'll do fine," he told me, giving me a once-over that made me uncomfortable.

I nervously stared at the clock, watching the minutes tick by until it was time for my part. Finally, it came.

"Valentine Denay is our guest today. She's here to tell us about the bazaar her church is holding." Mr. Cane turned to me with a ridiculing smile. The minute I saw it, I knew I was in for trouble. "Tell me, *Miz* Denay, why would anyone name their daughter Valentine?"

"Because I was born on Valentine's Day."

He gave me a smirk. "I suppose if you had been born on April Fool's Day your mother would have named you *Fool*."

I couldn't let him get away with such insolence. "I like my name, Mr. Cane. Could we please talk about Cooperville Community Church's Bazaar?"

"Sure. Maybe you could explain to our viewers why churches have to have bazaars to raise funds. Seems to me God, if there is a God, would let one of your church members win the lottery. It'd sure make life a lot simpler. Don't you think folks get tired of being asked to attend church bazaars and give their hard-earned money to buy tacky homemade trinkets?"

That got my dander up. The man was attacking my friends, my church, and my Lord. *Help me say the right thing, Father.* "The items we sell aren't tacky trinkets," I said, keeping a smile on my face. "They're well-made, one-of-a-kind, beautifully handcrafted items that anyone would be proud to have in their home. And as to God making someone win the lottery—why? Why would He want to do that when His children are more than happy to contribute their hard-earned money to the church through offerings or the purchase of our bazaar items? We're proud to do it. After all, isn't He the One who gave us our jobs and the strength to do them?"

"Are you telling me you actually believe that stuff?"

I raised my shoulders, lifted my chin high, and looked him squarely in the eye. "Yes, I do believe that *stuff*, as you call it. Why? Because I know the One who created the universe and holds the world in His hands. I have a personal relationship with Him. Maybe you should read the Bible for yourself, Mr. Cane. Though some people don't believe in Him, that doesn't make Him any less real." Not waiting for his response, I looked directly into the camera lens and, smiling as sweetly as I could, invited the viewers to come to the Cooperville Community Church bazaar, gave them the dates, the phone number, a few details that I hoped would attract them, and the Web site address. God must have shut that man's mouth for he never said another word. When I finished, I extended my hand and courteously thanked him for giving me the airtime to publicize our bazaar. I sat until the program ended, then made my way out of the studio as fast as my shaking legs would carry me.

I was halfway through the lobby when a man dressed in a business suit approached me. "I'm Tyler Sandler, the general manager. I'm so sorry, Ms. Denay. There's no excuse for Ryan Cane's rude behavior. I must apologize for him. Ryan has been drinking on the job for some time now. I came close to firing him last week but, being a fair man, I decided to give him one last chance. He blew that chance today. I can't tell you how embarrassed I am by the way he verbally attacked you. To make up for it, I'm giving your church a number of the available public service spots." His face took on an infectious smile. "I'll be attending your church's bazaar, too, and I'll bring plenty of money with me. I happen to like handcrafted, one-of-a-kind items."

My heart soared. Once again, God had taken evil and turned it into good.

I was so excited about Bitsy's new baby and what had happened at the TV station, I skipped lunch and went directly to the church. The place was a beehive of activity. I stood in the middle of the floor, stuck two fingers in my mouth, and let loose with a loud whistle, a talent I'd acquired as a child but rarely used now that I was grown up. All action ceased. "I have great news," I announced. "Bitsy Foster had her baby, a healthy little girl. Mother and baby are at home now and doing well. Bitsy's mother flew in from California, and she's taking care of her." Cheers and applause filled the basement.

"And I have more news. I don't know if any of you were able to catch my television interview at noon today—"

"I did," one of the women hollered out. "That guy was a jerk!"

"Well, because of that *jerk* and his rudeness, the station's general manager is giving us as many public service spots as we can use to publicize our bazaar!"

"We've got good news, too," Reva said, lifting her hammer high in the air as a victory sign. "All the booths are finished! The women on my committee did every bit of it. We never asked the men to do a single thing."

Again, everyone cheered.

"Help! Fire!" The ear-piercing screams from the kitchen area sent us all running to see what was the matter.

"Someone call the fire department! The kitchen is on fire!"

I rushed into the kitchen and found flames leaping almost to the ceiling. "What happened?" I cried out, my heart racing.

One of the ladies grabbed onto my arm and dragged me toward the stairway. "We have to get out of here! The grease is on fire!"

Panic seized me. "The fire extinguisher! Did you use it?"

"Yes, but it didn't help much!"

Within minutes, a fire truck roared into our parking lot and several uniformed firemen rushed down the basement stairs toward the kitchen with massive extinguishers in hand and ordering everyone to evacuate the building. Like robots we all obeyed, gathering in stunned silence in the parking lot. After what seemed hours, but was probably only about twenty minutes, they emerged. The fire was out.

I thanked the captain and tried to apologize for what had happened.

"All in a day's work, ma'am. Just tell those women to be more careful next time. I know several of your ladies suffered minor burns, but you're lucky someone didn't get hurt really badly. Even the smallest fire can turn deadly if given the right fuel. Hot grease is one of the worst. Just make sure everyone stays out of the kitchen until we make sure there isn't a chance of that fire flaring up again."

I assured him we would stay out until they told us it

was safe to get back in and promised him we would be more careful next time. After that, I answered the few questions he needed for his report.

"Oh, no!" Karen Marso, who was the first one back into the kitchen when they turned it back over to us, yelled out, her face an ashen white. "Look at our beautiful kitchen. It's ruined! We'll never get it ready in time for the bazaar!"

Collectively, all twenty-eight of us tried to push our way through the doorway to survey the damage. I couldn't help it. I began to cry. In addition to the gray siltlike film from the fire extinguishers that clung to every surface, pot, pan, the range top and wall, there was spilled grease, burned towels, water everywhere, and a horrible, horrible smell. But the worst part was the beautiful row of snowy white cabinets that had surrounded the big gas range. The men of the church had labored long and hard to build them for us not even a year ago. They looked pathetic with the wood charred and the lovely white paint now blistered to a dull, streaked gray.

Stepping into nearly ankle-deep water, Reva trailed her hand across one of the stainless steel countertops, then lifted it and stared at the thick gray residue on her fingers. "Guess this is what I get for bragging. I was so proud of what my committee had been able to accomplish, building those booths without the help of the men, but there is no way we women can get this kitchen back in shape by ourselves. It's too big a job. Unless the men will commit to working 'round the clock to help us and to rebuild the kitchen, it looks to me like the bazaar will have to be either postponed or canceled. The cleanup of the water alone is going to be monumental."

As I gazed at the damage that had so quickly been done, and thought of all the necessary hours of labor it would take to restore the kitchen to the way it was before the fire, I knew she was right. The kitchen was the hub of any bazaar. Much of the proceeds we had counted on would have come from the meals, snacks, drinks, and desserts we'd planned to sell.

Pastor Wyman rushed into the big room and let out a loud, "Yeeoww! What a mess!" After moving about the room and checking the damage, he explained he'd been in a meeting across town and had gotten there as fast as he could. "Looks like our bazaar is off, at least for now. It'd take a miracle to get this place ready in time."

"I think if we asked them, the men of our church could get it done in time."

We all turned to find Robert standing behind us, his eyes scanning the room, assessing the damage. "I'm sure our insurance will cover most of the damage. If we all pull together, I think we can actually get it done. I'll even head up the job if you want me to."

A sad expression on her face, Sally gestured toward the charred cabinets. "But there's so much to do and so little time. Maybe we could have it at another church in the neighborhood."

"She's right." Pastor Wyman stuffed his hands into

his pockets and stared at the grease blanketing the floor. "It's going to take a long time and a lot of hard work to get this place back to what it was before the fire. Maybe we should consider moving our bazaar to another location."

"That's a definite possibility," Robert said, "but think of all the hard work our women have put in preparing for this bazaar. They've been working for months. Some making the food and items to be sold in our booths, some, like Reva's committee, actually building those booths. Every committee has labored long and hard to pull this thing off. Are we going to let this unexpected fire ruin our dreams for a youth center? I, for one, would like to see our first annual bazaar held right here. I think it's about time we men chip in to do our part."

Pastor Wyman gave Robert a dubious look. "You really think we can get enough volunteers to get this place back in order that soon?"

Robert's smile was reassuring to all of us. "Say the word and I'll get a group busy on it. Besides, with our insurance coverage, we'll probably be able to get some professional help in here, too."

Pastor Wyman paused, as if thinking over Robert's offer, then glanced about the room, taking in each person's face. "What about it? You ladies are the ones who've done everything so far. Do you think we should ask the men to step in and get this show on the road? Right here in our very own church?"

A unanimous, "Yes!" sounded from each lady present.

Our pastor smiled. "Then go for it, Robert. You're the bazaar liaison. I'm turning it all over to you."

"I'll call my prayer team and get them praying," Wendy called out from the back of the group.

Reva stepped forward, hammer still in hand. "Since my committee is through building the booths and making the signs, we'll help with the cleanup and do whatever else we can."

Lifting his doubled fist high, Robert grinned. "I say, on with the bazaar!"

I wanted to throw my arms about his neck and kiss him. Without him and his contagious enthusiasm, and his desire to see the youth center built, our bazaar may have gone down the tubes, but thanks to him, it was going to happen.

With Bitsy's mother staying at Bitsy's house, and Barbie's Red Hat Babes caring for her, my time was once again my own. So for the next week, nearly every waking moment I spent either at the church assisting where I could, or doing another radio or TV interview, for lack of someone else who would do it. Nearly every interviewer asked me about the fire, which gave me a chance to tell how our faithful church members were pitching in because they loved the Lord and wanted to see His work furthered. And how everything would be as good as new in time for the bazaar, because the proceeds were all going to help build a center for our young people.

"Bet you never expected our Friday-night date to be spent scrubbing down these kitchen walls, instead of going to a nice restaurant and that community theatre production of *West Side Story*," Robert said as he gave me a wink and elbowed me. We were working side by side on repairing the kitchen with dozens of other volunteers. "To make up for it, I promise we'll do something really special when this is all over."

I nudged him back. "Actually, I'm kind of enjoying working alongside you. Do you really think we'll be ready in time?"

He cuffed my chin playfully. "With everyone working at it, I know we will."

As I lay in bed that night, my muscles screaming out in pain from the grueling week I'd put them through, Robert's words kept repeating in my head, and I knew we would make it.

When I went to check on Barbie the next day, I found the queen surrounded by her loyal subjects, just as I knew she would be, all dressed in purple dresses and wearing red hats, daintily sipping tea and eating tiny cheesecakes topped with red cherry sauce. "I didn't mean to interrupt," I told the group, most of which I'd met the night I'd attended the Red Hat meeting with her. "I just wanted to check on our queen."

"She's doing just fine," a lady, with nearly as many bangles and baubles as Barbie, said, offering me a cup of tea. "We've made out a schedule so at least one of us is with her at all times. Since today was the day for our regular meeting we decided to hold it here in her newly remodeled home. As one of our newer members, we were hoping you'd be here, too. Didn't you get my e-mail about today's meeting?"

Duh! I should have called and explained I wasn't planning to be there. "Yes, thank you. I did get it, and I do plan to attend a meeting real soon, honest."

For the first time since entering, I looked around. Barbie's house looked spectacular. The walls were no longer lime green but a deep burgundy red, nearly the same color as my living room walls. The carpet was a soft neutral beige, the same shade as mine. And the sofas were oversized, massive, and upholstered in soft beige tones and accessorized with plump matching pillows. Mine were the same color and style. On the mantel was an assorted group of gold Victorian-style candleholders, decked out with candles, and above the mantel hung a beveled mirror that reached the ceiling, exactly as mine did. On the carpet, beneath an ornate iron glass-topped coffee table, lay a gorgeous oriental area rug in shades of beige, burgundy, and gold. If I hadn't known better I would have thought it was the same rug and table I had in my house. Silk flowers, mostly roses, in varying shades of pink, coral, burgundy, and red were everywhere, tucked in vases, on wreaths, in baskets. There were even silk roses tucked into the tall green silk ficus trees that graced the corners of the room. Everything looked quite familiar. In fact, the entire room made me feel suspiciously at home.

"Barbie has such good taste," one of Barbie's Babes said, edging up to me with her teacup, her pinky sticking straight up in the air. I could never get mine to do that and hold the cup, too, without spilling the tea. I guess it took practice.

"She designed this room all by herself," another one of Barbie's Babes said with enthusiasm. "Selected the paint color, the carpet, the furniture, even the decorations. Don't you think it's lovely?"

I couldn't restrain myself. I gave Barbie a piercing stare then answered more directly to her than the woman who'd asked the question. "I think I could live in this room and be quite comfortable. It seems Barbie's and my tastes are more alike than I'd realized."

Ignoring my stare, Barbie smiled at me then at the woman. "A girl has to do what a girl has to do. When my interior designer was called out of town, I knew I'd have to step in and take over or my house would never get finished in time. I just put together the things I like and—" Her hand made a wide flourish, which caused me to wonder if her rib was still bothering her. "*Voilà!* This is the result!"

All of Barbie's Babes applauded and gazed at her with admiration. Funny thing though, I no longer felt an ounce of jealousy. I was actually happy she was feeling better and her home had become the showplace she'd wanted, even if it was a reflection of my home and my tastes. These were her groupies, her support team. She needed that, and I was glad they were there. These women were nice women, out to have a good time, and to enjoy one another's company.

"Can you stay?" one of the ladies asked. "Barbie is

going to give us a lesson on makeup."

Just what I need. I thanked her for the invitation, reminded Barbie to call if she needed anything, told her I hoped she was feeling healthy enough to be the welcoming hostess for the bazaar, waved good-bye to the others and left. Barbie was back to being Barbie, which meant, look out, Robert!

By late Wednesday evening, by the sweat of many people's brows, the work on the church kitchen was complete. Those of us who had been working on it stood gazing at the finished product, glad it was done but happy that we'd had a part in it.

Robert reached out his hands and asked everyone to join him in a circle, then lifted his face and prayed one of the sweetest prayers I'd ever heard. He didn't ask God why he had allowed the fire to happen, or remind Him of the extra expense incurred, or enumerate the hundreds of hours the volunteers had given. Instead, he praised Him for this unexpected opportunity to serve Him, a chance to make our church kitchen even better than it was before, and for the wonderful time of fellowship we'd all had working together. By the time he finished, I felt like passing the offering plate. He closed by leading us in the singing of one of my favorite songs, the one about there being a sweet, sweet spirit in this place. I knew right then our bazaar was already a success and it hadn't even started.

Barbie appeared in her doorway and waved as soon as I pulled into my driveway. "I just wanted you to know, despite my injuries, I'm still planning on doing my part for your little bazaar."

Little bazaar? "Good, we're still counting on you. Try to be there by eight o'clock. I'd invite you to ride with me, but I plan to be there about six. I doubt you'll want to go that early."

"No, I certainly wouldn't. I'll be there by eight. You'll love the new dress I bought for it! It was kind of expensive but well worth it. It's red! I look smashing in it. I think Robert will like it, too."

A dozen snappy retorts came to mind, but I squelched them all. "Your dress sounds nice. See you at eight."

Friday, the first day of our bazaar, was sunny and beautiful with a cloudless sky and temperatures in the seventies. I arrived at the church at six as planned, wanting to make sure I had time to attend to some things that could only be done at the last minute. By nine, everyone who was a part of putting on the bazaar, including those who were manning the booths, the kitchen helpers, the cashiers, the errand runners, our dazzling hostess, everyone, was in their place, making sure everything was just right and each display looked enticing.

I smiled at Robert then flipped the switch on the microphone and spoke into it. "Good morning, ladies, and you willing gentlemen who are assisting us. Welcome to Cooperville Community Church's First Annual Bazaar. We've come a long way to get here and in exactly one hour we'll open our doors to the public. I want to remind everyone that there will be many here today who may be looking for a church home. We want to make sure they feel welcome. While raising money for our youth center is the main reason we're having this bazaar, the second reason is just as important. What you say and do today could influence people for God. Let's help them see His love in us. I want to thank each one for the many dedicated hours you've put into this bazaar, and the many hours you've spent praying for its success. Would you join with me in prayer as we ask—"

The mike went dead and the lights went out, filling the entire basement with total darkness and murmurs from those gathered.

"Don't panic," I called out loudly. "Everyone stay where you are. I'm sure it's nothing serious. I'm going upstairs to check, and will bring back candles. Okay?"

"Go on," I heard Robert say. "I'll try to keep people calm."

Some of the noise died down, but as soon as I felt my way up the stairway, it started again. The entire church was in darkness. I could hear Pastor Wyman's voice somewhere off in the distance and made my way toward him, hoping he knew what had happened.

"Valentine, is that you?" he asked, shining a small pocket-sized flashlight in my direction. "Some guy in a big truck ran into the pole that carries the power line for the church and knocked it down. I've already called the power company. They're on their way. How are things going downstairs?"

"Not too bad, considering we have a basement full of

jumpy women, but Robert is with them. I'm going to grab some candles out of the supply closet." Despite the seriousness of the situation, I couldn't help but add a chuckle. "I promise we won't set the basement on fire again."

He gave me a generous smile then handed me the flashlight. "Take this, it'll help you find your way. I'm going outside to wait for the repair crew. Tell everyone to hang loose. Hopefully, they'll have the problem taken care of and the power back on before it's time for our bazaar to start."

I gratefully took the flashlight. "If not, it'll probably be the first candlelit bazaar in history. We can't let a little thing like being without lights and power stop us."

By the time I'd grabbed a box of candles and some matches to light them, the chatter in the basement had not only settled down, Robert was leading the women in a song about God lighting up our life. After I passed out the candles and they had all been lit, he changed the song to "This Little Light of Mine." *What a bunch of troopers,* I thought. Even Barbie joined in.

Thanks to the flashlight, I kept glancing at the time on my wristwatch. At exactly two minutes to ten the lights came on, the doors were thrown open, and a crowd of anxious shoppers rushed in. By five o'clock we were nearly out of the baked goods and snacks we'd allotted for that day and most of the booths had sold more than half of their items.

"You've done a great job, Valentine. I'm sure God is pleased."

At the sound of Robert's voice, I glanced up from my place at the cashier's table. Though he'd been in and out all day, I hadn't had a chance to talk to him. I couldn't hold back my smile. "Coming from you, I consider that a compliment, but this would never have happened if it hadn't been for you and your faith when we almost burned up the basement."

"Sure it would. With you at the helm, it was unstoppable."

"Then you had more faith in me than I had in myself."

He leaned in close and whispered, "I think we both deserve a break. How about having lunch with me after church Sunday?"

I grinned up at him. "I'd love it."

I was dead tired when I climbed into bed, but it was a good tired. The kind of feeling I had when I knew I'd given my best for something. The first day of our bazaar was over. Hopefully, tomorrow would be even better.

Saturday was every bit as beautiful as Friday had been. Most of the ladies arrived early, making sure the items in the booths and the food in the kitchen were attractively displayed and everything was in its proper place.

"How do you like my rose-colored dress?" Barbie spun around to reveal the low-cut backside as well. "Robert said I looked beautiful in it. That man can't keep his eyes off of me."

I wanted to say, *"No wonder! That dress is not only*

flamboyant, it's downright sexy!" but I didn't. Instead, I smiled and said, "You look great in rose," and she did.

"I safely put in yesterday's bank deposit." Edna told me, smiling as I joined her at the cashier's table.

It was so good to be with her once again. It had been weeks since we'd spent any real time together. She seemed different somehow these past few weeks, though I couldn't place my finger on what exactly had changed. She seemed happier than usual. Maybe she was still seeing the man she'd mentioned earlier, the blind date, though she never mentioned him. It would be nice if Edna found herself a man with whom to share the rest of her life. We all knew how lonely she was.

"Isn't it exciting that we had such a good day yesterday?" she said.

"The pastor did go with you, didn't he?" I asked her. "I sure wouldn't want you to go alone."

"Yes, he went with me. Otherwise, I would have been afraid, although the bank's parking lot is well lit."

I gave her slim shoulder a reassuring pat. "I'll make sure several of us go with you tonight. No sense taking any chances."

One minute before ten, I moved to the microphone and once again thanked everyone for their hard work and, this time, the power didn't go off. "Get ready," I told everyone. "In exactly five seconds we'll open the doors. Five, four, three, two, one!"

More eager shoppers pushed their way down the

stairs to our basement than had the day before. Even Bitsy, her mother, and tiny Valentine came to shop. My heart sang. Carter would be so pleased. If all went as it looked like it would, we would exceed the goal we'd set for the youth center.

Though a number of shoppers were still milling about the basement, checking over the very few items that were left, at eight o'clock that evening I stepped up to the microphone and declared our first annual church bazaar officially ended.

For the next couple of hours we worked at boxing leftover items, gathering up trash, taking down booths, cleaning the kitchen, sweeping and mopping floors, setting up tables and chairs for Sunday school, and a galley of other chores. By eleven o'clock, all traces of the bazaar had disappeared and the church basement was back to normal, ready for Sunday morning classes. The only thing left to do was escort Edna to the bank's night depository.

With a heart filled with gratitude, I glanced around at those who were still in the basement, some stacking boxes ready to be carried to their cars, some talking about the day's happenings, others walking about the room, double-checking to make sure nothing was left behind. After making sure all tasks had been completed, I headed toward the cashier's table.

"I'm going home now. I'm beat," I said.

I turned to see Barbie walking my way. She looked exhausted, too. "Thanks for your help," I told her. "You made a delightful hostess, and the decorations you made for the registration table and the entryway were beautiful." She seemed surprised that I'd complimented her, but she deserved it. She'd not only decorated and hosted all day, she'd even stayed to help clean up, something I'd never expected of her.

Dog-tired, I sat down next to Edna as she put the last few dollars into the bank bag after counting and recounting it. "Thanks for your work, Edna. I know keeping track of all that money is not an easy job. Your dedication is appreciated."

She proudly handed me a slip of paper bearing the grand total for the day. I nearly fell off the chair. It was above our goal and far more than I had anticipated. I handed it back to her and watched as she zipped the big bank bag shut. We visited about a few more things, things we thought would improve next year's bazaar; then she excused herself to go to the restroom. I was so tired I crossed my arms on the table and laid my head on them, closing my eyes to shut out the garish overhead fluorescent lights. When I heard Robert say my name, I lifted my head and stifled a yawn. "It's over, Valentine. You'll finally be able to get a good night's rest."

I stretched my arms and yawned again. "Thanks for everything, Robert. The board couldn't have picked a better liaison."

"Want to do it again next year? We made a great team."

I smiled up at him. "That we did, but I'll have to think about it."

"By the way, Pastor Wyman's brother-in-law gave

me a message a little while ago. He said Pastor Wyman was planning to go make the bank's night deposit with Edna. I hope you don't mind, but I told him the two of us would go with them. Safety in numbers, you know. I assured him I'd stay here with Edna and the money until he was ready." He glanced around. "Where is she? I thought she'd be here with you."

"She wanted to make a quick run to the restroom. She should be back any minute." I'd no more than said the words when Edna appeared.

Robert greeted her warmly. "Pastor Wyman said for you to wait here until he gets finished upstairs. Valentine and I are going with you two to make the deposit."

I stared at Edna. "Where's the moneybag?"

She gave me a look of sheer terror. "I thought you had it! I left it right here on the table next to you when I went to the restroom!"

"You did? I wish you'd told me. I thought you took it with you. I was so tired I shut my eyes for a few minutes!"

Robert grabbed hold of my hand. "Let's not panic yet. It has to be here somewhere."

The three of us frantically searched the area, but nothing turned up. Not even a stray penny that had fallen to the floor. In desperation, with the help of the few people who had still not gone home, we searched the entire basement and even rummaged though the church's two Dumpsters.

The moneybag containing Saturday's receipts was gone!

$\mathscr{C}$HAPTER 16

When the police arrived, we explained what had happened and how that bag had been accidentally left on the table, unguarded, for only a few minutes.

"It has to have gotten mixed up with the trash," one of the officers said. "But you never know about people where money is involved. Sometimes the opportunity presents itself and they succumb to temptation."

Even though we'd already checked them, it was decided every single thing should be removed from the two Dumpsters, in case it had gotten into one of the many empty boxes that had been placed there during the basement's cleanup. Floodlights were set up, and we began the tedious task of sorting through the massive amount of trash that had accumulated over the two-day period. Residue had been left in the hundreds of used food containers, paper cups, and pop cans and had spilled over everything, causing each searcher's hands to get sticky and soiled. Nearly an hour later, we gave up our Dumpster search. If that bag had been in either of those huge containers, we would have found it.

With a grim face, Pastor Wyman pulled his handkerchief from his pocket and wiped at his dirty hands. "It had to have been stolen."

His assessment set off a whole new chain of events as the police began their questioning of the few of us who remained. No matter how hard we tried to remember anything or anyone who might have caused the disappearance of that money, we came up blank. With the dozens of church members and their families who had stayed to help clean up, it could have been anyone. Finally, when all avenues had been exhausted, we were allowed to go home.

Hadn't Robert said I would finally be able to get a good night's sleep? How wrong he'd been. No matter how hard I tried to put it out of my mind, my thoughts kept going back and forth from the missing money to Barbie. I hated to even harbor the idea that she could have taken the money, but she had been there at closing and would have had the opportunity. And hadn't she told me she could have used the money Dirk and his father were to have given her?

When I saw her come out her front door early the next morning to pick up her Sunday morning paper, I rushed out to speak with her.

She gasped, her flattened palm going to her chest, as I told her what had happened. "The moneybag was missing? How terrible!"

"You were there way past closing time. Did you see anything, or anyone, that looked suspicious?"

She appeared thoughtful. "No, not that I can think of. Oh, Valentine, what a dreadful thing to happen, after everyone's hard work. Do the police have any idea who could have taken it?"

"No, not yet. We all helped search the grounds, but nothing turned up. I guess, until they find some kind of evidence, we're all suspects. Even you." I watched carefully for her reaction.

"Me? That's ridiculous!"

"You were pretty upset about Dirk and his father not paying you for the ring."

Her eyes narrowed as her face took on an angry scowl. "You *do* suspect me! I thought you knew me better than that. Your accusation makes me furious!"

"I didn't accuse you. I said we were all suspects. Even you."

Jutting her chin out, one hand went to her hip. "You are no friend of mine, Valentine Denay! As far as I'm concerned, I don't care if I ever see you again!" With that, she spun around, pulled her door open, and disappeared into her house, slamming it behind her.

I stood there, not sure what to do next. I hadn't meant to offend her, but she had been spending a lot of money lately, and with her constant boastfulness and the easy way she could lie when it was convenient, I never knew what to believe. But, I asked myself, how would I have felt if Barbie had confronted me in the same way? Made those same comments about me?

My answers to those questions made me see myself for what I was, and not at all what God intended me to be, and I was miserable. Gathering up my courage and readying myself to eat crow, I slowly approached her door and rang the bell.

No answer.

I rang it again. "Barbie, please open the door. We need to talk."

Again, no answer.

After several more unanswered rings and a few knocks on her door, with a heavy heart, I headed home. *I had tried to talk to her civilly, hadn't I?* But, in my heart, I knew I hadn't. In her eyes, I'd accused her of taking the money. I wouldn't blame her if she never spoke to me again. Why did I always botch things up where Barbie was concerned?

By time for our Sunday morning service to start, everyone had heard about the missing moneybag. Nearly half of the time that we usually devoted to singing hymns and choruses and getting into a worshipful mood was spent praying that moneybag would either be found or returned. Pastor Wyman even announced if the person or persons who took it were in the morning service, all they had to do was return it and there would be no charges filed against them. But no one responded.

I thought everything that could happen had already happened, but I was wrong. While Robert and I were eating lunch at a nearby diner, my cell phone rang. It was Bitsy's mother. She was crying so hysterically that I couldn't make out her words. My worst fear was that something had happened to the baby. In desperation, I asked her to settle down and speak slowly so I could understand her.

"It—it's Kevin. Bitsy's husband."

I froze and tightly gripped the phone. "What about Kevin? Has he been injured? Is he all right?"

"The man from the Army just left. Kevin has be—been

killed in action. A bo—bomb exploded in his face."

I felt as if all life had drained from my body. I tried to tell Robert what she'd said, but I couldn't get the words out. He took the phone from my hand and told Bitsy's mother we'd be right there.

Tears filled my eyes. I couldn't stop them. "Why would God take Bitsy's husband?" I asked, sorrow filling my heart. "She needed him. That new baby needed him."

Robert's strong arm circled my shoulders as he kissed my forehead. "Though we don't know why this tragedy has happened, we have to remember God makes no mistakes, Valentine. It's not up to us to question His will."

Not that I quit questioning, because I didn't, but Robert's words and his nearness were a salve to my troubled soul. Though at times I grumbled and complained, in my heart I was finally beginning to accept the fact that there was a master plan and I was a part of it. Carter's death was a part of it, even the loss of Bitsy's husband was a part of it but, sometimes, when my faith wavered, I had to be reminded.

The drive to Bitsy's apartment took forever. The distraught girl had cried so hard her eyes were swollen, and her mother wasn't much better. I threw my arms around her and hugged her close.

Bitsy lifted her tearstained face to mine, a gentle smile on her lips. "I'm so thankful Kevin and I shared the same faith. He'll be waiting for me and our baby in hea—heaven."

Robert held the sleeping baby while I hugged Bitsy. I wished there was something more I could do, but I had no idea what it could be.

"We're not sure when we can have the funeral," Bitsy's mother finally said softly, turning her face away from her daughter. "Bitsy wants it to be at the church, but we have no idea how long it's going to be before—"

Robert gave her an understanding smile. "I'll be happy to help, if you need it."

"Is there anything I can do?" I asked.

With sad eyes Bitsy's mother looked up at me. "You've already done so much. And, Valentine, I am going to do the housecleaning and ironing for you like I told you I would. You have no idea how grateful I am to be here with my daughter at a time like this. It would never have happened if it weren't for you."

"We'll talk about that later. Right now, just take care of Bitsy."

It was after six when Robert and I left Bitsy's home. Exhausted, the girl had finally cried herself to sleep. When we reached my house, Robert bent and kissed my cheek. "You gonna be okay?"

I nodded, feeling anything but okay.

"I can stay if you want me to."

I shook my head. "It's been a long day for you, too. A long week. Go on home and get some rest. I have a feeling this next week isn't going to be any easier."

I stood in the doorway until his car disappeared

271

down the street. I'd never felt so all alone. I'd really wanted him to stay. I needed him to stay. I had the unpleasant task ahead of me of calling Reva, Sally, and Wendy, and a few others about Kevin Foster's sacrificial death for his country.

After I made the calls and cried with each person, I climbed the stairs, walked slowly into my bedroom and stood at the foot of the bed, staring at the empty pillow, wishing Carter were here. Suddenly, the thought of spending the rest of my life alone seemed like a prison sentence. But would I ever be ready, truly ready, to share my life and my bed with another man? *Oh, Carter, though I seem to be busy every minute, my life is so empty without you. Is that why I'm turning more and more to Robert? Because I miss you? Or am I actually falling in love with him?*

Reva and Sally turned up on my doorstep early Monday morning. I'd just crawled out of bed. My mouth tasted like a fish bowl, my hair was standing on end, and I had mascara smears under my eyes and on my cheeks.

"I still can't believe it about Bitsy's husband," Reva said, stroking my arm. "At least part of him is still with her—that darling baby."

I fought back tears. "We don't know yet when the funeral will be."

"I've got a casserole in the oven, and Sally fixed a vegetable salad. We thought we'd take them over to Bitsy's apartment later."

I smiled a grateful smile at my friends. I learned long

ago, true friends were always the first to come through in a crisis.

Sally lovingly pushed a lock of unruly hair from my forehead. "Any word about the moneybag?"

I plunked myself into one of my kitchen chairs, leaned back and crossed my arms over my chest. "Not a word."

Reva gave my arm a pat. "It has to turn up somehow. I know God wants that money to go to the youth center."

Sally nodded in agreement. "Maybe we could do some sleuthing on our own. Ask questions of the people who live around the church. That sort of thing."

Weary of body and heavy of heart, I sighed. "I'm game. I sure can't sit here doing nothing."

"You got any plans for today?" Reva asked, rising to her feet.

"I thought I'd go spend some time with Bitsy later, that's all. Why?"

"Let's head over to the church and walk this thing through. Maybe we can come up with something. I know the police are investigating, but we know the church, the area, and most of the people who were there. There has to be something that would lead us to that money. That bag is too big and too heavy to have just disappeared or been misplaced."

I hurriedly dressed, applied a dab of makeup, and combed my hair while Sally put on the coffeepot. After a quick cup to rev up our engines, we headed for the church.

Pastor Wyman was outside scanning the area around the parking lot when we pulled in. "I keep thinking that moneybag will show up, but so far, nothing." He lifted his hands in surrender.

"We're going to canvass the neighborhood," Sally explained, bending to retie a shoestring. "Surely someone saw something suspicious or someone lurking about the church."

"I think the police have already done that, but it can't hurt to do it a second time."

We excused ourselves, then began our mission. After knocking on at least twenty-five doors and finding very few people at home, we sat down on the curb to commiserate. "Look at that kid on the skateboard," I said, pointing him out as he whizzed across the church's parking lot and jumped the board high into the air, landing on the sidewalk.

"Lucky boy," Reva said. "Probably doesn't have a care in the world. Oh, to be a kid again."

"He's good. I'll bet he spends hours practicing. Some church parking lots have signs posted forbidding skateboarding. I think it's kinda neat we don't do that at our church. Kids need a place to play," I said.

We looked at each other then back to the boy. "You don't suppose—" Sally said.

The other two rose quickly and nodded their heads. "It's worth a try."

The skateboarding kid must have thought he was in trouble by the look on his face when we motioned for him to stop.

"We just want to ask you a couple questions," I told him, forcing a smile so we wouldn't scare the child.

Eyeing us with suspicion, he stomped one foot down hard on the end of his board, causing it to pop up into his hands. "There's no sign saying I can't skateboard here."

"We know that. We think it's great that you play on your skateboard here. In fact, our church is going to build a youth center right on this block. It's not likely, but we were wondering if you were anywhere near the church late Saturday night, say around eleven or eleven thirty? We were having our church bazaar that day, and there were a lot of people in and out. We're trying to locate one of them." I decided not to mention the theft unless it became necessary.

He bobbed his head. "Yeah, I was here. I was going through your trash, looking for pop cans to sell. I'm not in trouble for taking them, am I? I didn't think anyone would care."

I gave his shoulder a gentle squeeze. "You can take all the pop cans you want from our trash."

"What's he look like? Or is it a woman?" the boy asked, his sober face taking on a smile.

"That's the bad part." Reva glanced at me, and I nodded for her to go on. "We don't know if it's a man or woman, and we don't know what they look like."

The boy frowned. "Then how am I supposed to know if I saw them?"

Good question. Sally stepped in. "The person we're looking for was carrying a large gray bag, kind of like

275

a big envelope, only made out of cloth, and they may have been in a hurry."

"Did the guy have a beard?"

We looked at one another quizzically. "We don't know," I admitted. "It's the bag we're interested in."

The boy cleared his throat and spat on the ground. I hated it when I saw kids do that. Men, too. It was so unsanitary.

"There was this one guy I saw. He had a beard. I remember him 'cause he came out of the church in such a hurry he ran into me and knocked me off my skateboard." He yanked up his sleeve, revealing a skinned-up place on his elbow.

"He didn't stop and help you up? Or say he was sorry?"

The boy shook his head. "No, just hurried on past me."

Reva, Sally, and I sent each other glances. "He sure had a neat truck. It was yellow and had really cool hub-caps."

I wracked my brain for anything else we might ask the boy. "Was he carrying anything? A big bag maybe?"

"Don't remember."

"You said he had a beard. Was his hair brown, black, blond. Maybe red?"

He scrunched up his face. "Brown, I think."

Reva's brows rose. "I remember you. You came to Vacation Bible School a couple of summers ago. You were in my class."

He grinned, obviously pleased she remembered him. "I'm Jimmy Wilford."

Reva stuck out her hand. "It's nice to see you, Jimmy. I hope you'll come and visit our church again."

"I might sometime. Thanks for letting me have your pop cans."

We watched as he whizzed off on his skateboard. With a heavy sigh, Sally leaned against a parked car. "Well, where do we go from here?"

I shrugged. "Other than telling the police about the man with the beard, I have no idea." We climbed into our cars and headed our separate ways.

I hadn't been able to get Bitsy off my mind. My heart ached for her. After a glance at my watch, I decided to drive directly over to her apartment again and see if there was anything I could do to help ease her pain. Robert's car was already there when I arrived. He opened the door when I knocked.

"Bitsy's mother has been holding the baby so I could help Bitsy with the funeral arrangements. It's been a trying time for her, but I think we have everything taken care of," he whispered, closing the door behind me. "I'm glad you're here. I don't think Bitsy has had a minute's restful sleep since we were here yesterday."

I hurried across the room and threw my arms around her and held her close while we both cried. I was a widow—I knew how it felt to lose the love of my life in death, but what could I say to a woman Bitsy's age, a brand-new mother, who had just lost her husband in such a terrible way?

Robert wrapped his strong arms around both of us, pressed his cheek against mine, and began to pray. His prayer was directly from the heart, and exactly what all of us needed. When he finished, Bitsy smiled up at him through her tears and thanked him.

Reva and Sally showed up a few minutes later. Reva, with a casserole, and Sally with a vegetable salad, and they'd brought one of Wendy's fresh-made apple pies. While they spread everything on the table and encouraged Bitsy to eat something to keep up her strength, I told Robert about our fruitless morning, including our encounter with the boy on the skateboard.

"The only thing he remembered was that some man had knocked him off his board, and the man had a beard. He couldn't remember if he'd been carrying anything."

"He didn't remember what the man was wearing?"

"No, but he was impressed by the guy's truck. He said it was yellow and had some kind of neat hubcaps on it. Leave it to a boy to remember those. I'm afraid he wasn't much help. No one was. Unless God intervenes, it looks like all that money is gone forever."

I gestured toward Bitsy and our friends. "I know you have things to do, Robert. Why don't you go on? We'll stay here for a while. Maybe we can get Bitsy and her mother to take a rest. I'd like nothing more than to take care of that baby for her."

He grinned. "You mean little Valentine Denay?"

I grinned back. "Yes."

After checking to make sure no one was looking our

way, to my surprise and delight, Robert bent and kissed me. "I do need to get back to work, but first I'm going to stop by the church and see the pastor. He's taking this whole missing moneybag thing much harder than most folks realize. I'll call you later."

I stayed at Bitsy's until nearly six, then headed back to my house. I glanced toward Barbie's house as I turned my car in off the street. Two cars were parked in her circular drive. One red. One purple. Apparently some of Barbie's Red Hat Babes were taking care of her as they'd promised. I parked in my garage then dragged myself out of the car. My bones ached. Even my hair hurt. All I wanted was a hot shower and bed.

Tuesday didn't bring any more news, other than the detective who had been assigned to the case assuring us he was diligently working on it.

After peering out my upstairs window late Wednesday morning, and finding no Red Hatters' cars in Barbie's driveway, I picked a bouquet of fresh flowers from my garden and made my way across our lawns to Barbie's house and rang her bell. She answered almost immediately, looking positively radiant in a deep turquoise pantsuit and the gorgeous squash blossom necklace and concho belt she had offered to loan to me. With that explosive halo of blond hair framing her beautifully made-up face she looked like an ad from some of those fancy Santa Fe boutiques I'd seen in women's couture magazines. "You're looking great," I told her. "You must be feeling better."

"Oh, I didn't realize it was you." She stared at me for

a long time, as if deciding whether to continue our conversation or slam the door in my face. "I am feeling better, thanks to my pain pills, but don't worry. I just need them until this rib is healed." Her eyes narrowed as she tilted her head and eyed the flowers in my hand.

"Oh, these are for you. I picked them from my garden." I swallowed hard. "Kind of a peace offering."

"Any word about the missing money?"

Ouch! "No, nothing concrete, but I do want to apologize for my rude behavior. I had no business even thinking you or anyone else I know would have anything to do with the disappearance of that money. I hope you can forgive me. My only excuse is that I was so upset and tired I could barely hold my head up."

Without saying whether she accepted my apology or not, to my surprise, she took the flowers then motioned me inside. "*Your* Robert was supposed to personally be supervising my landscaping, but I haven't seen much of him. I thought he would be a man of his word but, like all men, his promises mean nothing. He's stopped by a few times with some really outlandish excuses that I found hard to believe." She gave me one of her caustic smiles as I followed her into the living room.

"I doubt he's ignored you intentionally. I know he's been busy. First, the problem at church, then, only hours later, Bitsy got word Kevin died and Robert helped with the funeral plans." I gave her a shy grin. "Besides, he's not *my* Robert. I have no holds on him." *Yet.* "In fact, I thought you told me *you* were after him." I felt bad for downplaying Robert's and my rela-

280

tionship, but I wasn't ready to tell Barbie about my feelings for him.

"I wasn't aware he'd helped that nice young girl. What an awful thing to happen to her." She gracefully lowered herself onto the sofa, then, her expression taking on a mischievous grin, pointed me toward a nearby chair. "I have to admit that man turns me on. Now that I'm feeling better, you'd better watch out, Valentine. I plan on going after him again. Robert would make a marvelous husband number four." She gave me a wicked wink. "I wonder how he is in the—" She paused. "In the kitchen! Fooled you! You thought I was going to say something else, didn't you?"

I simply shook my head. I wasn't going to dignify that question with an answer.

"I'm pretty good at solving mysteries," she went on. "I once figured out who the peeping Tom in our apartment complex was. Maybe I should volunteer to help Robert find whoever took that money. Wouldn't that be something if I could figure out who the culprit was? They'd probably do a feature article in the newspaper about me. Maybe even an interview on TV."

Barbie figure out who the culprit was? Ridiculous idea, I thought to myself. *What could she possibly do that the police and the rest of us haven't already done? Did everything always have to center around her?* "It was nice of your Red Hat ladies to pitch in and help you like they did," I told her, needing to change the subject before I said something I shouldn't. "They're a nice group, and they looked so cute in their purple dresses and red hats."

"You must go to next month's meeting with me. We're having lunch at the Opryland Hotel, then doing a tour of the restored Ryman Theatre. One of the leading country singers is going to be our host, and he'll be signing autographs afterward. I'd tell you who it is, but it's supposed to be a big secret. I promised him I wouldn't tell, but I can tell you his initials are G. B." Shifting slightly sideways and crossing her legs at the ankles, she struck a pose that reminded me of one I'd seen Marilyn Monroe do in *The Seven Year Itch*. "He's coming as a special favor to me. You must bring Sally and Reva, too. I know they'll enjoy it."

I thought it over and decided to take her up on her invitation. With all that had been going on in our lives, we could all use a bit of fun, and from when I'd attended Barbie's Red Hat meeting I knew we would have fun. "I'll ask them. I've already told them what a great time I had at the last meeting. In fact, since that meeting, I've seriously been thinking of starting my own Red Hat chapter."

Her jaw dropped. "You have? Really?"

"Yes. I went to their Web site to learn more about the group and found they encourage anyone who wants to, to start their own chapter. I thought it might be fun to organize a new group from some of the ladies at my church since we have so much in common already, and many have expressed interest."

"You can belong to more than one chapter, you know."

I nodded. "Yes, I read that on the Web site. I really enjoyed my evening with Barbie's Babes, but I'm not sure I'll have the time to keep up with two chapters."

She batted those long lashes. "I might be willing to join your chapter, too, if you asked me."

"You're not a member of our church."

"I've been thinking about joining. I have a lot to contribute. The Sunday I was at your church, I noticed a good many of those ladies could really use some help with their clothing and makeup."

"Umm, we'll see. I haven't decided if I'm going to start a chapter or not. I'll keep you posted."

She waved her hand around the room. "I hope you're not offended because I used the same colors in my house, but I've always loved that deep rich burgundy red color with beige as a backdrop and figured why not?"

"I consider it a compliment that you would use the same colors." I did consider it a compliment, but of all the colors in the color wheel, why did she have to go with my colors? I'd thought her more original than that.

"Those colors are nothing like what that Myrtle person chose. In my opinion, she's a lousy decorator. I'm considering reporting her to that aid thing."

I frowned. "Aid thing? You mean the Association of Interior Design?"

She waved her hand through the air. "Whatever."

She stared at me for a long moment, which made me wonder what was going on in that head of hers. "You're a good friend, Valentine."

What? Me? A good friend? I thought the woman hated me!

"You're one of the few women I respect. You are what you are. Most people are nothing like what they want us to believe. Carter was lucky to have you."

I never expected to hear words like those from Barbie. Suddenly, I felt ashamed and very small. Sometimes, I'd been downright rude to her. I didn't know what to say, so I just stared back.

Pointing a long, manicured-in-flame-red nail at me, she grinned. "But don't think you're going to get Robert. I like that man and I want him. And whatever Barbie wants—Barbie gets!" Her grin turned into a full-fledged laugh. "So from this moment on, it's every woman for herself. If you want him, you're going to have to fight me for him! You might have gotten Carter, but you're not going to get Robert!"

I had to laugh, too. We sounded like we were still in our teens instead of grown women. "Did I ever say I wanted him?"

Her smile narrowed as that finger pointed at me. "You don't have to say it, Valentine. I can see it in your eyes every time you're around him."

I felt myself blush. Were my newfound feelings for Robert that obvious? "You're dreaming. I'm not sure I'll ever want to marry again, so why would I *go* after him, as you put it?" I couldn't let her know how attracted I was to Robert and his gentle ways. That would be like waving a red flag in front of a bull.

"Because you're crazy about the man, that's why. Go ahead. Admit it. You can't hide it, Valentine. Ask your friends. They'll tell you. It's written on your face every time you're near him. I'm sure he's noticed it, too."

I couldn't stand any more of this kind of talk. It was not only too personal, it was uncomfortable. I had to get out of there. I glanced at my watch. "Is it really that late? I have a ton of things to do today. I just wanted to check in on you, make sure you were doing okay. It's nice to see you up and about and not in pain."

She pulled a prescription bottle from her jacket pocket and waved it at me. "Like I said, these babies do wonders. You should try them sometime."

I backed toward the door. "Catch you later."

She gave me a grin that was almost mocking. "Too-dles."

I couldn't resist. "Toodles to you, too."

Though I tried to spend some time with Bitsy each day, most of the next week I spent at home. A good bit of my time was focused on the missing money and catching up on cleaning, gardening, and dozens of other things I'd let go while I'd been busy preparing for the bazaar. It seemed cruel that Kevin's funeral had to be put off for a week, but that was the way the Army said it had to be, so there was nothing to do but wait.

Robert phoned nearly every day, and we talked about Bitsy, the bazaar, the missing money, even Barbie. But he was as busy playing catch-up at work as I was, so we rarely saw each other. His crew had finished their landscaping job at her house, and she was more than happy with it, bragging about it each time I talked to her.

Finally the day of Kevin's funeral arrived. I'd gotten up early, planning to go to Bitsy's house, to see if I could help get her and the baby ready. As if she hadn't had enough to cope with, she hadn't been able to produce sufficient milk to keep baby Valentine satisfied. The child had begun to cry all hours of the day and night. The doctor said Bitsy's lack of milk was probably due to the stress she was under and told her she may have to give up nursing her baby, which really upset her.

"I can't believe this is happening, Valentine!" Bitsy threw her arms about my neck and sobbed into my shoulder when she opened the door to let me in. "My Kevin is really gone."

"But you'll all be reunited in heaven," I reminded her, hoping to add a little joy and expectation to her overwhelming sorrow.

We'd all been dreading this day. The day her dear husband's body would be lowered into the ground, to its final resting place. The day had started out rainy and bleak, an absolutely miserable day for a funeral, and it didn't get any better as the morning wore on. At Bitsy's insistence, I rode to the church in the limo with her, her mother, baby Valentine, and Kevin's parents who had arrived that morning. The distraught girl cried all the way there and through the entire service. At times, I thought she was going to collapse from grief.

The ride to the cemetery seemed to take forever. Since Kevin had been in the Army, it was to be a military funeral. After we were all seated under a tent of protection from the rain, six uniformed soldiers carried the American flag-draped casket into the tent and placed it on the bier. Then, taking the flag, they ceremoniously folded it into a perfect triangle and presented it to Bitsy. The entire precise process was awe-inspiring. It seemed everyone there held their breath.

I'd never heard Pastor Wyman give a better graveside message. At the conclusion, the soldiers who were a part of the gun salute came to attention then fired three volleys into the air. Those of us watching flinched at the sound of each shot. Then the bugler played "Taps."

Though I had planned to stay with Bitsy after the luncheon the ladies of our church had prepared, Bitsy urged me to leave, explaining she and Kevin's parents needed their privacy to grieve. I left word with her mother to call me anytime, day or night, if Bitsy wanted me there; then I left with Robert.

We rode along in silence all the way to my house, both emotionally drained from the day and its sad events. Hating to be alone at a time like this I invited him in, with the promise to make sandwiches and a pot of my famous coffee, though neither of us were hungry.

He sat in the living room while I made the coffee and put our sandwiches together. When everything was ready I carried the tray in and placed it on the table. I was going to sit in my favorite chair, but he patted the cushion beside him, so I moved to the sofa instead. I could tell he had something on his mind by the way he watched me.

"Valentine," he said, taking my hand and looking into my eyes, "today was a wake-up call for me. I realized I may live another forty years or I may die tomorrow. But, whatever time God allots to me, I don't want to spend it alone. I—"

He paused, and I was sure he could hear the pounding of my heart as it thundered against my rib cage.

"I—" He paused again as my front door opened.

Of course.

It was Barbie.

That woman. Why did she always show up at exactly the wrong time?

"Hi! Though I was tired from the funeral and having to stand at the cemetery, I decided to come over and keep you two company!" She flitted past me and scooted into the empty place on the other side of Robert. "I'm thankful my rib is doing so much better now. It certainly slowed me down there for a while, but I'm nearly back to my normal, feisty self." She went on and on and on, describing every incident from the fall down the stairs, which she hadn't had, to the moment she arrived at my door.

A half hour later, after we'd exhausted the subject of Barbie's made-up fall down the stairs and her remodeling and landscaping job, Robert excused himself and left, saying he had paperwork to do.

As soon as he'd backed his car into the street, she threw her hands up in the air. "Well, since Robert is no longer here, I guess I'll be going, too."

"You don't have to leave because he did. Barbie, I need to talk to you. I've been thinking—"

"Don't have time, sugar. My Realtor is coming over, and I need to change into something more—" She paused and gave me an exaggerated wink. "More— enticing."

"But this is important. I need to—"

"Sorry, whatever it is will have to wait." As she backed out my door, she let out an impish giggle. "I saw the two of you drive in together. Bet you thought you were going to have him all to yourself, but I fixed that, didn't I? Now Robert's gone and you're alone. I can set you up with one of my male friends if you like."

I let out a sigh. "It's been a long day. Don't even go there. Good night, Barbie."

I went to bed early with thoughts of Bitsy and what she must have been going through. I could just see her holding that flag to her breast and crying her heart out. I was sound asleep when the phone rang at eleven o'clock. *Who could be calling this time of night?* I thought about letting the answering machine pick up, but changed my mind, deciding it might be something important.

"I hope you weren't asleep. I knew you'd want to

hear this." It was Robert. I could tell by his voice that he was excited. "Pastor Wyman just called. Remember that boy with the skateboard who told you about the man who was driving a yellow truck with those fancy hubcaps?"

"Yes, I remember."

"I'd forgotten all about it until the pastor and I were talking in his office the other day. He said something about needing to get new tires and I jokingly asked him if he was going to get those fancy spinning hubcaps. He said they were too expensive for him, but his brother-in-law had some on his new yellow truck. Don't ask me why, but those words sent chills down my spine. When I told him about the boy with the skateboard and what he'd said about the man hurrying out of the church that evening right after our bazaar had closed, he got really upset. That brother-in-law had been at the bazaar at closing time. The pastor said the man has been in trouble most of his life, even served time for robbing a convenience store. It's a good thing you ladies talked to that boy. To make a long story short, Pastor Wyman called our Nashville detective who, in turn, got in touch with the Las Vegas police. They have a warrant and are on the way to the guy's home."

I couldn't help it. I burst into tears. I'd been so worried that money wouldn't turn up, yet it seemed the mystery of the missing money was about to be solved. Where was my faith? Why hadn't I trusted God?

"The way everything is falling into place," he continued, "we expect to hear from them any minute, telling us they've found the guy and he still has the money, and our plans for the youth center will be right on track."

A great relief flooded my soul. "This is such wonderful news. I'm so glad you called me. I hate to say it, but I was beginning to think we'd never find out who took that money."

"Valentine! I have an idea!" He sounded so jubilant I could almost see that infectious smile of his. "I think we should call it the Carter Denay Youth Center. I'm going to present the idea to the board. Whatcha think?"

Trying to contain both my sobs and my joy, I wiped at my eyes with the sleeve of my pajamas. "What a great idea. Carter would be so pleased. It'd be the perfect way to honor his memory."

"From what you and others have told me about him, I'd say his memory is worth honoring."

"You're such a good man, Robert. I consider it a privilege to know you." Why did I have this funny feeling in the pit of my stomach every time I talked to him or was near him? Was my interest in Robert more than that of a friend? Could I be deceiving myself? Like Barbie said? I stared at the empty pillow beside me. Or was I simply lonely and tired of being by myself?

"Valentine."

"Yes?"

"Nothing. What I have to say is too personal to talk about over the phone. I'll tell you when I see you.

Whoops, hang on. My cell phone is ringing and the pastor's name came up. Hopefully, he'll have good news."

I could hardly wait for Robert to come back on the line. Maybe this was the news we'd been waiting for.

But all the excitement was gone from his voice when he spoke.

"They found him, but not the money, and the guy claims he's innocent. Said he never even saw the moneybag. He may be lying, but the detectives were convinced he was telling the truth. We're right back where we started. Though the Las Vegas detectives are going to do some more checking . . ."

My heart sank and I felt faint. "There's one other person we haven't discussed who could have taken it," I said.

"Really? Who?"

"Barbie. She didn't exactly tell you the truth about her injuries . . . I promised I wouldn't tell. Let's just say she may look like she has plenty of money, but I'm not sure that's true, not after a story she related to me recently. I hate to think she could have had anything to do with it, but it might be worth checking out, just to clear her if for no other reason."

Robert seemed startled by my comment. "Surely you don't think she's capable of doing something like that."

I felt bad for even bringing up her name, especially after she'd been so upset with me. "No, I don't, but she was there when the bazaar ended. In fact, she stopped by the cashier's table to tell me she was going on home not long before Edna showed me that piece of paper with the day's total on it."

After a pregnant pause and with great concern in his voice, Robert said, "I'll talk to the detective first thing in the morning. If that money doesn't turn up soon, or they don't get any leads, we may all be bona fide suspects."

To say I didn't sleep a wink all night would not be an exaggeration. I'd been so sure that money would be recovered and it hadn't happened. Then my thoughts turned to Edna. I hadn't seen her since the night of the theft, but the stricken look on her face came to my mind. How selfish could I be? As badly as I was feeling, she must have been feeling awful! I hurriedly dressed, stopped by the bakery, and picked up a couple of those huge, yummy cinnamon rolls and two Styrofoam cups of coffee and drove to her apartment.

"Hi," I told her, trying to sound upbeat when she opened her door a crack. Without waiting for an invitation, I pushed past her and into her apartment. Something was amiss. Several large suitcases stood by the door and, instead of being dressed in her usual matronly, dowdy granny-type dresses, Edna was clad in a flame-red suit, her mousy gray hair now a harsh jet-black and coiffed in a new trendy style. To say I was in total shock would have been an understatement. All of those things made my eyes bug out, but what really sent me into shock was what lay on the table beside her purse.

CHAPTER 17

S everal tall stacks of bills that had to have amounted to thousands of dollars were lined up neatly, as if they'd just been counted.

I didn't even have to ask.

Edna's face told it all.

She was the thief!

"Why, Edna? Why would you do such a thing? You were a part of us. You worked as hard as the rest of us. I know it hasn't been easy living on your meager retirement, but to steal from the church? From God?"

The frazzled woman literally dropped onto the sofa, crying her eyes out. "I—I did it for him."

I moved quickly to sit down beside her, still having a hard time believing what I was seeing. "Him? Him who?"

Trembling, she shook her head. "My boyfriend."

"The blind date?"

"Yes, we've been seeing each other for some time now. He loves me, Valentine," she said between sobs. "He—he thinks I'm beautiful."

"I had no idea you were still seeing him. Why couldn't you tell me?"

She lifted her mascara-smeared eyes with the most pitiful look I'd ever seen. "I thought you'd all laugh at me. He—he's only forty-five."

"Forty-five? You're nearly sixty-eight!" I blurted out without thinking. "I'm sorry, Edna. What you and your boyfriend do is your business, but what about the church's money? What does your boyfriend have to do with that? I think you owe me an explanation." I gestured toward the stack of money. "And what are the suitcases for?"

"He's going to marry me, Valentine, as soon as he pays off his gambling debts."

"You took the money to pay off some man's gambling debts?" I shrieked loud enough for the next door neighbors to hear. "Just because he said he loved you and promised to marry you? Don't you watch television? Haven't you heard about men like him taking advantage of lonely women and getting them to do things they'd never do, because they believed his lies?"

She gave her head a shake. "If I hadn't gotten the money for him, some terrible men were going to kill him. I couldn't let that happen, could I?"

Furious at this woman's gullibility, I glared at her. "Where is he, Edna?"

"I don't think he'd want me to tell you."

I grabbed the cell phone from my purse and waved it at her. "You've done a terrible thing. I hope you realize that. But how did you do it?"

"I . . . lied to you that night. I didn't go to the restroom like you thought."

"Where did you go?"

"I—" She paused and lowered her gaze, as if to avoid looking me in the eye. "I slipped the moneybag into a large plastic trash sack, took it to my car, and locked it in the trunk, then I came back."

She almost seemed proud of what she'd done. I was so angry, for a brief moment, I wanted to slap her to bring her back to the reality of the severity of her crime. But I didn't. "Where is your boyfriend now?"

"He left the day before the bazaar. He's waiting for me in Phoenix. He thought it would be a good idea if I stayed around for a while, to avoid suspicion, before meeting him there." The nerve of the woman—she actually smiled at me. "He's going to buy me a wedding ring as soon as I get there, with a big diamond in it. I've never had a big diamond before."

I quickly moved to the door, the only way out of her apartment, and leaned against it, making sure she had no way of escape, and dialed 911.

CHAPTER 18

A nd you thought I was the one who took that money!"

I stood in my open doorway the next morning, in my nightgown, rubbing my eyes. "Barbie, what are you doing here? It's not even seven o'clock."

She pushed past me, then stood in the center of my foyer, arms folded across her chest, her face devoid of a smile. "You didn't even have the decency to come and tell me the thief had been caught. I had to hear it on the early morning news."

"I did come to tell you, right after we learned it was

Edna, but you weren't home. Didn't you get my note? I tucked it into your storm door."

Her expression softened. "I—I guess I didn't see it. I went into the house through the garage door."

We both turned to gaze at her house. Even from that distance the small white piece of paper I'd written on could be seen stuck into the opening of her door.

She gave me a sheepish grin. "I'm sorry, Valentine. I came out the garage door this morning, too. I didn't see it."

With a smile, I carefully slid my arm about her shoulders. "Why don't I make us a cup of coffee?"

She nodded, her hand reaching up to cup mine. "Good idea."

After the coffee began to drip, I sat down beside her at my kitchen table. There were so many things I needed to say to her, yet I had no idea how to begin.

Barbie gave her head a sad shake. "I'm sorry to hear Edna was the one responsible for taking the bazaar's money. I liked her. She seemed like such a nice lady."

"Yeah, I'm sorry, too. I think all she wanted was someone to love her."

"I guess that's what we all want."

It was time. I had to say what I needed to say. "Barbie," I began slowly, choosing my words carefully, "I owe you an apology."

"For suspecting me of taking that money?"

"That, and a number of other things. You and I have known each other for a long time and, I'm ashamed to admit, I haven't treated you as I should have." I reached out and folded her hand in mine, glad she didn't pull away. "We were rivals in high school when we should have been friends—"

"You never wanted to be my friend," she inserted quickly.

"You're right, and I apologize for it. I was—" This was even harder to voice than I'd expected. "I was—always jealous of you."

She pulled back and frowned up at me. "You were? Really? I was jealous of you!"

"Yes, I was quite jealous, but that's not the worst part. We were teens then, just beginning to grow into adulthood but, now, we're grown women and I'm *still* jealous of you." It seemed to me a slight smile curled at her lips.

"Because of Robert?"

I couldn't help smiling back. "Yes, because of your interest in Robert, but also your beauty, your gorgeous full thick head of hair, your incredible smile, your willowy figure, your winsome personality, and so many other things that I can't begin to list them all."

"You think I'm beautiful?"

"I think you're gorgeous. You're one of the most striking women I've ever known."

"I think you're beautiful, too, and you're such a nice person. Not many people would have taken care of me and put up with my childish demands like you have." She dabbed at her eyes. "It was fun dressing you up in my purple dress and red hat and taking you to that Red Hat meeting. You looked spectacular. I was so proud to introduce you to my friends."

"And I was proud to be the queen's guest. You make a great queen. It's obvious all of Barbie's Red Hat Babes adore you."

I slipped my arm around her shoulder. "I think it's about time we stopped this rivalry and began being friends. True friends."

She sniffled as a tear rolled down her cheek. "I'd like that."

A tear rolled down my cheek, too, which caused us both to laugh. "We've wasted too much time being enemies when we should have been friends," I told her, pulling several tissues from the box on my counter and handing one to her. "I'm glad you moved in next to me."

"I'm glad, too."

"Friends?"

She threw her arms about my neck. "Friends."

I sat beside Robert in church the following Sunday as our pastor rejoiced, praising God and explaining that most of the bazaar's money had been recovered. Fortunately, since Edna's boyfriend had left town before she'd stolen the money, the only part that was missing was what she'd spent on her new clothing and her outlandish hair change. Though we all hated to think of what lay ahead for Edna, due to her gullibility and her yearning for someone to love her, the plans for the Carter Denay Youth Center could go on as we'd all hoped. Was God good, or what? If He hadn't sent me to Edna's apartment that morning before she left town, we may never have known what happened. Dear, sweet, lovable Edna would have been the last person we would have suspected. *Amazing,* I thought as I stared at the empty space in the pew where Edna normally sat, *what some women will do for the love of a man, or at least what they think is the love of a man.*

After we all settled down, Pastor Wyman preached on marriage and how important that commitment is in God's plan. I caught sight of Barbie as she sat in the front pew between Sally and Reva, almost hoping she hadn't seen me come in with Robert. Now that she and I were friends, I didn't want anything to come between us. But with her determination to win him, I had to admit I had my doubts our new relationship would remain peaceful. I stiffened, afraid someone would notice, when he reached for my hand and held it securely in his. I had no idea where the two of us were heading. All I knew was I had feelings for this man that I couldn't explain, and I enjoyed every minute I was with him. Though I had no intention of *fighting* Barbie for him, I certainly wasn't going to roll over and concede. If God wanted the two of us together, then I knew, one day, it would happen.

Robert leaned toward me and whispered in my ear. "You're a beautiful woman, Valentine. I like being with you."

I felt a flush rise to my cheeks. "I like being with you, too."

"Maybe someday, you and I—"

I put a finger to his lips. "Shh. Let's not rush things,

Robert. Let's just take one day at a time and see where God leads us."

"Good idea. Slow it is. I'll try to be patient." He smiled that smile that always made my heart tingle and my knees go weak. "But if that bolt of lightning you told me about ever strikes on a cloudless day, I hope I'm the man standing in front of you."

"I hope you are, too," I answered in a tiny whisper, ducking my head after giving him a demure smile. I knew, if I ever were to even consider remarrying, it would be to a fine, godly man like Robert.

At the close of the service, we took time to greet our friends and other worshippers, then walked hand in hand through the double doors and out into the parking lot.

"What a magnificent day." Robert nudged my shoulder and gestured heavenward. "Look, not a cloud in the sky."

I smiled up at him with a sigh of contentment. Finally, things were calming down and life was good again. I was no longer angry with God for taking Carter from me. Like Robert had said, there were no mistakes with our Creator. His plan was perfect. Apparently, my husband's mission on earth had been accomplished.

Without warning, Robert suddenly spun around, pulled me into his arms and kissed me full on the mouth, right there in the parking lot, in front of dozens of church members. But did I pull away, tell him he shouldn't do something so foolish? Shouldn't behave like a teenager? Especially at our age?

No! I wilted into his strong arms, relishing the feel of his lips on mine, the intoxicating fragrance of his woodsy aftershave, the wonder of this special, unexpected moment. I still loved Carter and always would, but being held in Robert's arms, being kissed by him, felt so right.

Suddenly, off in the distance, we heard the roar of thunder. Pulling apart and gazing into each another's eyes, we threw our heads back, roaring with laughter as Robert shielded his face with his hand. "Quick, God," he called out loudly, still holding onto me. "Send that bolt of lightning so this woman will marry me!"

I almost said, *"Yes, I'll marry you, bolt of lightning or not,"* but I didn't. Not yet. Time. I needed time. Though I was almost certain what I was feeling for Robert was love, true love, I simply wasn't yet ready to give myself completely over to another man.

Almost.

But not quite.

In some ways, even though I knew Carter would want to see me happy, he and his memory stood like a barrier between us, keeping me from full surrender.

A sweet look of tenderness and understanding replaced the smile on Robert's face as he bent and lightly kissed my forehead. "I know it's hard, dearest. It's hard for me, too. You and I were truly blessed. We loved our spouses dearly and had happy marriages we wanted to never end. But, for some reason we can't understand, God decided to take my Lydia and your Carter to be home with Him."

Tears filled my eyes and trickled slowly down my cheeks. He was putting into words exactly what I felt.

"When I lost Lydia I thought my life was over. For months, I brooded and mourned for her. The only reason I moved back to Nashville and bought Mr. Miller's landscape business was because Lydia had wanted to be buried here, in the plot next to her mother and father. With my wife's grave being in Nashville, I knew I had to be here, too. Though Lydia was with God, her body—the shell in which she lived while on earth—was in that grave, and I wanted to be near it. I had a good job where I was, managing a landscape business for a national chain, but once my wife was gone, there was nothing there to hold me. I often questioned God as to why He would bring me here to Nashville, to a place where I knew so few people."

He paused, and with the pad of his thumb, wiped my tears away. "Now I know why. It was because you were here, Valentine. I know God wants us together, and I'm willing to wait however long it takes for you to be comfortable committing yourself to me. I love you, and I want to be your husband in every way, but only when you're ready."

I gazed up at this godly man who had come into my life. My heavenly Father had sent him exactly when I needed him. His laughter, his strength, his gentle ways, his willingness to do God's will, all gave me support and encouragement the very moment I needed them.

God's ways were truly amazing.

"Dearest Robert, I—I—" I swallowed at the lump in my throat. Trying desperately to get my emotions under control, I blinked at my tears. There was so much I wanted to say, but the words wouldn't come.

He kissed first one eyelid and then the other before pressing his cheek to mine and softly whispering, "I'm sorry, sweetheart. I didn't mean to make you cry. I just had to let you know how I feel about you. How much I love you."

"I—I love you, too, Robert." There, I'd said it. I'd actually said it and, somehow, voicing it, saying it aloud, made my love for him so real I wanted to shout for joy.

His grasp around my waist tightened. "That's all I needed to hear. As long as I know you love me, I don't care if it takes a week, a month, or a year until you're ready to become my wife. I'm a patient man, and you're worth waiting for." His lips formed a mischievous smile. "Just promise you won't take too long, okay?"

Deeply touched by his sweet words and his open expression of love, I stood on tiptoe, wrapped my arms about his neck, and slowly pressed my lips to his. "I promise."

Hooting and hollering sounded as a ring of fellow churchgoers, whom we hadn't realized were anywhere near, began to applaud. I guessed I should have been embarrassed, and normally I would have been, but there was something so sweet and precious that had happened between us, I wasn't. Instead, surprising both Robert and myself, I smiled, gave them a wave, then kissed him again.

$\mathcal{C}$ HAPTER 19

As usual, Reva, Sally, Wendy, and I all met at my house for coffee, doughnuts, and girl talk the next morning. I'd invited Barbie, too, but it was time to have her roots done so she declined, saying she would be over later.

"That was some display you and Robert put on after church yesterday," Sally teased the minute she crossed my kitchen. "I just wish I'd had my camera."

Reva tilted her head and eyed me with amusement. "Umm-um. I haven't been kissed like that since my Manny died. Remind me what it's like."

Wendy shook her finger in Reva's face. "Shame on you, girls. You're embarrassing Valentine."

Grabbing the coffeepot from the counter, Sally waved it through the air. "I wouldn't mind being embarrassed if someone wanted to kiss me like that."

I knew I was blushing, but I couldn't do a thing about it, and I wasn't even sure I wanted to. I had been walking on clouds ever since Robert had declared his love for me and I for him.

We all jumped when someone knocked on the door. It was Bitsy, and she was carrying her baby in her arms.

"I can't stay. I have an appointment to have Valentine's picture taken, but I wanted to stop by for a minute, to show off my beautiful baby in the darling outfit you bought her." She nodded toward me. "And I wanted to thank you for being such a good friend when I needed you." She blinked, and it was obvious she was fighting tears. "I love you. You're very special. I know if Kevin were here, he'd want to thank you, too."

We all crowded around the sleeping baby, ohhing and ahhing at her beautiful face and her tiny pink lips. She was perfect in every way.

"You'll always have a special place in our hearts," Sally told her, her fingers going to touch the soft fluff of hair on the baby's head. "We're all here for you anytime you need us."

"And my prayer team is praying for you every day," Wendy added in her own loving way. "I'm available for baby-sitting whenever you need it."

Bitsy's face fairly glowed. "Thank you, Wendy. You can be sure I'll be calling on you."

"We've all been there, Bitsy. We're all widows. We know how you feel and how hard it is to be without Kevin," I said. I could only imagine what the coming days would hold for that brave young woman and her sweet, sweet child. "Take it from me, you're going to have some tough times. Life won't be easy without him. You'll miss him and, some days, you'll wish you could have died, too. But God gave you that beautiful baby to care for and to raise for Him. And though your little Valentine can never completely fill the emptiness

306

in your heart, she will bring you joy and happiness to ease the pain. It was gracious of our God to give you this bundle of charms just when you needed her. Cherish her, for she is truly a miracle and a gift from Him."

I hadn't meant to get on my soapbox, but I knew from my own personal loss how Bitsy must have felt, and I wanted to do everything I could to comfort her. We all did.

"I'm grateful to have friends like you who have already been where I am and are willing to help me through all of this." Bitsy's face brightened a bit. "But I have good news. I've talked my mother into leaving California and moving in with me."

I was so happy I wanted to shout. "Oh, Bitsy, this is absolutely marvelous news."

"Now my daughter will be able to see her grand-mother every day. In fact, the three of us are planning a trip in a few weeks, to spend some time with Kevin's family. Losing their only son has been pretty rough on them, and with their bad health it's difficult for them to travel." Bitsy glanced at my wall clock. "Oh, I hadn't realized it was so late. I'd better be going."

We hugged and said our good-byes, each of us feeling blessed by her visit.

"Barbie's Red Hat Babes are having their next meeting at the Opryland Hotel," I told my remaining friends once we'd settled down and were seated around the table. "She wants the four of us to come." I reached into the paper sack and pulled out a doughnut.

Reva dunked her doughnut into her coffee without looking up. "Sounds like fun. Let's go."

Sally nodded in agreement. "I'm for it. I could use a little fun."

I turned to Wendy. "How about you, Wendy? You want to go with us?"

She shook her head. "I think I'm a bit too old for Barbie's group. I find it hard to think of myself as a *Babe*."

We all laughed. In our eyes, Wendy, though much older than the rest of us, was just one of the girls.

I glanced around the circle. "You know what? I've been thinking of forming a Red Hat chapter myself. Maybe one composed of just widows. All you have to do is go to their Web site and fill out a form, authorize a small charge to your credit card, and *voilà*—you have your own chapter."

"I'd join." Sally giggled, nearly spilling her coffee. "If you're the one who forms the chapter, wouldn't that make you the queen?"

"I hadn't thought about it, but I guess it would, since I'd be the one filling out the form and paying the fee."

Sally giggled again. "Oh, boy! I wonder how Queen Barbie would feel about that? You *both* being queens?"

"I want to join, too." Reva slapped at Sally's arm. "I'd sure like to be there when she finds out our Valentine is going to be a queen. What would we call her? Queen Valentine? Queen Denay? Queen Organizer? We've got to come up with a good name."

"Barbie already knows. I told her I'd been thinking

about forming a chapter," I confessed. "She wanted to join our chapter, too. She even talked about becoming a part of our church so she could belong."

Sally shook her head. "Wait a minute. I thought you said all our members were going to be widows."

"I did. I had originally thought we would limit our membership to widows, since those of us who have lost our husbands have so much in common, and I still feel that way. No one can really know our pain and the loss we're going through or understand us like another widow. Forming an official chapter made up of only widows seemed like the perfect plan—until Barbie mentioned joining us. I feel terrible excluding her when she so wants to be a part of us, but she isn't a widow. Her three ex-husbands are still alive."

"It's nice that she wants to join, but I'm not so sure we should change the focus of our chapter, simply because someone wants to be a part of it," Reva said. "I like the idea of restricting it to widows."

"I really like Barbie and I certainly don't want to hurt her feelings over this, but I agree with Reva. I think we should make this chapter what Valentine wanted it to be originally—a chapter composed of only widows. I don't know about the rest of you, but the time I share with women who have also lost their husbands is extremely important to me. I need it," Sally confessed.

"Sally's right." We all turned toward Wendy, who raised her hand. "I've been thinking about this and have changed my mind. I want to be a Red Hat Lady, too, if only widows are going to belong."

"Oh, Wendy," I told her, pleased by her announcement. "That's great. It wouldn't have been the same without you."

"It's been thirty years since I lost my husband, but I still hurt, and probably always will. Being with you women who have experienced the same thing is like a balm to my soul. You know I'd never want to hurt anyone, but I think we need to keep in mind your original reason for forming this chapter—widows, and their need to share with other widows."

The room became silent as we each evaluated her words.

Finally, I asked, "So we're all in agreement? We want to limit it to widows, right?"

A unanimous, "Right," sounded instantly.

"Then it's settled. Membership in our chapter will be limited to widows." I have to admit I was glad the decision had been made, and had been unanimous, but I still felt bad at having to exclude Barbie, especially since we had now become friends. I vowed to myself that I would do everything I could to make her understand, plus, she could still attend as a visitor occasionally.

"I hope Barbie wasn't wanting to join our church because she wanted to get her claws into Robert. Everyone knows he's interested in Valentine."

"Sally!" I protested.

Sally rolled her eyes. "Come on, Valentine. You're not fooling us. You two positively glow when you're together."

"We do not!"

Sally laughed out loud. "Methinks the lady protests too much."

Reva stared off into space, her face taking on a seriousness. "Do you realize how many widows we have in our church? Widows of all ages? I'm glad we've made the decision to restrict our membership."

I nodded in agreement. "None of us ever asked for, or expected, this new way of life that has been thrust upon us. We are a special breed, with our own set of heartaches. We need each other, not just to lean on, but to explore life with. To laugh with, have fun with, and yes, to cry with." I put my elbows on the table and leaned toward my friends, my excitement growing with each thought. "Think of the possibilities, girls. So many widows are hurting. We need to share the love of God with them, remind them that He cares."

Wendy reached out and touched my hand. "God loves widows. He has a lot to say about us in His Word."

"He even promised He'd be a husband to the husbandless," Reva added.

Wendy nodded. "That He did, and I take comfort from those words every day of my life."

"Wouldn't it be great," I asked, "to just go out somewhere on a monthly basis and have fun with a group of widows? Wear silly red hats. Purple dresses. Feather boas. Laugh and giggle like we haven't got a care in the world. That's what those Red Hat ladies do. Camaraderie, friendship, it's what their groups are all about.

311

No special projects to work on. No fund-raisers to labor over. Their only commitment is to enjoy one another and have fun. I want to do that, too. I need some real fun in my life."

"Are we going to limit our chapter to just the widows in our church?" Sally asked. "I know of a couple of other widows in our neighborhood who would love to be a part of something like this."

"I think I know which neighbors you mean. Seems a shame to keep them out," Reva added. "They'd be a great addition."

"I, personally, would like to see us open it up to any widow who would like to be a part of it," I told them. "What an opportunity to reach them for God."

Practical Reva asked, "What if our chapter gets too big? Sometimes it's hard to make luncheon or dinner reservations if there are too many in your group."

"No problem," I answered, pleased that my friends were really getting into this idea of mine. "We can just spin off another chapter. You know, a satellite chapter. I read on the Web site that happens sometimes."

"Too bad Bitsy is too young to be a Red Hat lady," Sally chimed in with a sigh. "That girl is really going to need some fun in her life."

I leaned toward Sally with a chuckle. "You and Reva are too young, too. Remember? Barbie told you about the Pink Hats? The ladies who aren't fifty yet and too young to be Red Hat ladies? Bitsy could do that, too, even though it will be long time before she'll be fifty."

Reva clapped her hands. "I love the idea! Let's do it! Maybe we can call ourselves Valentine's—ah—Vixens?"

I nearly exploded with laughter. This from Reva? *"Vixens?* I don't think so. Like Barbie's Babes—the alliteration is there—but vixens?"

Sally waved her hand in the air excitedly. "How about The Merry Widows, and Valentine can be The Queen of Merriment? That has a really nice ring to it."

"Umm, maybe." I gave Reva a playful nudge. "At least Sally's idea is better than vixens."

"Are you saying we should make our chapter name more spiritual?" Wendy asked, her brow furrowed.

Sally giggled then gave the old saint a smile. "You mean like Victorious Vixens?"

When we all laughed, Wendy actually blushed, something I'd never seen her do.

Now *I* held up my hand. "Whoa! I think we're getting carried away here. Let's not go that far. Since our goal is to have fun, I think we need lighthearted titles, but Victorious Vixens? I don't think so." I smiled at my three friends.

Sally peered into the sack before pulling out the last doughnut, breaking it in half and placing the smaller portion on my plate. "I'm really excited about this. When are we going to have our first meeting?"

"How about one week from today?"

Everyone turned to stare at me, their eyes widened. "That soon?"

I nodded. "Sure. As far as I'm concerned, the sooner

the better. Starting a Red Hat chapter isn't rocket science."

Sally broke a small chunk off her doughnut half and waved it at me. "What'll we do? I mean, don't you have to make plans or something?"

"I'll make all the plans for the first meeting. After that, we'll take turns. It'll be a surprise, but it will definitely include lunch, so bring money. All *you* have to do is show up. We'll meet at my house and, wherever I decide we'll go, we'll carpool."

Wendy raised her hand. "Are those of us who are over fifty going to *have* to wear red hats and purple dresses to all our meetings?"

"Absolutely, that's part of the fun."

"How about those purple feather boas?"

I smiled at Wendy, trying to imagine what she'd look like dressed like that. "Only if you want to."

Wendy grinned. "That's a relief. I'm afraid I'd look like a floozy in one of those ridiculous things."

"In fact," I went on to say after we'd had a good laugh at Wendy's expense, "no one, other than those under fifty who must dress in their colors, will be allowed to attend unless they're, at least, wearing a purple shirt or blouse and a red hat. The hat could even be a ball cap, just so long as it's red. How else could you be a Red Hat lady?" I well remembered the night I went to Barbie's Red Hat meeting. Probably twenty-five of us women walked into that restaurant wearing purple dresses and red hats. Quite a few, even the feather boas. Boy, did we turn heads. But what fun it was.

"You know, girls," I said, realizing how disappointed Barbie would be when I told her we decided to limit our chapter's membership to widows. "I really feel sorry for Barbie. She wants so much to be liked, but she goes about it in ways that turn people off. God has been dealing with me and convicting me about my attitude toward her. I admit I've had a difficult time accepting her the way she is, and the way she seems to go out of her way to irritate me, but He's shown me the problem isn't with Barbie. It's with me. I've been envious of her beauty and jealous of the way she flaunts herself around Robert. I've even told her so."

I lifted my doubled-up fist into the air in a victorious salute. "But no more. From now on, I'm going to do everything I can to befriend her. When she looks at me, I want her to see God at work in me. He loves Barbie every bit as much as He loves me, or Reva or Sally or Wendy, or any of us mortals. We're no more special in His eyes than anyone, except that we are one of His children who call Him by name. As my friends, I'm asking you to hold me accountable. Anytime you see me behaving in a way that would be displeasing to God, you have to promise to call me on it, especially if it involves my association with Barbie. With His help, I want to love her into His Kingdom."

Reva rose to her feet and applauded. "Bravo. Well said. I think we've all been a bit standoffish where Barbie is concerned. Like you, Valentine, I want God to use me to win Barbie to Him."

Sally rose and added her applause. "I, too, say well

said. Count me in. I'll do everything I can to let Barbie know we love her. Our God is so good, we need to share Him."

For the next several minutes we talked about ways we could include Barbie in our lives. Then our conversation returned to our newly formed club.

"Being a widow and needing the support and understanding of other widows, I'm glad we're going to keep our membership limited to widows," Wendy added.

"Just because we're a widows-only group, that doesn't mean we can't bring a guest once in a while," I told them, glad the consensus was what is was. We needed to be concerned about Barbie, but we also needed to be concerned about the many widows and their needs, too.

"So we can invite friends and neighbors to join? Just so long as they're widows? Even if they aren't members of our church?"

"Sally," I said, snickering at the ring of powered sugar that rimmed her smiling mouth, "as far as I'm concerned, you can invite as many widows to join as you'd like. Just make sure to call me the day before our meeting so I can add their number to our reservations. The more the merrier. And make sure they understand we're out to have fun and they're paying their own way. Also, they need to know this isn't going to be a pity party. Anyone who shows up with gloom and doom on her face will be ousted immediately. Smiles and laughter are required."

Trying to mask her own smile, Wendy leaned toward me. "Reservations to where?"

I pointed an accusing finger in her direction. "Ah ha! I'm up to your tricks. You thought you were going to catch me, didn't you? If you knew where I planned to call, you'd know where we were going."

"I've got it!" Sally screamed out so loudly we all jumped. "I know what we can call Valentine. The Queen of Hearts! Our queen has a real heart for God, and with her name, it'd be perfect."

The room became silent as three sets of eyes focused on me. "What about it, Valentine?" Reva asked, looking enthused. "Do you like it?"

My heart was so touched by Sally's comment about me having a heart for God, I found it difficult to speak. Though many times I questioned God and couldn't understand why He did the things He did and the way He did them, I did have a heart for Him. I wanted Him to have His way with my life. I smiled at my friends. "I'd be honored to be your Queen of Hearts. It's the perfect name."

All three women clapped their hands.

"I really like it," Sally said. "With our queen being the Queen of Hearts, we could even wear heart pins on our dresses."

"Okay, now we've got that settled. Let's go ahead and talk about a name for our chapter. If we're going to have our first meeting next week, maybe we'd better have a name. I've been thinking, since we're going to limit our membership to widows, why don't we simply call ourselves The Widows' Club?"

"The Widows' Club? I love it!" Jumping up from her chair, Sally began to dance around the room, clapping her hands and laughing loudly. "This is going to be so much fun. I can hardly wait!" She latched onto Reva's hand and pulled her to her feet. "Come on, Reva, smile, giggle, wiggle! Dance with me! We're part of The Widows' Club!"

The two began doing a silly jig, kicking up their heels and swinging their hands about wildly.

I stood, bowed toward Wendy, then extended my open palm. "How about it, Wendy? Are you ready to have some fun? Shall we join them?"

Her face shining, Wendy reached out her gnarled fingers, rose, and gripped my hand. "I never thought I'd see myself dancing, but yes! I'm ready!"

Thus was born The Widows' Club.

Center Point Publishing
600 Brooks Road ● PO Box 1
Thorndike ME 04986-0001 USA

(207) 568-3717

US & Canada:
1 800 929-9108